C000160987

THE ALCHEMY PRESS BOOK OF

HORRORS 3

A MISCELLANY OF MONSTERS

ALCHEMY PRESS ANTHOLOGIES

THE ALCHEMY PRESS BOOK OF
HORRORS 3
A MISCELLANY OF MONSTERS

Edited by

Peter Coleborn & Jan Edwards

The Alchemy Press

The Alchemy Press Book of Horrors 3
© Peter Coleborn and Jan Edwards 2021

Cover art © Daniele Serra

Frontispiece "Brown Jenkin" © Randy Broecker

Other artwork © Peter Coleborn

This publication © The Alchemy Press 2021

Published by arrangement with the authors

First edition

ISBN 978-1-911034-11-7

All rights reserved. The moral rights of the authors
and illustrators of this work have been asserted by them in ac-
cordance with the Copyright, Designs and Patents Act1988

No part of this publication may be reproduced, stored in a re-
trieval system, or transmitted, in any form or by any means without permission of the publisher.

All characters in this book are fictitious and any
resemblance to real persons is coincidental.

Published by
The Alchemy Press, Staffordshire, UK
www.alchemypress.co.uk

CONTENTS

ACKNOWLEDGEMENTS

A Song for Christmas © Ashe Woodward 2021

Black Spots © John Llewellyn Probert 2021

Build Your *Own* Monster!!! *Guaranteed* to Scare the *Whole* Family!!! © Bryn Fortey and Johnny Mains 2021

Cuckoo Flower © Tom Johnstone 2021

Dream a Little Dream of Me and My Shadow © Adrian Cole 2021

Dreamcatcher © Pauline E Dungate 2021

Echoes of Days Passed © Mike Chinn 2021

Inappetence © Steve Rasnic Tem 2021

Memories of Clover © KT Wagner 2021

Redwater © Simon Bestwick 2021

Songs in the Dark © Jenny Barber 2021

Sun, Sand, Stone © Marion Pitman 2021

The Beast of Bathwick © Sarah Ash 2021

The Daughters © Tim Jeffreys 2021

The Head © Garry Kilworth 2021

What the Snow Brings © Ralph Robert Moore 2021

In memory of Bryn Fortey
A fine writer and the best of people
1937–2021

"Here there be monsters"

"Not all the monsters have fangs."
—Jack London

"O brave monster! Lead the way"
—William Shakespeare

"I have seen many strange things, but such a monster as this I never saw."
—Jacob Grimm and Wilhelm Grimm

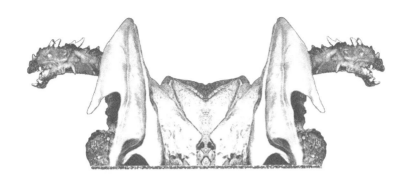

BUILD YOUR *OWN* MONSTER!!!
GUARANTEED TO SCARE
THE *WHOLE* FAMILY!!!

Bryn Fortey and Johnny Mains

There were five charity shops in Effingham-on-the-Stour – the obligatory Oxfam bookshop which opened over the road from Binky's Books in 2014, forcing the closure of Binky's in less than a year.

Dame Jackie's was on Rudkin Street and without doubt the best charity shop in the county – a massive warehouse with as much furniture, clothing, sporting goods, CDs, DVDs, records and books as one could hope for. On the outskirts of town, four minutes away from the recycling centre was Lisa's Light, a small shop run by the family of Lisa Helrunar. She had been struck by a malignant cancer when she was only thirteen years old. The family had been running the store for five years and have made a bit of cash for various cancer charities.

Then there is Effingham Dog's Trust, run by the Millward sisters, both in their seventies and as vivacious as they come. The back of their building had seen many of the town's teenagers throughout the decades have their first sexual experience.

Lastly, the charity shop that's most overlooked by those seeking a cheeky bargain is Hildebrand's off Roxburgh Street. It's a pain to walk to, being at the top of the steepest hill in Effingham, but it's a place that's usually well stocked. The Hildebrand name will be forever linked with Effingham: when the last resident with that name was murdered – Primrose Hildebrand – the shop was set up in her memory, with all profits going to the many local church-based causes she volunteered for.

~~~

Emily Vaught knew none of this when she visited their shop two weeks after lockdown was lifted. She was just glad to be out and about. She was living with her brother, who was a year younger than Emily, and was driving her crazy. There was only so much she could take hearing a 40-year-old man play *Zombie Bollock-Chomper* and *Kill all Coppers* on his PS4, and not lift a finger to help her. He was quite happy to be furloughed, and in his words: "Getting paid to stay at home and do bugger all, it's fucking amazing!" He didn't care that she still had a job and needed complete silence to do it.

Emily worked as a copyeditor for a local publisher. When lockdown began she was told to work from home. Electronic proofs were sent to her online and she'd spend as much time as she was allowed checking for typos and errors before returning them. She was rarely, if ever, thanked in the author's acknowledgements but at least she was sent a copy of every book that she had corrected and her "shelfie", as she liked to call it, had ten books she had worked on.

Emily had just finished a job, a 300,000-word manuscript for a screenwriter turned "serious science fiction author", and it had been quite a task. She needed time to gather her breath, a slightly ironic turn of phrase given the times everyone was now living in, but more, she needed an escape from reading about "bug-eyed skull-monsters" that fed off "mind-planets" as they zoomed through the infinite blackness of space. Retail therapy was in order.

And so Emily was more than happy to get a bit of exercise. She was also desperate to go back into a shop and buy something that she really wanted that wasn't considered an "essential" item. To have human contact with someone other than her grunting half-witted ape of a brother was another plus.

~~~

Emily visited the Millward's shop first of all, waiting in a line for ten minutes before being allowed in. She rubbed her hands with a slightly cloying antibacterial liquid – slimy and sweet scented that lingered even after washed her hands three or four times when she finally returned home. She was in and out of the shop quickly after buying a couple of CDs – Dory Previn's *Mythical Kings and Iguanas,* and a replacement copy of Madonna's *The Immaculate Conception.* She almost bought a horror anthology called *Poe* by Ellen Datlow for her brother – hoping it would distract him from the PS4 – but she saw that it was his own copy: *Jason Vaught* was scribbled on the first page.

She then popped into Oxfam's. The person on the till was revelling in the officiousness of it all and Emily nearly walked straight back out. Luckily she hit paydirt: two Nick Drake CDs and a signed copy ("to Carla, beware the crabs!") of Robin Ince's *Bad Book Club.*

Emily considered taking her purchases home but since it was a pleasant afternoon even the uphill slog to Hildebrand's was preferable to having to listen to Jason's loud and noisy warmongering games. So she undertook the steep climb, taking her time and pausing whenever she felt the need.

As it turned out, there was little in Hildebrand's to interest her on this visit. The one thing that caught her eye was a mixed bundle of American magazines and comics from the 1950s and 60s. They weren't her sort of reading material – *Famous Monsters of Filmland, The Vault of Horror, Tales From the Crypt,* and so on – but her brother used to be an avid collector when younger. Surely these just might tempt him to turn off his console for a spell and give her some peace.

~~~

The ploy worked but only in a limited way. Jason thumbed through some of the comics, muttering that they were nowhere near as good as he remembered them before losing interest.

"And those adverts at the back," he barked, jabbing an accusing finger, first at the pile of comics and then at Emily, as if implicating her in some unethical practice. "Do you remember that time when Dad used to buy me the *Beano*? I sent off for a pair of those X-ray specs once, remember? I was really angry when all I got was a cheap cardboard frame with flimsy plastic lenses that didn't work. That was a whole fortnight's pocket money wasted and I still couldn't get to see Abby Wyngarde's knickers! A fucking rip off!" With a dismissive wave at both the comics and his sister Jason turned back to his console.

Emily remembered her brother falling for a "guaranteed to increase your height" scam which he had found in a copy of *Viz*, smuggled in past Mum and Dad when he was sixteen, paying good money only to be sent two pieces of wood to insert in his shoes – but she thought it best not to mention it.

Instead she picked up a copy of *Horror From Beyond* and flicked through the pages with a bored disinterest as Mr Hyde seemed to win World War II on his own by ripping off all the top Nazis heads and playing football with them. It wasn't her cup of tea, never had been, but she had to admit that the adverts *were* amusing. How gullible youngsters must have been back then, falling for such claptrap. Kids were much more sophisticated today, she thought.

One advert grabbed her attention:

BUILD YOUR *OWN* MONSTER!!!
GUARANTEED TO SCARE THE *WHOLE* FAMILY!!!

it proclaimed loudly in capital letters, with a special introductory offer of only $1 for Part One, followed by monthly payments for subsequent issues of the do-it-yourself kit.

Emily had a couple of dollar bills tucked away upstairs, a keepsake from an American holiday of some years before. On a sudden whim, and maybe to distract herself from the bangs and explosions of her brother killing zombies, she filled in the order form and cut it from the back of the comic, before fetching one of the dollars from the pages of a photo album, and addressing an envelope. If she hurried she might catch the Post Office still open – and it *would* get her out of the house for another little walk.

Of course Emily knew it was just an amusing but pointless exercise. The comic, and therefore the advert, was nearly 65 years old. The chances of the company remaining in business ranged from slim to impossible, leaning strongly towards the latter. But it gave her a private smile or two. When she got back from the post office, still smarting at the price of sending a letter to America, she checked online to discover that the company went out of business in the 80s, and the letter was soon forgotten.

~~~

Some weeks later a letter from Plastic Moulds of Famous Faces Ltd arrived. It was a genuine surprise.

Dear Emily Vaught,

We are in receipt of your $1, but unfortunately Build Your Own Monster Inc went out of business many years ago. Their warehouse was mothballed and lay empty until our company, Plastic Moulds of Famous Faces Ltd moved in early last year.

When they left, Build Your Own Monster Inc had cleared the building of everything – except for one sealed packing case which was found behind a collapsed wall in one of the cellars. We tried to contact anyone involved with the old company but the solicitors that dealt with the company's insolvency folded fifteen years ago. The building was owned by the bank until we moved in.

We are hoping soon to expand into the British market and are preparing moulds of your country's great icons: Boris Johnson, Tony Blair, Winston Churchill and Tommy Cooper.

As a goodwill gesture we are going to forward to you, at our own expense, the packing case that Build Your Own Monster Inc left behind. We hope that its contents, whatever they are, will satisfy your needs. Maybe at some point in the future we could discuss using this gift in a publicity campaign.

Yours etc,

Sam Herbowitz,

Company Director

Plastic Moulds of Famous Faces Ltd

Emily did not like the sound of the publicity campaign but was intrigued as to what might be coming all the way from America. She most definitely did not want Jason to know what she had done. There would be no end to his moaning and mickey-taking. Fortunately, there was a large garden shed that he never went near. When the packing case arrived, if it actually did, she would store it there.

The previous owners had converted the shed into a workshop,

and so it was fitted with lighting, power points, a bench, and smaller table that was home to dozens of tins of paint that had been there for years. There had been a time when Emily considered converting it into a summer house, some place she could retreat to and escape the constant noise of Jason's games. But her brother had objected; even though they had been left equal shares in the house, Jason seemed to think that he was the lord of the manor.

"You talked me into a new washing machine last year," he had pointed out, "We are not made of money, you know." Plenty for childish computer games, Emily had thought, but did not say.

Despite Jason being her brother she was becoming more and more annoyed with him, and arguing with him was a pointless exercise.

~~~

When the large packing case finally arrived sometime later, the rather overweight delivery driver and his painfully thin helper reminded Emily of Laurel and Hardy, but without any of the comedy. They huffed, puffed, and complained constantly while manoeuvring the box on a two-wheeled trolley through the rear entrance and into the shed.

Finally the box was positioned exactly where she wanted it and Emily gave the two men a five-pound note each for their help, however unwillingly it had been given.

"All that for a measly fiver," muttered the fat one as they departed, leaving her alone with the oversized box that had come all the way from America. Whatever it was it was clearly worth more than the single dollar she had sent. She thought about the back that Sam Herbowitz wanted scratched but she certainly had no intentions of taking part in any advertising for Plastic Moulds of Famous Faces Ltd. Maybe she would send him an email thanking him for the box and then ghost him.

It would soon be time for lunch and Jason would grumble non -stop if it was late. He never offered to make it. Emily went back to the house to prepare the meal, which she hurried through keen to get back to the intriguing box with its unknown contents.

~~~

Selecting a rusty crowbar and making use of aching muscles

she'd forgotten existed, she jimmied the crate open, stumbling back in horror as the lid slipped away and clattered onto the floor revealing what appeared to be a jumble of body parts.

But no, they couldn't be real, could they?

Quickly overcoming her initial reaction, Emily prodded the pieces that lay at the top. They had a soft latex-like feel, sort of rubbery – and not dissimilar to flesh.

Removing a piece at a time she laid them out on the workbench and the hastily cleared table. Some appeared to look human and the others animal, with long limbs covered in coarse fur. According to a number of enclosed leaflets, Build Your Own Monster Inc had once offered a wide choice of both humanoid and creature-feature monsters, and the packing case apparently contained leftover remnants from a variety of monster kits. There were also Meccano-like sets to be constructed into metal frames, plus a pack of different sized bodkins, a dozen balls of strong twine, and some sort of neck apparatus that enabled heads to be bolted in place. Build Your Own Monster Inc seemed to have thought of everything. Emily was rather impressed but then—

"Emily! Emily! What are you doing in the shed?" An angry Jason was halfway along the garden path.

"Sorry," she apologised, rushing out and shutting the door firmly behind her.

"Where's my bloody dinner?"

"Just tidying up. I didn't notice the time."

What his sister did was of no concern to Jason as long as the house was kept tidy and his meals prepared on time. He's such a lazy so-and-so, thought Emily.

~~~

It barely registered with him over the following days that Emily was spending so much time out of the house.

Build Your Own Monster Inc had apparently offered versions of a Vampire, Zombie, Werewolf, Frankenstein's Monster, as well as King Kong, Godzilla, the Creature from the Black Lagoon, and the Hound of the Baskervilles. After cataloguing the parts Emily didn't think there was a complete kit for any one of them, but there were enough bits and pieces for her to create a pick 'n' mix something, like an oddball jigsaw puzzle. The whole idea of constructing weird things occupied her every spare moment, even invading her dreams at night.

There were enough metal rods to enable Emily to build two skeletal frames upon which to build her monsters, one vaguely human and the other some type of a creature. The rubbery fleshy parts had to be added, fixed, and sewn together; then the heads could be bolted in place according to whichever monster she desired.

~~~

Emily was very pleased with what she had achieved, and quite proud of herself. It surprised her that Build Your Own Monster Inc had gone out of business; the quality of the kits they were producing all of those years ago was to be applauded. They must have looked so lifelike and wouldn't have been out of place in a modern horror film.

They also had a sense of humour. One notice enclosed in the packing case gave a *WARNING!*

It has been pointed out to us by the scientists who developed the synthetic flesh used in our product that it will incorporate life-enhancement properties if allowed to lie dormant for 50-plus years. If this amount of time has elapsed, under no circumstances allow your monster any contact with electricity. Build Your Own Monster Inc will not be held responsible if you find yourself besieged 50 years from now! YOU HAVE BEEN WARNED!

Emily smiled at such an outlandish suggestion, but couldn't help being a *bit* curious.

It was a poor substitute for the thunder and lightning of old Frankenstein films, and she felt rather foolish for even trying, but, after fixing the Vampire and King Kong heads on two bodies she attached crocodile clips onto the sunken bolt on the back of their necks. In turn, long strands of copper wire were attached to a car battery that was stored in the shed. She wasn't particularly expert with electrical matters: the big flash that lit up the shed, and a sharp smell not unlike burning flesh, demonstrated. Emily kicked open the door letting smoke billow out. She hoped that Jason was too preoccupied to notice.

When the smoke cleared one of the creatures grunted "Me, Kong" and beat a rhythmic punching on its chest. Emily fainted.

"Drink, Madam."

She allowed a little liquid to dribble in through partly open lips before opening her eyes, then nearly fainted again. It was the Vampire holding the cup of water.

~~~

However strange it might be, it seemed the WARNING notice was completely genuine. Emily discovered that each head possessed its own set of peculiarities when attached to a body. All were monsters, presumably with terrifying and blood-curdling abilities. Luckily for Emily they viewed her as their saviour, calling her "Madam Creator" (the Vampire) or "Momma" (King Kong) or "Mother" (Herman Munster). They also promised her their total obedience to her every whim.

~~~

All her life Emily Vaught felt she had been ill-used and under-appreciated. Even her parents, who had loved her, especially before their split, held the old-fashioned opinion that a girl's only function was to be a good and supportive daughter, sister, and eventually a wife. Jason had been given, and mostly wasted, all the opportunities she would have welcomed. When neither of the siblings had married, and after their mother had died, Emily unwillingly found herself cast in the role of housekeeper. As well as working as a copyeditor, she was head cook and bottle washer for an ungrateful and overbearing brother who treated her more as a skivvy than a sister.

"The place is looking dusty, Emily. Needs a good polish. You've been letting things slide lately. *Digit extractum*, Emily, *digit extractum...*" Then, not waiting for her to reply he turned back to his latest video game or whatever selfish occupation caught his attention. One day, Emily thought, he is going to push me a step too far.

Having made sure her lazy lump of a brother saw her flicking a duster around the room, Emily escaped to the shed.

"What is it, Madam?" The Count was always sensitive to her moods. In all his previous incarnations he had possessed the Vampire's mortal fear of sunlight, but in this shared body he was finally able to enjoy the daytime. His gratitude to Emily was doubly increased. She was amazed at how *fluid* his movements were, that when he spoke there was no mechanical jarring of the jaw. He was as real as she was.

"You seem distressed."

The Hound of the Baskervilles rubbed up against her leg, looking to be stroked, and her mood improved as it always did when with her monsters.

"No, it's nothing," she said. "Just my brother being his usual obnoxious self."

"You really should let us deal with him for you," suggested the Count, stroking her hand. "From what you tell us, George would be the one to sort him out."

The Zombie head had been so named by Emily as a tribute to George A Romero for his *Dead* canon. It would be rather fitting, she thought, a little malicious spark lighting her mind, very fitting indeed.

"A tempting idea," she murmured, more to herself than to the Count. The house would be hers alone, she considered. And no more bangs and explosions from his blasted non-stop video games. She'd finally have peace.

"Do it, Madam Creator. Rid yourself of the unwanted turnip."

The Count's silky tones floated like oil on water. Without really thinking, Emily removed the Vampire head and replaced it with the Zombie's.

"I overheard your conversation," said George. "You have an unwanted brother and I am in need of feeding."

"I could make you a sandwich," suggested Emily, a little panic upsetting her equilibrium.

"You've read the stories and seen the films, Madam," replied George. "I can only be satisfied by a living brain."

"But Jason only has one the size of a peanut. Probably."

"It will suffice for now. Stand aside, Madam, and let me solve both our needs."

"Please try not to damage the furniture," whispered Emily as the Zombie stepped onto the garden path and stomped his way to the house.

~~~

Jason suddenly became active for the first time in years when a real zombie shuffled into the room. He leapt to his feet. He was an expert at killing undead hordes of the pixelated variety but facing a real one was a completely different situation. Especially since George's shuffling gait was only an act in order to mess with his head.

Jason had no time to consider the unlikelihood of a real zombie invading his home. He was too busy fighting for his life. As unfit as he was for physical endeavour, desperation drove him on, but it was an encounter he was bound to lose.

George grabbed his arm and wrenched it downwards, pulling it free from his body. A huge wave of blood erupted from the unexpected wound in his torso. It fountained over the wall like someone throwing a bucket of paint. Jason opened his mouth to scream but George slapped him hard and he fell back, trying to use an arm that he no longer possessed to stop him from collapsing.

Even while sitting in the shed, with the door closed and fingers in her ears, Emily could hear the shrieks and screams of her brother, along with the crashing sounds of battle from the console.

"You should have been nicer to her," George said, his voice sounding as if it was full of grave dirt. The Zombie knelt on Jason's chest – his mind by now flown the coop – and leant forward and ripped out Jason's throat with dirty broken teeth, munching on the flesh and gristle as if it was a strip of biltong. Once George was satisfied that Jason was dead, he looked for something heavy to crack the skull open, and it wasn't long before the Zombie was feasting on brain, relishing the fattiness of it and not minding in the least when one oyster-like chunk exploded in his mouth. A glut of slick juice dribbled down his chin and onto the floor. The place was messy enough as it was.

After George had finished eating the Count was sent in next. He drained Jason of his remaining blood. He, in turn, was followed by the Werewolf, the Hound of the Baskervilles and then Godzilla, all feasting on Jason's corpse. They tore at the flesh, munched internal organs, and crunched the bones, until nothing of Emily's brother remained except for a large stain on the carpet and those bloody marks on the walls, which would need to be cleaned later. The Count, however, said he would like to try his hand at cleaning the wall when Emily fetched the bleach. The smell of the liquid made the Vampire's nose tingle with delight.

~~~

"Did I hear mention of a possible sandwich?" asked Herman, who was a carbon copy of Fred Gwynne's character in *The Munsters*. "We are not all suited to a cadaverous diet," he continued, chuckling away. "Fruit would be best for Kong and any sort of sandwich will do for me, while the Creature from the Black Lagoon likes only fish. However, you'll have to be careful to give those bodies you attach our heads to time to digest, or they might explode."

Back in the house, Emily tidied up where the earlier struggle had knocked over chairs. She squirted carpet cleaner on the stain, by now the only thing remaining of poor Jason. In the kitchen she found apples for Kong, made cheese and pickle sandwiches for Herman, and fried some fish fingers for the Creature. Once the Count entered, happy that the walls were back to their normal state, she detached his head and placed it on the table, all the while he was talking about how he might like to have a shot of the video game Jason had been playing before his demise.

"No more of those, they're going straight into the bin," Emily warned.

Emily was going to be busier than ever, catering for all their appetites, but faced the prospect with a smile. They appreciated her, and that made a big difference. She might even think about moving them from the shed into the house so they could become one big happy family.

"Is there anyone else you would like us to deal with?" asked Herman, between dainty bites of his cheese and pickle sandwiches. "Your enemies are our enemies now, Mother. Anyone or anything – you just have to say the word."

Emily had initially felt quite squeamish over the killing of her brother but now she found it much easier to consider other targets for her monster family. There was that rather unpleasant woman in the Oxfam shop, for instance, so superior and snooty, revelling in her position, playing at being a boss. She would be no loss at all and her absence would actually make shopping a lot more pleasant.

"There is *someone*," Emily whispered.

"Tell us the name and location," Herman said. "Just give us the word, Mother."

All the heads nodded in agreement, the Count cursing as he nodded too vigorously, tipped over and fell off the table. Emily picked him up laughing. The Count gave a sheepish smile, his sharp fangs perfect and beautiful.

~~~

Effingham-on-the-Stour has an odd history and a strange aura had always hung over it, but it was nothing compared to what it was about to experience. Meek and mild Emily Vaught was about to run riot, her every wish backed up by her new Monster family.

A month later Emily received a letter from Sam Herbowitz, the Company Director at Plastic Moulds of Famous Faces Ltd. In it he said that he would soon be in the country, lockdown permitting, and would she like to meet up? He was really looking forward to what had been found in the box. She read the letter out to her family and the Zombie squealed with delight as he was starting to get very hungry again.

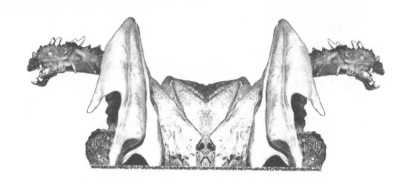

THE HEAD

Garry Kilworth

"You've made a right cock-up of this. You there, mate?"

"Yes, Pete."

"Where exactly are you?" His voice had lost the censure now.

We were communicating by satellite phone, my emergency contact with the outside world.

"I'm not sure," I said. "I was heading south-east. You can get the position from my signal, can't you?"

"And you ran the *Aphro* into a bloody reef?"

"Hey, it's me who should be having the hissy fit. It was night, man. The wind was howling so loud I didn't hear the breakers. The yacht's a dog's breakfast. So, would you please move your arse and come and get me." Pete was a brilliant sailor, thank God. "But listen, I don't want anyone but you to know what's happened. You know how important this is to me. I need to get to Hawaii on my own, without any modern navigational devices, otherwise the media will have a field day."

"Tangaroa wasn't much help, was he?" Pete asked, with a surprising lack of sarcasm.

~~~

Before setting out for Hawaii, I'd told Pete what I'd done. Tangoroa's carving was up on the prow, but I'd also placed alongside him one of Maui, the trickster god.

Pete had said, "You're having me on. Tangoroa's a heavy. You're making him stand next to that little cut-up Maui? How's that going to work?"

I have a fondness for the trickster god. "Maui's more interesting. Mate, I love the story where he changed heads with his wife to walk through a village, just to get a reaction – villagers gawping or laughing like dolphins. Anyway, you're no more use than Tangoroa. You have to come and get me."

"What about all the gear? And what happens to me?"

I sighed with impatience. "I'm not expecting you to sail blind. Come with the minimum that you need to find your way and we'll leave the stuff here. We can always collect it at a later date, if necessary. And as for you, I'll drop you off somewhere before I reach Hawaii."

It was Pete who gave with the heavy sigh now. "With mates like you, who needs—"

"Yes, I know," I interrupted him. "If the position was reversed, you know I would do the same for you. Listen, you'll have to use *Circe*. It's got to be the twin sister of the *Aphrodite*. We can change the name on the way to Hawaii."

"Listen, I'm not hanging over the edge of a boat at sea, painting a new fuckin' name on it."

"I'll do it."

"Too right, you will."

We had been friends for half a lifetime, having gone to the same school together, and then into business as partners in a boat building firm.

"All right. I'll leave Silv in charge here. However, it's going to take over a week to get to you. Can you survive all right? Water? Food? Shelter?"

"I'm good," I said. "Don't rush it. If something happens to you, we're really stuffed."

"No worries."

"And don't even dob me in to Silvia. I don't want anyone to know about this, even my wife. Say you're going to Perth to sell the *Circe*. By the time we come back, it'll be the *Aphrodite*."

"You'll have to doctor the log, mate."

"Too right."

~~~

There was a camera strapped to the mast. A video diary of the voyage was obviously a must for any future lectures. It had always been an ambition of mine to be invited to address the golden three – the Australian Geographic Society, the Royal Geographical Society, the National Geographic Society.

"September 23rd, 2013. The direction of the ocean swell, certain stars embedded in the darkest sky you could imagine, and scattered cloud banks to port tell me I'm somewhere west of the Solomon Islands. Now, it would probably be more authentic if I were a Kiwi," I said, one hand on a stay and half-facing the camera, "but I'm an Aussie. I'm not a Maori, not even a New Zealander, but I am passionate about the Polynesian migrations and the bravery of those early islanders who criss-crossed the Pacific in their twin-hulled pahis looking for a new life elsewhere. It's my intention to emulate the voyages of those sea-faring peoples using the same navigational aids."

I stared out over the vast ocean, giving the camera a profile angle.

"Those wonderful navigator kings set off over this vast ocean, voyaging from atoll to atoll, from island to island, with no charts or instruments, and even without any knowledge of where they were going or what they would find once they got there. Can you imagine such courage? Bamboo craft with pandanus, crab-claw sails carrying families numbering up to a hundred people on each craft, perhaps in convey, emigrating from their birthplace, shooting out over the wide Pacific, the greatest of earth's oceans."

I turned back to face the camera again. You need to keep changing position, I'm told, in order to retain the audience's attention.

"They left the island of their birth because of overcrowding or rivalry between princes, carrying taro and coconuts, and picking up flying fish and small squid on the way. On board, besides the humans, were dogs, pigs and domesticated birds. No doubt also a rat or two, or three or four, or maybe more."

I grinned to reinforce this attempt at light humour.

"And how did they find their way, because they didn't just drift around until they hit land? Well, as I've said, no charts or instruments, just the gifts of the natural world. They used the direction of the ocean swells, the paths of the stars, the colour and temperature of the water, the sun, moon and prevailing winds. In order to find a new island they searched the sky for a cloud with a greenish tinge to its base, indicating that down below was a reflecting lagoon. They would put a pig in the water, whose marvellous snout would pick up scents from land miles and miles away and swim towards it. They would follow the direction of sea birds that they knew were looking for a place to nest. They picked up hints from flotsam: palm leaves and other flora."

Oh, they were a canny set of mariners, those Polynesians, who had no written language. And what joyous warm-wind voyages they made, yes, anxious ones, but full of hope for a new life on a fresh new island. They danced, they sang, they saw the wonders of the blue world – whale sharks perhaps, dolphins, massive lion's mane jellyfish, manta rays – they sailed under skies encrusted with diamonds, the roof of their voyaging. Stories would be told around the fires at night and love affairs and marriages would spice their free hours. There would be rivalries, there would be fights, there would be deaths, but it was life on a tiny floating island.

I went back and turned off the camera and stared at the direction of the swell, and took the tack suggested by the Pacific marine expert I'd talked to before leaving Darwin. Not exactly my expertise, but what the hell. There was also the colour of the waves and the temperature of the water to take into consideration but I'm no "Feeler of the Sea" as those *kahunas* were called, so these were not prime nav aids for me. Instead, I waited for the night and the star paths to appear. The Southern Cross and companions were much more reliable. I had a modern copy of the ancient Polynesian compass rose of winds, which I didn't consider cheating since the early mariners used it. I suppose in the old days they didn't have written words on the rose, but they would have learned from their grandfather what each thorn was pointing to.

Once more I stared up at the firmament and got a bit emotional, which always turns to lyrical with me trying to express my feelings.

"Oh, bright star, would I were as stedfast as thou art!"
Was that Wordsworth or Keats? It didn't matter.

I remained gazing on a sky encrusted with bright stars. They took my breath away, those distant suns, especially out here where the light pollution was non-existent. I looked for the single diamond that I needed to fix on and then waited for others to rise, one after the other, so that I could follow their path and find the direction of my destination: Hawaii.

Thoughts of those incredible mariners still flowed through my mind when I went off to my berth.

Those early Polynesians couldn't write but they had incredible memories. They could accurately recount any voyage on a crab-clawed canoe that took them through an unexpected odyssey. That was real navigation.

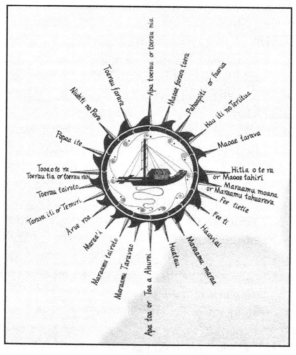

So here I was, in my modern yacht, eschewing the use of satellite devices, or any other modern form of finding my way over the Pacific. At first, all I felt was exhilaration. There's nothing like being barefoot on the warm deck of a sailing boat, cutting through blue water, the wind impregnating the jib and the mainsail, the sun scattering diamonds on the surface of the sea. I could feel the sun on my browned body, smell the salty spindrift in my beard. Free. Free as dolphin, or a frigate bird. This was real life, not dealing with shitty paper in an office, or even with the physical work of boat building. Standing behind the wheel on a sloping deck, shooting out into the unknown. Hell, it filled your whole body with the intense pleasure of experiencing a great passage.

Silvia would sometimes ask me whether this or that would make me happy. "Once we get the new house, will that make you happy?" I didn't believe in happiness as something you bought and kept, like a flash car. Happiness is fleeting, ephemeral, will-o'-the-wisp. It touches you with light fingers, then it's gone up into the ether. I rarely got that feeling while on land, but out here, with the vast vault of the blue sky above and seemingly borderless ocean stretching to infinity all around, happiness came as passing birds on wings of joy.

It was surely how those early Polynesians must have felt, embarking on a journey into the unknown over the earth's largest ocean. I wanted to be like them, do like them, and maybe even come across an uninhabited island I could claim for myself on the way. An adventure in the later years of my life.

And what I got for myself, was a shipwreck on a coral reef.

~~~

I managed to get ashore with quite a few of my stores and possessions, but because I had set out without electronic aids I had no means of knowing *exactly* where I was. At that point in time I wasn't greatly alarmed. I did have the satellite phone terminal, which was for a dire emergency only (I'm not *totally* crazy), but the camera containing my precious videos was still on the wreck, which was half out of the water. I decided I could get that later, once Pete got here. If in the meantime it went under or got damaged by a storm, I still had the log which I carried always in my backpack. I would need some sort of record of the voyage when I got to Hawaii.

My latest star-path reckoning was that I was somewhere near the Micronesian Islands, specifically the southernmost island,

Guam. I had seen two Red-tailed tropicbirds heading north-west – and they surely wouldn't be far from land? The terminal gave me a position, of course, but without charts that position just told me I was somewhere in the middle of the Pacific.

Past the sands I found a beach shack. It was one of those beachcomber or surfer's huts made mainly out of sea-bleached driftwood with a palm-leaf roof, and decorated with shells and coral. Inside, the furniture, such as it was, had been knocked together again out of driftwood or local wood, but seemed quite sturdy, mostly bound together with strips of tree bark and raffia. There were even pictures on the walls, faded pages of photographs cut from magazines, of Polynesian outriggers, and there was one of a marlin hanging from a fisherman's line.

Someone had lived here, though a quick survey of the island revealed that it now seemed deserted, despite the fact that the shack looked as if it had been vacated at a moment's notice.

The island was not part of an atoll, but a single green smudge on a lapis lazuli sea. It was about a mile long and half-a-mile wide, jungled interior, with signs of animal and bird life. I had trained myself in survival techniques in the event of just such an accident. I had the means of making fire and a small solar-powered desalination unit in case the rain failed me. I would not be wholly comfortable, but in the last resort I would – *inshallah*, as a friend would have it – be able to signal any passing vessel in an emergency.

Besides, I told myself, the oceans of the world are full of craft these days, especially pleasure craft like that wreck I had left on the reef. Some seas you couldn't sail without running into them when you wanted solitude.

On the second morning I was scanning the horizon with my binoculars when an object along the foreshore caught my eye. It was a mound of something quite dark. I couldn't quite make it out with the heat haze, but it appeared to be an item that had been washed up. From the wreck? I didn't remember leaving anything of use behind, not of that size, anyway. I shrugged and put the binoculars down. I would go an investigate later but for the rest of the day I wanted to fish and maybe hunt for fresh food. There were plenty of coconuts around, but meat or fish would be welcome. It did occur to me, however, that there were no strong currents or waves in the lagoon. Plenty out beyond the reef, but the lagoon was calm and placid. So how did such an object wash up so high on the beach? Then I thought, maybe it had been there when I arrived and I just hadn't seen it before that morning.

Towards the evening, I set out to walk along the beach.

As I got closer to the thing which had intrigued me earlier, my stomach suddenly began to churn. I slowed my pace, unable at first to believe what I could see. Finally, I came to a full stop some thirty metres from the object. I felt very uneasy and not a little bewildered. There on the sands, covered with small red pelagic crabs and its hair matted with strands of seaweed, was a human head. It had very long black hair which ran in thick knotted strands well below the roughly severed neck. The face was skywards, staring at the perpetual cloud that hovered over the island, the nose a great arching ridge. But the one aspect of the head that filled me with queasiness was its size. It was at least three times larger than any natural human head. Had a lengthy time in the water swelled it to its present ugly proportions?

The thing about being on or near the equator is that there's no twilight. One minute it's daylight, the next it's night. No comforting gentle slip through the gloaming, one into the other. As I hurried back to the beach shack, I stumbled and faltered in my efforts to put distance between myself and the monstrous *thing*. I could hardly breathe. Flying foxes – fruit bats – flapped over me on their way to roost in the palms, creating a thrashing din. Somewhere out in the darkness a pig squealed and set my heart racing even faster. Finally, I made the shack and leapt up the wooden steps into the safety of four walls.

Once two or three whiskies had gone down, I managed to rationalise my fears. Why was I being so stupid? I hadn't even checked to see if the head had been made of flesh. It could have come from a polystyrene model of some kind, possibly having been tossed or fallen from a cruise liner. That was a much more realistic scenario than an actual human head. A giant manikin? Of course. I laughed and turned down the lamp. I had been wasting power to keep my mind from being unhinged. Absolutely pathetic. By the time I went to bed I was almost completely myself again. Not comfortable, but calmer. I finished the bottle, which had only been a third full when I started.

In the middle of the night I woke with wide eyes and stared at a cockroach travelling across the moonlit windowsill.

Why were there crabs all over the head if it wasn't flesh?

Once morning arrived, I knew I had to go to the head again. Feeling a lot braver in the bright sunlight, I ran over all sorts of other possibilities in my mind and these began to settle my anxiety. As I approached the head, from a distance I could see it had rolled over to one side and was now facing me. Perhaps some animal had nudged it in the night? A pig or large lizard? Then once again I slowed my pace. I realised it was now higher up the beach than before, and the sand leading down to the lagoon was showing marks where it had travelled. The hair had left striations on either side of a shallow trench. The crabs were gone but the large-boned skull was still decorated with weed.

Then a shrill noise came from the mouth of the head.

I turned and ran with all the speed I could urge from my shaking legs back to the shack again.

What was happening here? Had the sound actually come from the head? I knew from my days of photographing birds in the wild that they could effectively throw their voices. You think a bird is in one bush and it turns out to be in another a few metres away. There might even have been a living creature inside the head's mouth, but what that could be I had no idea. All I could keep telling myself was that it wasn't possible that the head could speak.

That night the air felt heavy and oppressive. I knew what was coming. Two hours later a tropical storm attacked the island, filling the sky with sheet and forked lightning. Thunder smashed through the darkness and the crashes came one after the other with a physical force that shook the island to its subsea roots. Rain hammered on the palm-leaf roof and soon forced its way through, making pools on the floor. A tropical storm is nothing like those in temperate regions. The noise is unrelentingly ear-shattering and painful. My head hurt as each bang punched the belly out of the sky. It carried out its usual frustrating cycle, moving away to the distant horizon where I witnessed a scores of jagged strikes all at one time, then returning to hammer the island.

Finally, just before dawn, it went far away out to sea, to harass any shipping.

In the middle of it all I tried to contact Pete, which was utterly foolish because I got nothing but white noise and static. In the morning the beach was littered with rubbish. Plastic oddments and other manmade crap covered the sands. There were molluscs and fish too, that had been caught too close to the water's edge and so flung up onto the shore.

Of course, I told myself, that's how the head got washed up! A tremendous tropical storm. There were many such wild tempests in the Pacific. And when I used my binoculars, I could see that the giant head had vanished from the beach. Probably washed out to sea again. Relief flooded through me. It had gone. It had gone. I wasn't crazy. I could settle down, read one or two of the books from the previous owner's shelves. As I said, it seemed he or she had left in a great hurry. There were cans of food in the cupboards and signs of once-fresh food that had been devoured by the ants and cockroaches and anything else that managed to squeeze through cracks.

I was comfortable with life on the island until I came across a passage in a book on Polynesian mythology.

It was believed that there were many supernatural dangers facing those stranded on unfamiliar islands. One of them was the Head of the giant Ulupoka, severed in a battle with the sky god Rangi. It roamed the sands of certain islands, bringing disaster and death. The Head found its way to a human and its bite on the neck, or even the feet, was fatal. It could mimic any sound and would attract an unwary man by copying the sound of a dog or pig. The Head could smell the presence of seafaring men on its shore. Mingling with the sea-bottom odour of drying weed, shellfish and crustaceans coming from an exposed reef, the thick cloying perfume of trumpet blooms, the sometimes-unbelievable stench of rotting mud in the mangrove swamps. It could smell groin sweat, oiled skin and hair, and the stale breath of a lost sailor. When the Head was scuttling and creeping over the landscape, palm-rats sensed the presence of evil and stiffened in their climb. Birds in the frangipani trees stared down with fearful eyes at the strange tracks left upon the coral sands. It seemed the Head travelled from island to island, borne by the waves, ever seeking fresh victims.

"Fuck!" I slammed the book down on the rickety table.

I stared out of the window at what was left of the dear old *Aphrodite* and studied the big ocean waves crashing round it on the reef.

A Polynesian giant? A fucking fairy tale? This was a hoax. Someone was screwing with me. I had a good idea who it was, too. The bloody owner of the chair I was sitting in. The man who built this salt-stained sun-bleached wooden hovel. He had fashioned some sort of model and was using it to fuck with my mind. What kind of sick bastard would do a thing like this? Maybe someone with a grudge against rich white yachtsmen who had the audacity to make a landfall on his island? *His* island!

I could hear his voice in my head.

Who did they think they were, these Johnny-come-lately Europeans, taking over his ocean? Going where they pleased without a by-your-leave? He would make them wish they or their ancestors never left the shores of Europe.

I leaned back in the creaking chair and almost toppled over, but my blood was up. I would find that bastard islander and make him wish he'd never left the place where he was born. I filled my backpack with water, biscuits, and sun-dried beef, grabbed a hat and a machete, and set out to scour the whole landscape, inch by inch. Although I had already done a cursory inspection of the hinterland there was an area of high igneous rock in the centre of the rainforest, the island being of volcanic origin. Some of the rocks had been carved into strange figures and perhaps a cave had been hollowed out. He could be hiding in that area, or maybe even in the rainforest itself, keeping one step ahead of me?

I went to the rocky area first but I was so unsettled and twitchy the stone carvings gave me the frights. There was an eerie feeling about the place so I left after a cursory inspection. I didn't want the islander, if he was a Polynesian, to complain later that I had been desecrating a place where his ancestors or gods were held sacred. I wanted no excuse to get in the way of my righteous wrath.

After four hours I was exhausted and trudged back to the shack. Some of the rainforest had been thicker than I first thought. I had to hack my way through thorny acacias and lawyer vines, which left my forearms bleeding and my pants shredded. There were great hanging loops of those tree-parasites, lianas, as thick as my thigh, and the trees grew so close in places it was impossible to squeeze between them. There were boggy places too, especially where the mangroves grew. I hadn't found the perpetrator of that foul practical joke and I was completely depressed by the whole episode. All I wanted to do now was get off this hellhole and out into the Pacific again, where the air is fresh and the scent is of salt water on a cedar deck.

I got to the shack about five o'clock and rummaged in one of the cupboards. I had seen a bottle of liquid in there not long after arrival and on sniffing it I knew it was kava, the favourite hooch of Polynesian islanders. It's supposed to relieve anxiety and induce feelings of relaxation and calm. I needed all of those and sat on the steps of the porch, without even taking off my backpack. I sat quietly sipping away and staring out to sea hoping to find a yacht on the horizon.

Then…

…the Head came out of the surf and up the beach with incredible speed.

It used its hair like flails, which it flung forward to grip on logs and coral lumps, anything, even the raffia bedstead I used as a sun lounger. It came tumbling forward with an intensely eager look on its immense and pockmarked features, the cavernous nostrils flaring, the dark eyes wide and glinting with anticipation, the thick brutish lips curled back, its tongue-tip protruding between the two rows of even yellow teeth. It was huge and hideous, and the shock of its swift progress was almost petrifying. I froze but only for a second before leaping up and snatching the machete from the step beside me.

It was almost upon me, its wide mouth open, its teeth clattering, when I struck it a blow on its forehead. The slavering eagerness vanished from its expression and it screamed, shrilly, loudly. Terrified, I managed to hit it once more and its high annoyance turned to pure fury. It lunged at me and gripped my shirt for a second, but I grabbed a handful of sand and flung it into those red-rimmed eyes, forcing it to release me. I ran in panic for the trees.

My shaking legs carried me straight back into the rainforest and along the narrow track I had cut for myself earlier that day. The Head tried to follow me, but its momentum was halted when its hair became tangled in the thick undergrowth. The fiend let out a bellow of rage before retreating, leaving strands and red clumps of its scalp hanging from bushes and tree bark.

Whimpering with shock and disbelief, I made my way back to the middle of the island to hide. There I stayed for three days. I drank dirty water from a pool, which made me retch, and ate berries that I was sure were going to kill me, but thankfully only gave me stomach cramps. In the night I went as high as I could up the jagged volcanic rock, hoping that if the Head did manage to reach this place it would have trouble climbing. Sleep evaded me most of the time, both through the fear and the pain from sharp stones. In the end I was so ragged and unwell, I decided to go back and face my fate. With the machete still in my possession I set off hoping to find the Head gone.

When I reached the edge of the rainforest, I peered out and to my immense relief I could see a familiar yacht moored beyond the reef. There was a yellow dinghy floating in the shallows. Pete had arrived! I could see his footprints leading up to the shack. I almost wept with joy. I had managed to stay alive and now we could kick this infernal island into the past and leave it there for good. I ran to the shack, one eye on the surf for any sign of the monster. The lagoon was clear, however, and nothing lurked there.

"Pete, Pete," I cried, running up the steps. "We have to get away from here. We have to—"

Flinging open the door, the next word jammed in my throat.

There he was, my best friend. Or at least there was half of him. Just the legs and part of the torso remained on the blood-soaked floor. The Head looked up from its meal and stared at me as if I were a trespasser. Gore hung from its lips and it quickly licked the filaments away, before going back to eating Pete.

I turned and ran, leaping off the porch. The beach sped under my feet, weary and weak as I was, my strength surging from a well of deep horror. The dinghy took my weight as I flung myself in it and shot out into the lagoon. Once on the *Circe* I cast off. I sailed away from that miserable island and only found time to mourn my friend when that ugly lump of dead coral was safely out of sight below the horizon.

When I believed I was two days away from my destination, I dumped all the electronic equipment overboard. Then I moored on a shoal and changed the name of the vessel from *Circe* to *Aphrodite*. They hailed me as a hero when I hove into Pearl Harbour, and I soaked it up. I soaked it up without a conscience. I deserved that bloody adulation. I had earned it ten times over. I had already mourned my friend on the final leg of the voyage.

Pete was thought to have been lost at sea. He had left Brisbane, ostensibly for Perth, and hadn't contacted a soul since then. On average, two thousand lives are lost annually at sea, so his death was not thought suspicious nor was it investigated. It was widely assumed he had got into difficulties and had gone down with his boat. I mourned him – he was a good mate, a loyal friend – but I didn't do so without being plagued by nightmares.

I still worry that the wreck of the original *Aphrodite* will be discovered, along with my camera containing videos of the voyage to that infernal island. I could be defrocked even now. That particular scenario bothers me only a little, however. The thing that really does upset me is a visit to a wild, lonely shore. Can't do it without a panic attack. I get jumpy and nervous and if Silvia's with me, my dear wife, she sometimes looks at me with deep concern. Then there're the nightmares – when I wake up screaming. She tells me I've changed since the voyage, and she's right. She asks what really happened and I want to reply, "There are more things in Heaven and Earth, Sylvia..." But I don't.

We live too close to the shore.

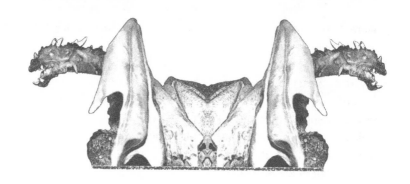

INAPPETENCE

Steve Rasnic Tem

They slipped from the shadows to monitor his decline. Impatient, they moved forward to taste the light. All the world was hungry it seemed, except for him. Even the thought of food repelled him.

Guy stared at the spoon his daughter Ann had shoved up to his face. The yellow glop sitting there glistened with a pre-digested sheen. "I can't." He turned his head away.

"He's just like Princess was," a small voice said. One of his grandchildren, he wasn't sure which. One of the girls maybe. "She didn't eat anything for over a week. And then she— The vet took her away and we never saw her again."

"Inappetence. That's what the vet called it. She couldn't eat. They look at the food but they can't eat the food. They're just not interested. It was because of her teeth. Are Grandad's teeth okay? I know he doesn't have them all, but he has some. But how are the rest of them? Maybe his mouth hurts and that's why he won't eat."

That was Tony, who'd just started college. Tony was a bright kid, and Guy loved him, but the boy always had an explanation for everything. Young people needed to learn how to listen. You can't listen if you're always talking. Guy didn't talk much anymore. But he was listening all the time. He turned his head and looked forward again, but kept his mouth clamped shut in case his daughter tried something sneaky with the spoon.

His vision was blurry. They were all standing there, he thought, at the foot of his bed and around the side, so many of them. He and Cassie had raised a huge brood. Their bodies were far brighter than anything else in the room, except their faces which were shadowed or blurred – he wasn't sure – at least out of sync with the rest of them. He couldn't make out individual facial features, so he was unable to tell them apart.

"Let Ann help you, Dad." That was Robert's voice, his oldest. Jimmy was somewhere in that bunch as well, and Jimmy's wife. They all let Ann take the lead. Ann was like her mother, always taking charge when someone was sick.

He loved his children and grandchildren, all of them. But he had no appetite for them right now, or anyone else. He had to figure out what was going on with him, with his world, and it seemed he didn't have much time. He might not understand a lot of things, but he recognised when time was running out.

He felt an itch somewhere on his right leg, but he couldn't pin it down. Even if he knew its exact location, he had no way to scratch it. He imagined his skin was breaking down, little bits of it falling off everywhere. It was the sort of thing you normally didn't think about. But at this stage of his life most of the things he thought about were entirely new to him.

Ann held his hand. "Dad, if you can't eat your doctor will put you back in the hospital. I know you don't want that. None of us do."

He shook his head. "Water. Please."

A straw poked at his mouth. He grabbed it with his lips and sucked the cool liquid in. So delicious. When he was done, he pushed the straw away with his tongue. His eyes cleared momentarily, and he saw it was one of the boys, Jude, who was holding the glass. "Good boy." He smiled and Jude smiled back. Such a handsome boy. Guy didn't think he had ever been that handsome even for one day. Why Cassie agreed to marry him he had no idea.

He began to choke. He couldn't catch his breath. Things went flying out of his mouth and he felt intensely dizzy. He heard a couple of the children crying and a rush of activity. Someone propped him up and held a cloth under his chin. Something came out of his mouth, mostly phlegm, but maybe something else. He wondered if he'd lost a piece of tongue, some bit of throat lining, a tonsil perhaps, or something deeper. Did he still have his tonsils? Probably not. At the moment he couldn't remember exactly what tonsils were.

The sudden trauma cleared both his head and his vision, and apparently the room, as only his daughter and Tony remained. "What? Did somebody die?"

"Dad!" Ann leaned forward in the chair by the bed, her cheeks damp and her eyes shadowed with exhaustion. Beside her was the table stacked with his vast repertoire of pills and other medicines.

Tony's face looked stricken. Guy felt terrible. "Oh, I'm sorry kiddo. That was just a stupid joke. I meant no harm."

"S-okay," Tony said. He was trying to smile but failing. Guy imagined the boy didn't want to be there, but he was sticking to his guns, acting like an adult. Good for him.

Guy shifted his head and gazed at his daughter. "Could I rest a while, honey? Try again at dinner? Some Jell-O maybe?"

"Dad, that *was* Jell-O."

"Maybe a different colour then, if we have it."

"Sure. We've got all the colours of the rainbow down there." She kissed him on the cheek and they left the room.

He wasn't sleepy. He wanted to be by himself for a while. He couldn't look at their eager faces wanting him to be better. He couldn't tell them he was done.

He had a big house and didn't mind they'd moved in downstairs. In fact, he wished they'd done it sooner when he'd been healthy enough to enjoy their company. Most days he could barely hear them. The murmur of their conversations might as well have come from next door or even down the street.

Sometimes there were gentle vibrations emanating from below. He liked to imagine they were from children joyfully playing. Sometimes cooking smells drifted up the three flights of stairs and into his room. These were not welcome as they triggered nausea almost instantly. Guy couldn't even think of food. Everything meant for consumption seemed poisonous now.

This room at the top of the house had windows all around. It was octangular and clung to the corner of the structure, hanging slightly above the third floor. When he and Cassie bought this place, they called this room the lighthouse. Sometimes when they took walks at night they'd come back and see its windows from a block away, all lit up and showing them the way home. "It looks so full of life," Cassie would say. "I bet some very happy people live in that house."

She'd used this room as her art studio. That was her painting hanging high on the wall above the foot of the bed: a natural bower of trees by a stream rendered in layers of olive green and umber and russet shadow. Every day Guy stared at the painting and thought he saw something different arriving in the gloom beneath the trees. This disturbed him, and yet he often thought about lying down in such a place and waiting for whatever was to come. Something stealing out of the shadows. Something rising out of the water along the bank. It unsettled him to think this way, but he couldn't help himself.

Several of the windows were open to facilitate a nice cross breeze. Cassie had liked it this way and Guy wanted to recreate at least some of the ambiance. He had plenty of blankets on the bed, but his daughter complained he would get too cold. He let her close most of the windows at night rather than argue.

He heard a car door slam. Probably Ann's husband Mark coming home from work. He was a good man and treated them all well. He told Guy tales of the progress he'd made with various household repairs and remodelling, because he recognised this was news Guy would appreciate hearing. But death embarrassed Mark, and of that they did not speak.

He could hear the kids playing outside, the crisp sounds they made as they stepped on the first fallen leaves, the random exchanges between neighbours he hadn't talked to in months. He might have been able to get himself up with the walker and use it to get over to the window and look out, maybe even call down a word or two, but he might fall, and ruin the evening for everyone. Besides, he didn't want to see how the colours had changed, how activities were still taking place without him, how life still maintained its same, inevitable pace. The world outside was still hungry. People were still starving to do things, to eat their time away. But Guy had no more appetite.

Late afternoon shadow slipped into the room and spread across the floor. Despite its placement high on the house, this room went dark first due to the placement of the nearby trees. But it was the beginning of autumn, and once the leaves were off the trees and spread across the ground, he'd see bare limbs and the steel clarity of winter light again, assuming he lived that long.

He wouldn't mind getting to hear the crunch of all those leaves again, the kids kicking them swish swish swish as they came home from school. He'd always enjoyed that particular sound, and the explosive crush when one them dived into a thick pile.

Ann came up with a plate as it turned dark. He saw the shiny green of the lime Jell-O, and at least his stomach didn't react. She sat next to him and asked if he wanted to feed himself. He sat up, but his hand was too weak to securely hold the spoon. He hadn't expected that and didn't know how to feel about it. She fed him a few spoonfuls, and he relished the slight tang of flavour, but then his stomach clenched. She pushed the emesis basin under his chin just in time.

After she'd cleaned him up and he could speak, he said, "We'll try it again in the morning." He tried to smile but didn't know if he had actually succeeded at creating one.

She kissed him on the forehead. "Light on or off?"

"On for now. But could you check on me later? I mean, if I should fall asleep, you could switch the light off. I hate wasting electricity. The planet, you know?" He didn't want her to know he was scared, but perhaps she already did.

"Of course, Dad." The sounds of her descending steps went on for a long time.

He thought about the creamy white stuff they fed you in the hospital, when you couldn't or wouldn't eat. They filled a thick plastic bag with the stuff and hung it from a pole. They inserted a line directly into your chest, and the white stuff ran down the tube and fed you through there. He didn't want that. He tried to imagine eating without tasting or smelling, without using his mouth or nose at all.

He wanted to talk to Ann about Hospice, but he didn't know how to bring up the subject. Ever since she was a little girl, he'd always hated disappointing her. The look on her face broke him every time.

The wind picked up. Cassie's painting rattled against the wall. He thought he saw movement inside the bower, something coming out to the stream to drink, or going back into the shadows to hide. But the painting was shaking, the wind trying to lift it off the wall, so possibly that was all.

He could hear the trees outside creaking and bending, the branches shaking, the sharp crackle of dead leaves as more began to fall. The yard must have been swimming with them. Both the open and the closed windows were clattering within their frames.

He began to smell the corruption. He was sure it wasn't him. He'd worried a great deal about his personal hygiene during his illness, whether they could help him stay clean enough so he wouldn't stink. He didn't want his grandkids to remember him as a smelly old man. He didn't know exactly what the odour was but it wasn't any smell he knew a human body made. The stench was somewhere outside the window.

He heard them moving through the leaves. He thought he might have been hearing them for several minutes but he'd been focused on the wind and Cassie's painting. He had no idea how many of them there were. The crunching leaves made it sound like an army.

Guy couldn't understand why they were so impatient. Perhaps he wasn't meant to understand. But they could have waited until he stopped breathing. Maybe people who were dying gave off a particular scent or emanation that drew them. Maybe they couldn't help themselves. That was what he wondered when he first saw one, the one bony shoulder and the side of its pale unformed face in the open window a few weeks ago.

He'd had a suspicion, so he asked Tony to read to him from a couple of books in his lawyer's bookcases. They would be Tony's eventually, along with everything else in the cramped office space which had been his retreat for decades. He'd made that clear to Ann even though she struggled as much as possible not to talk to him about the *after*. "He can use some of the supplies at the university, and maybe later he'll want to dig into my library, maybe even build one of his own," he'd told her. "I know he likes to read. He's a smart kid. I'm proud of him, tell him that. Tell him he can have anything in my office he wants. It's all his."

Tony was not the most patient lad, but he seemed to enjoy reading to Guy. He'd read well, with no stumbles. "From Arabic mythology. Ghoul or Ghul. Ghouls feed on human flesh, drink blood, rob graves, prey on corpses, etc. It also refers to a person who revels in the loathsome and revolting. I think I know some people like that."

"I think we all do. What does the other book say?"

"There are some pictures, but they're all over the place in terms of conception and approach. Your basic hideous creature, I guess, whatever that means to you."

"That's okay. I can use my imagination. Anything else?"

"Um. Drinks blood, we already knew that. Steals coins. Wait. 'Shape-shifts into an ostrich'."

"You're making that up!"

"No Grandad – it's right here." He started to hand over the book.

"I'll take your word for it. I'm not seeing that well these days. Go on."

Tony skimmed the page with his finger. "Sometimes preys on lonely travellers or children."

"What does it say about that?"

"That's all. It's the last line of the article. Maybe if it can't find a corpse it eats whatever's handy. If you like I can see if I can find out more on the internet. Why are you interested in this Dungeons and Dragons stuff anyway?"

"I remember hearing the word, and Halloween's coming up. Have you picked out a costume yet? You could go as a ghoul or whatever."

"Grandad, the last time I dressed up for Halloween I was twelve, and even then I was embarrassed."

Guy remembered smiling at that bright and lovely boy. There was probably nothing to worry about. When the body was stuck in bed the mind had nothing better to do than to imagine the worst things possible. In any case, that was folklore. Even if he had seen something to worry about, the reality was likely far different than the human interpretation.

He heard scrambling on the brick outside. He began sweating profusely. He was being ridiculous. He knew prolonged bed rest sometimes resulted in psychological stresses besides the usual physical complications. Decreased concentration, orientation, and intellectual skills. Anxiety, depression, irritability – he'd experienced all those. Occasional hallucinations.

Then there was the smell again, originating from some rotten mouth, a corrupted gut. He hated to think Cassie might have experienced any of this during her final days. With all his being he hoped not. She'd been unconscious most of her last two weeks. Of course, he didn't know what she'd dreamed about during that time. He liked to think it was of a peaceful afternoon under the trees beside a stream, with nothing hiding in the shadows except more green.

The light went out. Had Ann come up and flipped the switch? Had he dozed off? He listened for footsteps on the stairs but heard none. From the spirited sounds of the wind, possibly they'd lost power. He wondered if she would try to check on him.

A shush of sound, and maybe something sliding over the windowsill. He felt an anxious itching in his extremities with no apparent location, a vague sort of nibbling.

A scramble and a crawl and he thought he would scream. He stared at the foot of the bed. The painting hanging above was swallowed in shadow. He had no taste for this. He wasn't cut out for it.

They stood up with all their blank faces, hairless bodies emaciated and vaguely doglike, their long fingers ending in sizable claws. He listened again for footsteps on the stairs and hoped not to hear them. He needed his family most of all to stay away.

For a moment his brain skipped, and he was back in the hospital bed with no appetite left for anything, the doctors towering above him, discussing his case as if he weren't there. He'd wanted to shout and tell them he could hear every word.

Then back in his own bed, in the lighthouse at the top of his world, the blank faces looming closer, then as if to tease him, the faces becoming his own, except with the hunger returned.

"Just do it!" he shouted. "Do your damn job!"

And they did.

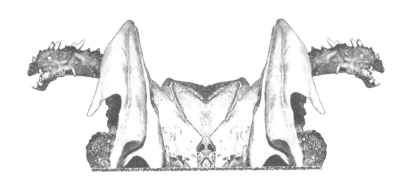

SONGS IN THE DARK

Jenny Barber

My father never approved of Pedrick. Not because of Pedrick's free trading, never that. The island is too small a place to have concerns about any bounty wrought from the sea, and Pedrick is one of our most successful traders. So successful, in fact, that most suspect he has the favour of a mermaid.

When asked, Pedrick admits to nothing save being blessed with the luck of the sea and fair friends in foreign ports, and from there he swiftly falls into a story of a close call with a Revenue ship, or the follies of the harbourmaster in St Peter Port.

Pedrick charmed me with stories of his travels, and showered me with many beautiful gifts – lace from Spain, silk from France, a porcelain dinner set from far-off China, and eventually there was a ring, and permission asked and grudgingly given. And now we are married, and in his delight at finally winning me he has brought me to this place. Here to see the caves in which he stores his treasures, far from the roving eyes of the visiting Revenue agents. Here, where he can plan new ventures away from those who might steal his glory. Here, where *she* lives.

Her name is Meliora, he says. He won't say how he won her favour, only that she is a helpful transporter of the treasures he has built his fortune on and here is where she calls home.

He rows us into a hidden sea cave tucked into the north shore cliffs and ties his boat next to a rock ledge, and there, with a gentlemanly offer of an arm, we begin the tour of his empire. We follow the narrow ledge around a twist of rock where it accompanies the sea channel down a sloping tunnel and brings us to the main storage cave. As the water joins a large pool in the centre of the cave, the ledge climbs and joins a raised stony shore that brackets the sides of the pool. Many boxes and barrels are stacked high along the rock, a damp tideline showing how close the water creeps at high tide.

"Mermaid magic keeps the water from my stores," he tells me with a careless shrug, as if such things are commonplace.

Higher still are baskets and bags crammed tight into the niches that pock the walls, but while his storehouse is interesting enough it is the markings inscribed on the walls that catch my attention. Constellations of spirals and circles and crescent moons are scratched in scattered clusters around the cave while long lines of deeply carved runes, bordered with twisting serpents, stretch high and low. I have often wondered at similar designs on the standing stones and ancient barrows that dot the island, but have never taken the time to learn their secrets from the wise women who know such things – something I now regret given the abundance of sigils inscribed here.

"There have been mermaids in this cave for centuries," Pedrick says. "Though my Meliora will not tell me if she was one of them, or even how old a mermaid gets."

I shutter away the brief wave of jealousy when he calls her his, then recall that I am the one he is wed to, and with more confidence demand to meet her.

He takes me deeper into the cave, following the path of another sea channel that leads from the pool into more tunnels, with only narrow strips of uneven rock to tread on. This is, undisputedly, mermaid territory – the water not wide enough for a boat to paddle through, the rock not wide enough to comfortably walk without clinging determinedly to the wall, and each small cave we pass through is filled with pools and branching streams that lead deeper into the dark. I know not how long we pick our way over such an unfriendly path, but feel a sense of relief when we finally arrive at the last cave. *Her* cave –

where rags and rubbish fill the hollows and only a few small rocks here and there give solace from the treacle-dark water that otherwise fills the entire space.

The water looks cold and unfriendly, fit for drowning the unwary, and as I watch something glitters in the water. With hardly a sound she breaks the surface to greet us.

"Who have you brought me?" the mermaid asks. She is pale as a wraith, with a mass of lanky seaweed-like hair draped down her head, and scales that glint silvery in the lantern light. As she floats in front of us there seems to be something of the snake about her movements. I glimpse curved fangs in her mouth, and I wonder if they are as small as they look or if, like the cobra, their true size will only be revealed when she opens her jaws wide enough to feed.

And I wonder how Pedrick can stand to do business with such a thing as her.

"This is Elowen," Pedrick says. "She is dear to me and I would have you two be friends. Elowen this is Meliora, a veritable goddess of the sea."

"I am no goddess," Meliora says. "I would never dare such arrogance. Welcome Elowen. I trust we can be as bosom companions as are my darling Pedrick and I."

"I hope so too," I say, "for a wife must be on good terms with her husband's friends."

"Ha, I am no wife." Her low savage laugh echoes around the cave and has me cringing as it whispers to the primitive animal within me that here is danger. Had I looked at Pedrick then I might have seen some sign on his face that would inspire me to caution, but jealousy returns to my heart and I speak firmly to assert my claim. "*I* am his wife," I tell the mermaid. "Newlywed this Sunday past." And with those words, surely doom us.

She stills her movements, eyes wide and black. "Are you—?"

"I was going to mention—" Pedrick starts.

She turns to him with a low hiss. "You were going to mention— Are your promises of love and undying devotion as fleeting as your stamina? How long?"

"How long what?" Pedrick asks.

"How long have you courted this human's affections. How

long have you been whispering sweet words to me while chasing another?"

"I..." he says, mouth gaping.

"Had you asked," she continues, "I would have shared our pleasures with this one. Instead, you broke your vow to me."

His face then, the terror, the contortions wrought from trying to think of an acceptable excuse, tells me more than whatever hastily spoken words he might have managed.

"Pedrick—" I begin.

"We should go," he says, pulling me away. All I can think of is how much water lies between us and where our dinghy waits – and how fast sea folk are said to travel.

She screams then, a long howl that reverberates around the cave and ices my blood and mind alike. I cannot move nor speak, can only watch as she lunges towards me, an act of seconds drawn out to hours, and I am pulled firmly, relentlessly, off the rock and under the water with her.

There is dark. There is cold. There is the cloying deep salt taste of water sucked into my lungs, and a burning in my throat as my scream is drowned before it can begin. And there is music: many voices woven in eerie concert, melodies intertwined into something transcendent, with words that dance on the edge of perception, their meaning just out of reach.

From somewhere distant I feel a sharp pain. From somewhere distant there is fear – impatience, longing – and a need to sink deeper into the song. And then I am hauled from the water and time restarts.

Pedrick babbles non-stop, his words as out of reach as the sea song was. In haste he pulls me down the tunnel but my wet skirts tangle my legs and I tumble into the water, only to be dragged out again by Pedrick, who grumbles and swears in constant litany. He digs his fingers hard into my arm and pulls again, and still we run, and still I stumble and slip, and am dragged back to rock again, over and over, through tunnel and cave and tunnel and cave, until we reach the large pooled cavern that lies between us and our escape.

It is then, of course, she strikes again.

First there is a deep base hum that vibrates through my very bones, then it swells into an aria that is louder, higher, harsher, hammering my ears with a great and terrifying noise that cannot be muffled.

Around us boxes and barrels shake free from their stacks, crashing to the floor with such force that wood breaks and lids leap free of their fastenings, spilling pungent brandy and dark tealeaves across the floor.

And the walls – the walls spit stones at us, the floor judders until we fall, our attempts to stand thwarted by the tipping and tilting that catch us always at just the wrong moment.

There is a deep and implacable roar, and the rock walls to either side of the narrow passageway that is our escape close in, merging together until all ahead is solid stone. All save the smallest crack high above where we cannot reach.

Her voice whispers through the crack. "You can have eternity together." And then it is gone and we are left in silence.

Pedrick calls out for Meliora, apologising, making bargains, cursing. As his voice grows hoarse he stomps around the cave holding up the flickering lantern to every piece of wall, searching for a flaw, a larger crack, any unnoticed way out, but none are to be found.

I dare not move much, save to make use of the light that reflects from the lantern to inventory the crates we are trapped with. There are boxes of tobacco and tea, salt and silk, fine porcelain that match in pattern the dinnerware he had gifted me, though none of these will be much use to us now. There are casks of brandy that have survived the shaking intact, which will give us something to drink that isn't sea water. And there are fish and crabs in the pool so we will not be short of food for a time.

While Pedrick rages and storms from cave to cave I huddle near the small fire we made from broken boxes and packing straw, shivering in my under-things as I wait for my clothes to dry. And as I wait I try to recall all that I know of mermaids, their delights and their dangers, their curses and their blessings, and their charms that can go either way. And songs, always their songs.

I begin to sing. At first soft and then, for wont of anything more useful to do, I sing louder, perhaps hoping to get the mermaid's attention, wherever she swims beyond the walls of our prison. I sing the shanties my father and his workmates sing on the boats. I sing the lullabies the women croon as they put the babes to sleep. I sing the hymns carried over from the mainland by those who have fallen under the spell of the priestly folk.

I sing, and at some point I think I hear a voice outside the cave join me in chorus, but I dare not stop, not until my voice dries up and the air grows so muggy that I drift and sleep, and when I wake the fire has gone out and it is full dark.

~~~

Always dark, and even now I am not sure how long we have been here.

There's a grumble of a snore from not far distant and I call my husband's name. He sleeps on oblivious to our plight, and perhaps that is best for now. The lantern is out of oil and no use to me. I try to rekindle the fire but Pedrick's tinder is ruined now by sea water.

All I have left is to sit in the dark, and wait. Soon there is a soft melody carrying through a crack in the wall. I close my eyes and I listen to the haunting song. There is something in it that speaks of freedom and swimming in the moonlight. It summons a deep longing in me. I clench my fist and feel sharp nails digging into my palm. Nails longer than they should be. Could I have been here that long? Foolishness. All things seem more in the dark.

The water in the pool makes only the slightest of shushes as water rolls across the edges of the surrounding rock. No doubt the fish discovering that they too are prisoners of the cave. Hunger aches in my stomach. With no fire left to us, what food we can claim from the pool must be eaten raw and I'm not that desperate yet. But soon – soon.

I feel so wretched. There's a throbbing at the base of my neck – and an incessant itch on my arm from an injury that I cannot recall. Everything has been such a blur since the mermaid's scream that I have the overwhelming notion this is all happening to someone else. Yet I can feel the hardness of scabs forming on my wound, overlapping like scales with sharp edges that nip at the softer skin of my fingertip when I rub them back and forth.

I should feel afraid. I should feel angry. I should feel …

something, but as the music rises around me all I feel is calm acceptance, as if this is where I have always meant to be. The water calls to me, inviting me into its embrace, and I cannot help but crawl towards it, seeking, perhaps, to touch the life within. But once I reach the water, reach down into it, all there is ... is water, cold as winter to my touch.

The singing becomes louder and closer, as if emanating from the pool itself. I reach again to the water, stretching down deeper until the wound on my arm is submerged. It's oddly soothing and the crawling itch in my skin is gone, so there I stay until it becomes too awkward and I must take out my arm and settle into a more comfortable position.

The music shifts into a lullaby that cushions my descent into sleep and when I dream it is of a brighter, more welcoming cave, its resident mermaid swimming peacefully in the pool, no sign of anger or malice – or anything else to be concerned about.

The cave becomes brighter and in the light she is not so frightening, her skin pearlescent and speckled with glinting flecks of silver that blend into the sparkling scales that cover the curves of her body. Her hair now shines a deep obsidian, far from the seaweed I first thought it was. Her eyes contain the universe. Now I can see why he would turn to her. Now I can only wonder why he would need to marry a mere human when he could have a goddess such as she. She beckons me into the pool and I, without fear of retribution, go to her, sinking into water warm as a summer's sea. We float there, she and I, and the air is filled with a new music that hints of secrets and promises wondrous things.

She approaches, her mouth on my neck, kissing gently, briefly, then with a savage strike she sinks her long-curved fangs into me. She suckles at my throat, catching stray drips of my blood with her darting tongue. This is when I know that my life is in the most danger, and yet instead of pain and terror there is pleasure, and peace, and rightness.

In her arms I drift for a time, her tail tangled around my legs, her talons trailing against my skin in unreadable patterns. She softly croons in my ear, and by and by the music dims and with it the light. And so I wake. Alone. In the dark.

No, not alone. Not quite. Pedrick still snorts and snores, and in his restless sleep knocks an empty bottle across the rock floor with a sharp clink that jars me out of my daze.

I rub my arm, feel an ache that throbs like a heartbeat under rough scaly skin. The cave is hot, too hot now that it is shut off from the sea air, and it takes but a moment to peel off the last of my clothes. But still it is not enough and I am reaching for the water again. The chill that had so shocked me earlier is no more, and while not warm the water is cool and pleasant and a most welcome thing.

I slip into the pool, sink down slowly until all but my head is submerged. I can feel the movements of fish flitting hither and yon around me but none brush close enough for me to grab. A pity, as hunger has taken firm possession of my belly – and I crave fresh meat.

I swim to the centre of the pool, then on impulse I dive deep and reach out to the shapes that move near. I manage to catch one, spear my nails in it, holding firm against the squirming fish, and before it can escape I take a bite through scale and flesh. I do not wonder at the ease with which my teeth tear my prey, nor the satisfaction at the taste of this uncooked meal, only accept that this is as it should be. The meat ignites a wild hunger inside me, and one bite becomes two and three and more, until what little is left of the fish is distasteful bone and quickly discarded.

I remain in the water, floating, feeling safe and at home, and there I stay until Pedrick wakes. He calls for me, of course, in a voice that jangles my nerves and sparks brittle irritation in me. When I tell him I'm in the water he demands I leave it so we can work on a new escape plan, or perhaps just so he can have the benefit of close human comfort.

I hesitate, tempted to stay where I am, but the echoes of a good wife's obedience still have their hold over me and so I comply, finding my clothes in the dark and dressing silently, my movements automatic. But oh how I resent him for it. The ground is hard and coarse, the air stifling, and the water is, by far, the better option.

It's not long before he's shouting again, first calling for Meliora, then for help from some unknown other; but these caves were chosen for their isolation from the homes scattered on this side of the island, and that is not going to change just because he wishes it. When his rage subsides into sullenness he talks low and long with promises of rescuing us both, of revenge against the mermaid, of moving to the mainland, of a big house far from the sea. These promises are not nearly as appealing as he seems to think they are, so while I make such small noises of agreement as are appropriate, I volunteer no further words and by and by his voice fades to a trickle, then halts altogether.

The silence is a balm, and relief settles in me until I hear water falling from above. First in rhythmic belches, then a steady surge, as a small waterfall runs down the wall and pours into the pool bringing the scent of fresh saltwater with it. A high tide, I think, and wonder how many high tides it would take for the pool to escape its constraints and the cave be filled to the brim, and if we will starve before we drown. I think back to my underwater hunting and the sweet taste of blood and flesh in my mouth. No, I will not starve, not so long as there are fish to be had. Pedrick will not be so lucky, I think.

When my husband's silence shifts once more to the grunts and grumbles of sleep I slip back to the water, to swim and to feed, then to float without care. After a time the music returns and a dim light glows from within the water pouring through the crack. I think I hear a solid splosh, as of someone diving into the pool, but Pedrick still sleeps and I cannot sense anything larger than fish in the water. My heart sinks, I had hoped perhaps… But no, *she* swims in other waters and I am still alone with him, and anything else is but some strange dream brought on by too much brandy.

I close my eyes and let the dream take me away to better places, places filled with moonlight and freedom, of swimming the wider ocean, with Meliora at my side. We hunt fish, great and small, chasing the boats on their early morning search for the day's catch; and when all is done we return to our cave, one that is ours alone and not some smuggler's storehouse, and there we play in the pools and sort through our treasures.

I wake to Pedrick calling my name. I peer through the twilight gloom of the cave to see his dim shape fumbling along the wall and stumble towards the boxes and more of the brandy.

"Elowen!" he calls.

"Swimming," I say lazily. "Floating nicely, thank you."

"The water's freezing," he says.

"The water's lovely," I respond. "You should try it."

"Come out of the water, Elowen," he says. He is still feeling his way around the crates until he finds one with bottles still left inside.

"I am perfectly fine," I say, paddling further away from him.

"Do as I ask woman," he snaps, "you're not in your right mind. Get out of the water, right now."

"I'm perfectly fine," I repeat.

He lurches towards my voice and trips over shattered wood, falling to his knees on the floor. I float in silence, waiting to see what he will do. He's close enough to the edge of the pool that he could tumble into the water easily but despite my invitation to join me, the prospect of his invading my new world is not one that fills me with pleasure.

But no, when his scrabbling brings him to the edge he ignores the water in favour of sitting, feeling around him until he grasps a rolling brandy bottle and stashes it in his shirt. He then shuffles slowly backwards until he finds the wall and pulls himself upright. With one hand on the wall he guides himself back to his nest.

"Come out of the water, Elowen." He sounds tired now, his head turning this way and that as he searches for me. "Follow my voice. There's no shame in being lost in the dark."

"I'm not lost," I say, and his head snaps in my direction. His eyes, I realise, haven't adjusted as have mine.

"You're something..." he mutters, then louder, "this isn't proper wifely behaviour. Attend to me and perhaps we may yet find our escape..."

I remain silent, floating on my back allowing the air to pebble my skin. Then I roll and dive under the water, cutting off Pedrick's latest demands. While he no doubt babbles on I swim in the pool until I chance on an exit well beneath the surface. I follow the tunnels and caves towards Meliora's pool and there I spend a pleasurable amount of time investigating the treasures she hoards.

Had I thought them rags and rubbish when first I saw them? A folly of the poor light and the distraction of a mermaid, no doubt, for closer examination reveals better their quality. The clothes she has collected are nearly new with only a few rips here and there to mar their perfection, and no signs of suffering from the damp climate of the cave. The silk smooth as when it had first been cut from cloth, the buttons an adventure in shape and texture, and the colours – not so well seen in the dimness but I have no doubt they too are not faded.

There is a niche full of glassware – bottles of thick glass and thin, some curving sensuously, others as solid and straight as a parson. There is a recess in the wall so full of jewellery that I can sink my arm down to the shoulder and still not reach the end, the gems cold, the metal colder, but not unpleasant to my skin. There are shells and rippled stones and what could be bones. I feel the edge of a blade and knock metal into metal with a harsh clatter as I discover a cache of tools stolen from a fisherman, if I judge the shapes right. It is a hoard full of endless sensation and my fascination is unending.

I return to the water – it is warmer here, by far, than the pool in the cave where Pedrick still surely grumbles. I gain a new appreciation for Meliora's choice of home. It won't hurt to stay here a while longer, floating; avoiding my husband's company is something with much appeal.

I try humming a run of notes, then a few lines of some nonsense verse, and can't help a giggle of delight at the sound as it bounces off the walls. Not quite a mermaid's song but not bad. Not bad at all. As if in reply, a true mermaid song finds its way through the tunnels to this sanctuary, and I hum along in harmony, drifting in the water, blissful and at rest.

Whether I sleep or not is difficult to tell as what dreams I have are now filled with naught but a growing hunger, yet I cannot find fish in this pool and so must return to the main cave, where Pedrick waits for me, to hunt.

I swim, and the water is as clear as if lit by a hundred lanterns. I dive and chase fish, not quite their match in speed or agility, so I turn to cunning and sink to the bottom of the pool, my long strong nails digging into the ground to keep me down, and I wait. I wait as curious crabs scuttle near me but their shells do not appeal so they are allowed to go on their way. Then the fish come dancing around me in jerking movements as they test the water for danger. I am patient despite the hunger burning inside me. When one is close enough I grab it and eat, and catch another and eat, greedy and relentless in my frenzy – but still they are not enough. I need more than fish.

I start to rise and the sound of choral song thunders and thrums along with the blood in my veins, pulling me to the surface, and onwards to the rocky shore where a bigger meal waits. I leave the water and crawl quietly and quickly over the hard cruel stone towards him, my mouth wide, my teeth long and sharp. Pedrick turns in his sleep, his neck bared, his heartbeat loud and inviting.

Mine.

I lunge. I bite. I tear chunks of flesh from my prey, my new talons ripping away his useless clothes so I can reach the softer meat. If he wakes, if he fights, if he makes any noise, it is not for long, and I am by far the faster, the stronger, the better. I eat and finally, when I've eaten my fill, I return to the water and float and doze.

As I doze I hear a distant song, growing louder and louder, harmonising with the rumble of rock that moves, as the crack in the wall widens, letting the sea pour in. The water in the pool rises higher and higher, drowning body and boxes and barrels alike.

"Come, sister," Meliora sings, "it's time to swim."

And through the opened wall I swim, out into the wider sea to hunt, a new tail thrashing behind me.

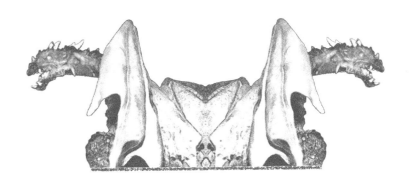

THE BEAST OF BATHWICK

Sarah Ash

"One and two and—" Gwendolen Beattie tapped the side of the upright piano, whispering the beats as eight-year-old Susan Jermyn fumbled her way through Ernest Newton's *The Woodpecker's Dance*, the jaunty rhythm mangled and lumpy when it should be light and playful. The child's jaw was clenched tight, Gwen observed, as she struggled on, getting slower and slower. Susan eventually reached the end and Gwen noted the girl's stiffened shoulders and tense posture as she scowled down at the keyboard.

"It's coming along nicely," she said encouragingly. "But you still need to work at the left- and right-hand parts separately. Here—" She leaned forward to circle one problematic bar in the bass stave. "And here." Susan heaved a sigh and glanced up at the clock on the mantelpiece, obviously longing for the lesson to be over.

The door creaked open and a sleek black shadow slipped into the room. Susan's shoulders relaxed as she stretched out one hand to the cat. "Balthazar!"

"Who said you could come in?" Gwen rose to scoop up the cat but Susan was already on her knees on the fireside rug, stroking him; and proud Balthazar was allowing her to pet him. *I could have sworn I closed the door. How did he manage to open it? Ah well…*

The sound of purring filled the room.

Gwen sighed and sat down to finish writing her instructions in the girl's notebook for the next week's practice. *Susan's mother will be here any minute now and the child's too distracted to concentrate any longer. Besides, I need time to get ready for the auditions tonight.*

There was a ring at the doorbell. "Someone at the door!" shrilled Gwen's mother from the dining room even as Gwen hurried out into the hall.

"On my way," she called back, opening to see Susan's mother on the top step, holding out a folded copy of the *Bath Evening Chronicle*.

"I coincided with your paper boy. I couldn't help looking at tonight's headline," Mrs Jermyn said, wiping her feet on the mat as Gwen stood aside to let her in. "Gave me the shivers! Have you seen the photo, Miss Beattie?"

Gwen opened the newspaper and read *Beast of Bathwick Strikes Again!* Beneath was a very indistinct photograph with twin pinpricks of light that might have been eyes glinting in the darkness – but could also have been car headlamps penetrating a thickly swirling fog. "It must be a hoax."

"The police say that's the third sighting this week," continued Mrs Jermyn. "It might be a panther – or even a puma."

"In Bath?" Gwen was sceptical. "The nearest zoo's in Bristol, up on the Downs over a dozen miles away. If a wild cat had escaped, surely they'd have caught it by now."

"That poor motorist – he swerved to miss it and drove into a ditch. Could have been killed."

"Mummy, you're late." Susan appeared, cramming her notebook into her music case.

"Remember Susan, twenty minutes' practise every day and…" Gwen's instructions faded to silence as mother and daughter retreated into the damp twilight.

"Has the *Chronicle* come yet, Gwen?" Mother sounded more fractious than before. It must be time to make the tea. "That paper boy's getting later and later."

Gwen checked her watch, making sure she had left herself enough time to get ready. Tonight was audition night!

The Woodpecker's Dance had been endlessly playing in her head since Susan's lesson but as Gwen changed out of her teaching attire another tune slid in to replace it. A lilting, lyrical waltz, one of Sir Arthur Sullivan's finest: the soprano audition piece for tonight. She hummed the melody to herself as she opened the jewellery box and took out her grandmother's black Art Deco enamel brooch, fashioned like a sleek panther with diamante eyes. "My lucky brooch," she murmured as she pinned it to the blouse, because it always seemed to bring her the roles she wanted when she wore it. She didn't really believe in such superstitions but her brief heady experience of backstage life in a London show had rubbed off just a little before Father's sudden death had shattered her dreams of a career onstage.

The doorbell chimed. It must be Ken come to pick her up. Gwen grabbed her coat from the stand, pausing to peer at her dim reflection in the hall mirror, checking her lipstick was not smudged. "I'm just off out, Mother," Gwen called, hastily buttoning her coat, knotting the cashmere scarf around her throat to keep out the damp of the misty evening – so bad for a singer's vocal cords, as her college singing teacher used to tell her.

As she opened the front door, something silkily furry wound itself around her ankles. She nearly tripped, clutching at the door frame to steady herself.

"Steady on, Gwen." Ken grinned at her as Balthazar shot out and down the steps, disappearing into the darkness.

"That cat—" Gwen recovered and closed the door behind her. Now Balthazar was out he'd have to stay out until she returned. Mother would not remember to let him in, no matter how loudly he mewed.

Ken held open the passenger door for Gwen then walked around to sit beside her at the wheel. As he revved the engine, Gwen looked up and down the road for a glimpse of Balthazar and just for a moment she thought she saw the cat. But surely it was far too large to be Balthazar; and then it had vanished into the dark.

"Don't worry about Balthazar," Ken said as he pulled out and headed toward the main road. "He'll be back when he wants his supper."

"Yes, he does like his food." Gwen thought of Balthazar's

piteous mewing that would be heard halfway along the road when he returned home, demanding to be let in. Heard by everyone except Mother.

"He's grown so much. What've you been feeding him?"

"It seems only yesterday he was a tiny kitten." Gwen smiled, remembering bringing Balthazar home in a wicker cat carrier, not sure whether she'd adopted him to keep Mother company, or herself.

The little green Austin A30 was a snug fit for two people and as Ken changed down a gear to cope with the steepness of the hill, his hand brushed against her knee. She felt her face grow warm and hoped that he couldn't see her blushing. He was, after all, a happily married man. Gwen and Ken had been friends for a dozen years, meeting as junior church choristers before the war and still singing together five years since it had ended.

Ken was that rare treasure in amateur music groups: a true tenor. Like Gwen, he made up for what he lacked in physical stature in the power and timbre of his voice. Unlike Gwen, he hadn't left Bath to go to music college in London, working instead as a draughtsman for the Admiralty – where he'd met Lynne, his wife. Who didn't sing.

"So, we're doing *Ruddigore*, this year? The one with Sir Ruthven Murgatroyd?" Ken pronounced the title with a dramatic roll of the "r's" like a pantomime villain and making Gwen laugh. He always had the ability to lighten her mood. "It's an unusual choice, straight out of a silent movie, isn't it? Bad baronets, ghostly ancestors and an evil curse. No wonder it isn't often performed."

"And a chorus of professional bridesmaids." Gwen stared out of the window as they drove through Combe Down. She felt pangs of sadness as she recognised something of that perpetual bridesmaid in herself.

"If I get the tenor lead – the dashing sailor Richard Dauntless – I don't end up with the soprano at the end," Ken said. "Rose Maybud marries the bad baronet instead."

"WS Gilbert's satirical sense of humour again, I suppose?" Gwen said.

"And you'll be playing Rose."

Gwen turned to him in surprise. "I can't assume I'll get the role, Ken."

"But you're the best light soprano in the company."

Gwen laughed the compliment aside but she felt herself blush again, with pleasure this time. "*Others* are auditioning."

"Who? Not Myrna Barclay, surely?" Ken quirked one eyebrow. "Isn't she a little—" and he hesitated "—mature for Rose Maybud?"

Before Gwen's return to Bath, Myrna had been the soprano lead in the society, taking the main roles in *Iolanthe*, *The Yeomen of the Guard*, *The Pirates of Penzance*... But in spite of her glamorous frocks and immaculate appearance, Myrna was no longer a young woman and her voice was becoming noticeably more suited to mezzo roles, whereas Gwen's light soprano navigated the highest notes effortlessly.

They pulled into the carpark of the senior school where the cast met to rehearse in the main hall. A faint misty drizzle hung in the air. Gwen stumbled getting out the car – and Ken caught her arm, righting her.

"Sorry. I missed my footing." She glanced up, grateful for his attentiveness. It would not have done to turn up at the audition mud-splattered and with laddered stockings.

"Careful how you go – there are too many potholes. It's hard to see them." He let go of her, locking the car. "Do you want to take my arm?"

"Oh, I'll be fine." Gwen was relieved for once that the car park was so ill-lit, that the darkness hid her third blush of the evening, embarrassed to be so clumsy.

~~~

"*If somebody there chanced to be who loved me in a manner true,*" Gwen sang, her voice floating out light and clear in the school hall. "*My heart would point him out to me, and I would point him out to you.*"

She had been nervous when Hugh, the accompanist, struck up the introduction but the instant she opened her mouth she remembered how much she loved to sing – and how well this charming waltz melody suited her vocal range. She could not make out the faces or expressions of the rest of the society members listening at the back of the hall. She was already immersed in the role of Rose Maybud, the sweet seventeen-year-old heroine. When she finished she was greeted with enthusiastic applause and she instinctively acknowledged it with a bow, one hand resting on the piano – before mouthing, "Thank you" to Hugh and going to the back of the hall as the next hopeful went up on the little stage.

"Well done." Ken gave her the thumbs up. She nodded, still caught up in the warmth of the reception, as the piano began again.

When she first joined the society, she had been alarmed by their practice of holding open auditions – open in the sense that everyone listened. "You'll all have to sing in front of each other on stage anyway," Jim Herbert, the music director, had explained to them, "so why not start as we mean to go on? That'll dispel any early butterflies in the stomach and get you all used to performing together."

~~~

Gwen went to fetch her camel coat from the little cloakroom and was hurrying out again when her way was barred by Myrna Barclay. "You're a sly one, Gwendolen Beattie." Myrna smiled with crimson-slicked lips but her eyes were cold and accusing. "It's always the quiet girls, the 'nice' girls... Who'd have thought it?"

"Thought what?" Gwen had no idea what Myrna was implying but she instinctively took a step back.

"You and Ken. I saw you in the car park." Myrna advanced, still smiling. Her heels clacked on the tiled floor. "Did you think because it was dark that no one would see?"

"I— I don't know what you're—" And then Gwen realised. Myrna must have witnessed that purely innocent gesture, Ken helping her out of the car, her losing her balance, him steadying her, the two of them laughing embarrassedly. "That? I tripped and almost fell and Ken was only—"

"Did you know that Lynne and I are friends? We went to the High School together. Such a sweet soul. She'd be heartbroken if she knew what was going on."

Gwen shook her head, wanting Myrna to stop with her

hurtful insinuations. "You've got it all wrong. Ken and I are old friends too. There's nothing between us. Nothing—"

"And yet he always brings you here, you always go home together. A married man?"

"He gives me lifts because he only lives a few streets away. I don't have a car."

"Couldn't you ask Wendy? She lives much closer to you than Ken." Myrna took another step closer, almost pinning Gwen against the cloakroom wall. "Here's what we'll do. I'll forget what I saw in the car park and you will withdraw your name from the contenders for the role of Rose."

"Th— That's blackmail." Gwen heard her own voice as if from far away.

Myrna shrugged. "Your choice. You know how people blab in tightly knit little societies like ours. Once word got out…" She stood aside to let Gwen pass. "Well then, Jim's still in the hall. Off you go."

~~~

Most of the society members had already left and Hugh was turning off lights as Gwen re-entered the hall. Aware that Myrna was watching her from the doorway, her arms crossed, Gwen hurried over to Jim Herbert who was still seated, pencil in hand, re-reading his notes.

"Jim – can I have a word?"

He looked up and smiled at her over the rim of his tortoiseshell-rimmed glasses. "Lovely audition, Gwen. One of your best."

"Thank you." Gwen swallowed hard. "It's – it's just – I've had second thoughts. About taking on such a big role. It's Mother." She heard herself weaving excuse after excuse. *Perhaps I'm not such a bad actress after all.* "She's becoming more … confused. I don't like to leave her alone for too long." It wasn't entirely a lie. "And with all the extra rehearsals involved for the leads…"

"I'm so sorry to hear that. You're my first choice for Rose."

She forced a smile. "I'd had loved to play her. Perhaps another time."

He leaned forward over his notebook, hesitated a moment, then crossed out her name.

An autumn fog had settled over the city and the headlights of the little Austin barely penetrated the thickest swirls. Even when they reached the top of the hill, wisps of mist still wreathed across the road.

"What did Jim want?" Ken asked after a while.

"I'm sorry I made you wait after the others had left. Were you planning on going to the pub?" Gwen tried to change the subject. Myrna's threat still lingered in her mind, tainting her every thought even though by the time she left the hall Myrna was nowhere to be seen.

"Not tonight. I've an early start tomorrow. Some bigwigs down from London."

They reached the top of the hill and turned onto the stretch of road where there were no streetlights and he flicked the headlamps to full beam. Gwen peered out at the misty darkness, the indistinct shadow-forms of tree branches overhanging their way. Amongst them the outline of the derelict Claverton Farm came and went.

She remembered that the paper said this was where the Beast of Bathwick had last been seen. *So when did Claverton Down become Bathwick?* she wondered.

~~~

It roams through the night, padding on silent paws through the bracken. Lights pierce the misty darkness, accompanied by the unfamiliar roar of engines. Humans in their noisy vehicles crossing the open hilltop on a wide roadway. This is its territory. They have no business here disturbing its nocturnal hunting, scaring away the rabbits, hares and deer.

Prey. My prey.

~~~

"Isn't this where your Balthazar was found?"

Gwen started. She'd been going over in her mind what had happened earlier – wondering if there could have been any way to stand up to Myrna, and failing – when her thoughts drifted. *I'm such a pushover.* She peered out at the road and recognized their surroundings as Ken slowed down to turn right off Claverton Down Road. Streetlamps appeared once more through the drifts of mist.

"Why, yes. He was heard mewing, poor little mite, in the barns back there. He must have wandered away from his mother and got lost. He was taken to the Cats and Dogs Home and that's where I first met him. He was such a tiny little scrap of a kitten, half-starved. You wouldn't know it to look at him now."

"Is that why he's always hungry? He's a real fatty now. Are you sure he isn't visiting the neighbours for extra dinners?" Ken asked as he turned into Gwen's road and pulled up outside her house.

"I wouldn't be surprised."

"Same time next week?" he called as she closed the car door.

She nodded – "Same time" – and waved as he drove away. But all the joy and anticipation had drained out of her. When she had left the house earlier that evening she was full of dreams and hopes for the new production. Myrna had shattered every one of them.

She felt something caress her legs and looked down to see Balthazar weaving around her.

~~~

Gwen shut her bedroom door, sank down on her rose-pink candlewick bedspread and sobbed. She'd not cried in a long, long time. Since Father died and she came back home to look after Mother there had been no time for tears. She'd just had to get on with her new life and forget the disappointments.

Mother was listening to some variety show on the Light Programme. Raucous laughter and applause issued from her mother's room and Gwen was glad of it – it would drown out the sound of her sobs. She knew she could never begin explain to Mother the reasons for her distress. *Your daughter has just been accused of an adulterous act and is being morally blackmailed by a rival soprano over the lead role in the new production.*

The door opened. Startled, she looked up to see Balthazar. He blinked his jade-green eyes at her and she blinked back instinctively in greeting. "Come to keep me company?"

He merely blinked at her again. She patted her lap and he leapt up, balancing his large body on her knees. His warmth was comforting even though it took him a while to settle, turning round and round.

"It's not just the other society members," she told the cat as it began to purr, a deep-throated sound that resonated through his whole body and into hers. "Bath is such a small city. People talk and I need my piano teaching at the high school. Any whisper of a scandal and I'll be sacked. I can't take the risk."

But it was her own guilty feelings that troubled her almost as much as the loss of the leading role. Did Myrna know her more accurately than she knew herself? Was she harbouring feelings for Ken? He'd been such a good friend all these years. She always felt at ease in his company. Perhaps too comfortable with him?

Balthazar chose that moment to rise, to bump his cool moist nose against hers. She was surprised by this uncharacteristic gesture of affection: almost a feline kiss.

"Gwen? Are you home?" Mother was calling. "Put the kettle on."

"Sorry Balthazar, we're back on duty." Gwen went to stand up and he leapt off gracefully, following her, ever hopeful, as she made her way to the kitchen.

~~~

The following Tuesday, Ken arrived to pick Gwen up at the usual time. It was another dank autumn evening and the windscreen wipers squeaked noisily as they drove off into the drizzle.

"I got the letter today with the full rehearsal schedule," Ken said after a while. "I see that Jim has cast Myrna as Rose."

"I— I don't like to leave Mother on her own for too long these days." Gwen felt that some explanation was required. "She's getting more confused. She forgets to turn off the gas. You know. That kind of thing…"

"Couldn't one of the neighbours come in to sit with her? One of her friends?"

"I don't like to impose. And you know how touchy Mother can be." The excuse sounded weak but Gwen hoped that Ken would take the hint that she didn't want to discuss the issue anymore.

"But Gwen, you deserve to play that role."

I know. And I'm glad that you believe in me, Ken. I just can't take the risk. She nodded, aware that if she spoke her voice would betray her.

"You know what I think? Myrna's got her sights set on Jeremy."

"Jeremy? But he's been cast as the bad baronet—" Gwen began and then she understood what Ken was saying. Jeremy, a local solicitor, had a fine baritone voice and was very popular with the female members of the society. "Rose and Sir Ruthven end up together at the end of the show. And if I'd been playing Rose..."

"As you should be," Ken said loyally.

Had that been Myrna's ploy all along? To make sure that she could play opposite her latest crush, eliminating all potential rivals?

"It's only an operetta," Gwen said, more to herself than to Ken. "I'm just happy to be a part of it." Which was true; the instant she was caught up in the glorious music and the light-hearted frivolity of the plot she forgot about her troubles at home.

~~~

"And this is when, bridesmaids, you all enter again with Jeremy, stage left." Maureen, the producer, rose from her chair, her notebook open in one hand, flapping the other to show the chorus where to come on. Chalk lines had been marked on the scuffed hall floor to show the dimensions of the stage at the Theatre Royal.

"Jeremy? You mean the bad baronet," called out Gwen's friend Coral.

"But Rose doesn't know I'm the baronet yet – let alone bad!" Jeremy said in tones of mock offence and everyone laughed.

~~~

Gwen wandered about the house until she was certain Mother had gone to bed. She was unable to calm her thoughts about Myrna. Maybe someone else was stirring behind the scenes, someone who had also heard Myrna's threats that evening cloakroom? Or was Myrna feeling insecure about her role in the production and was determined to take out those feelings out on her?

Gwen forced herself to set the table ready for breakfast the following morning and checked that Balthazar was in for the night. Before climbing into bed, she closed the bedroom door, but not long after she'd pulled up the eiderdown and switched off the bedside lamp, she heard the door creak open and the soft pad of paws. Next moment a furry weight settled on her and the purring began.

"No, Balthazar," she said sleepily, "you're not allowed to sleep on the bed. Get off." The purring merely grew louder. Yet the cat's weight was reassuring, as if he sensed her sadness and had come to comfort her in the only way a cat could, just be being there.

~~~

It roams through the night, padding on silent paws through the bracken. Humans in their noisy vehicles crossing the open hilltop on a wide roadway. This is its territory. They have no business there, disturbing its nocturnal hunting, scaring away the rabbits, hares and deer.

Prey. My prey.

A rustle in the grass, a twitch in the undergrowth. It freezes, scenting food. A rabbit makes a run for it, tearing toward the winding roadway, launching itself across.

Follow the prey. Hunt it down. Starting at a slow run, breaking into a faster lope as the rabbit careers across the road, illuminated suddenly in dazzling light as a fast-moving metal box appears.

Too late to stop. Hungry. Ravenously hungry. Time to pounce. Launching across the road into the dazzle of light, springing on the terrified rabbit as the strange stench of the roaring metal box fills the air.

A jagged squealing, screeching – and the box overturns, falling into the ditch in a deafening explosion of sound. The lights are extinguished.

I pause – then lope onward, my bloodied prey wriggling in my jaws, looking for a quiet place to eat my fill.

~~~

Gwen awoke with a gasp, sitting upright in bed, heart thudding. Balthazar was nowhere to be seen. From Mother's room she could hear the pips on the Home Service announcing the news. Seven o'clock and still dark.

"I hate autumn mornings after the clocks go back." She put one hand to her head, trying to recall the last fleeting tatters of her dream. What did it mean? Chasing rabbits in the dark?

Was I sharing Balthazar's dreams?

"Make us a pot of tea, Gwen dear," Mother called.

Gwen pulled on her dressing gown and shuffled into slippers, stifling a yawn. She hesitated. After the dream she could not help wondering what Balthazar had left outside on the step last night: a mangled mouse, a dead bird ... or even a rabbit?

~~~

Today was their first day in the theatre. It was unusual to have its use on a weekend before a week's run of performances, but the Agatha Christie mystery play had already moved on to its next venue in Cheltenham.

Gwen almost tripped over Balthazar who instantly wound himself around her legs, loudly demanding food. "There'll be no peace till you're fed." But even as she forked strong-smelling cat food into his bowl and placed it on the floor, her mind was still mired in the darkness of her dream.

Fiercely feral. Sharp white teeth tearing into fur and raw flesh. The taste of warm blood... So different from the domestic cat she was watching enthusiastically eating his way through a bowl of brown goo that stank of pilchards.

~~~

"Bridesmaids: you enter as soon as the introduction begins," Jim called from the pit. "And I want to hear every word. *Fair is Rose as bright May-day.* Ar-tic-u-late!"

Gwen, waiting in the wings, felt a frisson of excitement as the orchestra struck up. The musicians were a motley assembly, cobbled together from players in the city brass and dance bands, mingling with teachers and pupils from the local schools, yet they brought Sullivan's music to life with gusto. The odd squeak or missed note didn't matter – this was a real live rehearsal in the Theatre Royal and she was instantly swept up in the atmosphere, eager to start singing.

But just as the bridesmaids made their entrance, the music came to a jagged stop.

"They've *what*?" Jim's voice was uncharacteristically harsh. He laid his baton down on the music stand. "Sorry everyone, can you take five? Something's come up."

Gwen and the other chorus members stood around on the bare stage staring at each other. In the pit some of the players began to tune their instruments again in a desultory manner.

"I hope nothing's wrong," Coral said to Gwen. "*Ruddigore* isn't one of those shows with a bad reputation, is it? Like—" and she hesitated, her voice dropping to a whisper "—like *The Scottish Play*?"

"I don't think so," Gwen said, gazing out into the empty auditorium. "Although with all the ancestral ghosts haunting the bad baronet..."

Jim reappeared at the rear of the stalls with Maureen. "Can you get the whole cast out on stage?"

"Myrna and Jeremy have been in a car accident," Jim announced when he reappeared. "The good news is that they're both alive, but apparently Jeremy's car is a write-off."

"What happened?"

"From what I can gather they were driving across Claverton Down very early this morning when something large ran out right in front of the car. Jeremy swerved to avoid it – and they ended up in the ditch."

"Something large?" Gwen heard herself repeating aloud. "Was it ... a deer?"

"It was big, that's all they know at the moment. The police are investigating, of course."

"It's the Beast of Bathwick," one of the basses said in a dramatic voice and some of the men snorted with laughter.

"What were Myrna and Jeremy doing in a car together in the early hours this morning, anyway?" Coral murmured to Gwen from behind her hand. "They're both married – to other people."

"Are they all right?" Ken asked.

Maureen glanced at Jim before answering. "Both in shock, naturally, and I understand Myrna has cuts to her face and neck. They were both taken to the Royal United to be checked over so I'll go round to see her when we've finished the rehearsal today."

"That will be good of you, Maureen," Jim said. "In the meantime, as they say in the pictures, the show must go on! Gwen: can you take over as Rose Maybud today? Ronald, you're playing Sir Ruthven until further notice."

Gwen heard Jim's words as if from faraway, her mind wandering. It was as if she had been back on the top of Claverton in the drizzly darkness before dawn, seeing again the distant headlamps of a car penetrating the fog…

It has to be a coincidence.

Behind her she could hear Wendy organizing a collection to buy flowers for Myrna.

"All right, Gwen?" Jim beckoned her to the edge of the stage; she knelt down so she could hear what he was saying. "We'll find someone to sit with your mother. Until Myrna's fully recovered, I don't think anyone else is right for the role. It's short notice, I know, but you're a quick study."

~~~

In the ladies' dressing-room the bridesmaids were helping each other into their pink-and-white dresses and arranging the little coronets of silk roses in their hair.

Myrna's costume was hastily shortened to fit Gwen, who was a good seven inches shorter than the statuesque lead soprano. The bodice still gaped at the front, however; Gwen had no alternative but to pin it securely with her black panther brooch.

Maureen popped her head around the door. "I thought you'd like an update on Myrna. She's been allowed home but she's been ordered to rest for the next few weeks."

After Wendy entered the room Gwen became aware of a chorus of horrified whispers cresting as the bridesmaids surrounded Wendy, until she could hear all too clearly what was being said.

"They were both lucky not to be killed."

"Lucky?" echoed Wendy. "Depends what you call lucky."

"You delivered the bouquet?"

"Myrna sends her thanks. But her face. Her face!"

"What d'you mean, Wendy?"

"She has terrible lacerations."

"That must have been broken glass from the windscreen."

"That's what the doctors say, but they looked more like claw marks to me. It looks like she'd been attacked by some wild creature. *Mauled.*"

Before Gwen could process what Wendy was saying, a crackle of static made everyone glance up. The stage manager's voice came over the tannoy. "Orchestra and beginners, please. Five minutes to curtain up!"

No time to think about Myrna any more. Or the Beast of Bathwick, for that matter. I have to go on stage and do my best. The show must go on!

"You're wearing your pretty brooch again today, Gwen," Coral said, reaching out to touch the glossily enamelled panther, as they waited in the wings. "The old wives' tales must be wrong because that black cat has brought you good luck."

The old theatrical superstitions arose in Gwen's mind. She glanced up at Cora and placed her finger over her lips. "Hush. Don't say that backstage – it's break a leg."

Cora let out a little gasp. "Sorry."

And then they both shared a conspiratorial little smile and chorused, "Break a leg!"

~~~

Author's Note: This story was inspired by the appearance (never proven or disproven) of The Beast of Brassknocker Hill, reported in 1979.

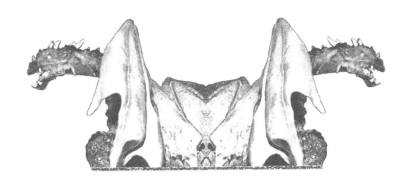

CUCKOO FLOWER

Tom Johnstone

14/04/22: 06.43
Always Use the Correct Nozzle, Lucy!

Yes, it sounds a bit obvious. I should know this by now. But sometimes I still need reminding, especially at those times when I haven't been sleeping too well.

So here's a recap on the importance of using the correct nozzle in my line of work. Full cone for spot treatments, deflectors for overall coverage. You wouldn't catch me using one of these for fungicide or insecticide work, especially not after I'd used it for weedkilling. That way madness lies. Not to mention, killing the patient. You can triple rinse, quadruple rinse, quintuple rinse, and there's still a chance there might be some herbicide left in the knapsack and on the nozzle. Maybe just a single droplet, but at the strength I'm using the consequences could be catastrophic.

In any case, that would be the wrong sort of nozzle. You use *hollow* cones for fungicides and insecticides, for a finer droplet spray.

For this job, I'm using an air induction nozzle, also known as a bubble jet. It draws air into the liquid stream, reducing the number of smaller droplets and aerating the larger ones to aid their dispersal. I need maximum coverage for this job, with as little drift as possible. The last thing I want is off-target application, especially given the product I'm using, but I do want to make sure I hit the target crop.

Hard.

This time I'm going to kill it outright.

14/04/22: 07.12
The World According to Terence Quick

I remember the man who taught me all I know about nozzles and knapsack sprayers.

Terence Quick, with his round pink smiling face: a cricket ball with steel-rimmed spectacles. That was how I thought of his head, the smile curving around it as though following its circumference. Grey fleece over a shirt and tie, above grey Sta-Prest slacks. After each pearl of wisdom had dropped from his lips he'd sit back in his chair and clasp his hands over his stomach, smile that satisfied smile, and ask the assembled students in his gently modulated Devonshire lilt the rhetorical question: "Are you happy with that?"

How I hated him.

But I did so in the same way as I hated my driving instructor, a man I came close to punching on one occasion.

And like my driving instructor, he got me through the test.

14/04/22: 07.46
Pre-Start Checks, Lucy!

I'm out into the jungle again soon. When I say "jungle", I mean the polytunnel.

But not before I've carried out the pre-start checks. Again this is kindergarten stuff which I nearly forgot in my eagerness to get cracking.

First, having donned the Operator's Protective Garments, white disposable coverall, teal nitrile gloves, steel-toe-capped rubber boots, mask and respirator, you depressurise the tank to make sure no residue of a previous application lingers in the lance, which would leak out when you remove it to check the filter inside the hose.

Then you proceed to the dry checks. Examining the outside of the tank for cracks or abrasions, checking the pump handle is working correctly, removing the lid to examine the filter and the inside of the tank, including the pressure chamber as well as the lid itself. When replacing the lid, it's important to ensure you don't cross-thread it. To do so would mean leaks and possible contamination, to yourself, the ground around your feet, and quite probably the water table beneath, too, especially if you're carrying out your checks near a drain, as well you might be.

Because next come the wet checks.

You fill the tank with six litres of water and re-pressurise the tank. This should reveal any leaks you haven't spotted with your visual inspection. Assuming there are none, proceed to the pattern check, spraying a sample into a measuring jug with the nozzle in a vertical position so you can see if the water's fanning out evenly. If it doesn't, if it splutters and makes a mess of the whole thing, it could mean there's some blockage in the system and you need to go back to the drawing board. If not, you're good to go for a practice swathe on the concrete to ensure it's giving a good even spread. But first you have to pick the tank up, shaking it at a forty-five-degree angle to see if the water splashes out from any hitherto undetected leaks.

You are now ready to calibrate your applicator!

Are you happy with that?

The way I'm going I won't be started before eight—

15/04/22
A *Round-Up (Get It?)* of the Arguments For and Against Glyphosate

I didn't rule out glyphosate to begin with. Arguably it is effective against *Reynoutria japonica*. That's Japanese knotweed for any lay person or persons who might read this. I say "arguably", because there is a 2014 report by Rosemary Mason suggesting the notorious weed has developed resistance to Monsanto's flagship product. The report's full of wild claims and political rhetoric amid some pertinent arguments, at one point asking, somewhat bizarrely, "Why does David Cameron hate Wales?"

I imagine Terence Quick's response to such a document. His lips would curl upwards at the corners until his smile curved around the contours of his face like the stitching around a cricket ball. Perhaps he'd make some quip about tree huggers or knotweed fanciers, and we, his students, would all laugh along. We were there to learn how to use such substances after all. He'd raise a hand to still our laughter, reminding us there *are* dangers associated with such chemicals, even comparatively harmless ones like glyphosate! Such hazards, he'd go on to say, are the reason why we must take extra care to follow the COSHH assessments, check the specifications on the product label, carry out the right calculations on the calibration charts, fill in the application records, et cetera. Blah blah blah. Never mind the COSHH assessments, I felt well and truly under the cosh when I underwent the training under Quick's tutelage.

Returning to the 2014 report.

While Mason may sound like a tin-foil-hat-wearing crank from my previous comments, she does have letters after her name and so I don't dismiss all her findings out of hand, despite some of her more eccentric outbursts. The main thrust of her argument goes something like this: glyphosate was originally patented as an antibiotic, but it also kills off beneficial bacteria in the guts of human beings. Hence her concerns about traces finding their way into the food chain via spraying on or near vegetables. Then there's the issue she raises about Japanese knotweed's resistance to this herbicide, leading to its re-emergence as a "super weed". After a concerted large-scale attempt to eradicate the plant using glyphosate in Adirondack National Park, Upstate New York, persistent regrowth despite the treatment led to experiments on rhizomes from historically treated and untreated sites. These trials, recorded in August 2015 at the ESA Centenary Annual Meeting in Baltimore, seem to confirm this pattern of resistance.

When I tried glyphosate on the as-yet-unnamed plant I discovered in the Philippines, the results were initially most satisfactory. A polytunnel containing about two thousand square metres (that's roughly half-an-acre in old money) of lush shining vibrant green plants with their unusual red globe-like flowers, slowly turning to brittle grey-brown husks.

Well, that was easy, I thought.

It may well be asked, why was I so keen to find a way of destroying this plant in the first place, to the extent that I brought back specimen samples with me to England in order first to cultivate it, then subject it to various herbicides.

I'm not sure I can answer that one, except to say I was fascinated by the plant.

During my field trip to the Philippines, I noticed the invasive nature of the plant, which the locals called the "Cuckoo Flower". Its ability to overwhelm and suppress all the other competition made Japanese knotweed, let alone bindweed or old man's beard, look like a timid shrinking violet by comparison.

Cultivating it under test conditions was not a problem. I soon found it had easily colonised the polytunnel.

And the glyphosate seemed to have done the trick when it came to killing it off.

Or so I believed.

Plants Playing Possum?

I went in there six days after the application to remove the withered stalks, which were shrouded in a fine powdery mist of dead, decaying plant matter. That's when I noticed the patch of green under the dead brown skin of one of them, peeling away like a flake of paint as I began to tug it out.

I stopped pulling before the roots became loose, not that this would have happened easily. I could feel the plant resisting my exertions, as if the harder I pulled, the stronger the roots held on, pulling back with equal and opposite vigour, my sweat-slick hands sliding off the slippery stalks in the intense humidity in there. At first I dismissed this as my imagination, until I saw the green.

Perhaps I should have gone ahead and ripped it out then and there, the others too, piled them onto a bonfire and turned a flame thrower on them. Then again, I'm not certain it would have done any good.

All my wrestling with one of the plants seemed to make it

greener. I wondered if the plant was reviving. Then I realised it was worse than that. It wasn't coming back to life as I pulled. It was just that more scraps of dead brown skin were falling off as I did so, exposing the green underneath.

It had never died. It just wanted me to think so. The brown shrivelling, the grey dust, they weren't symptoms of chemical poisoning.

They were a disguise. It's a phenomenon known in the biological lexicon as thanatosis, a concept from zoology rather than botany.

Or to put it another way, the things were playing possum.

Maybe they sensed that if they did this I'd go away, leave them alone long enough for them to, I don't know -- it seems insane when I write it down -- make their escape.

As soon as they sensed this stratagem had failed, the scales fell away. All five hundred or so gorgeous abominations emerged in their luscious treacherous glory. I'm aware my language is becoming somewhat unscientific, but those words came into my head as I watched them standing there, stately and triumphant, like a phoenix from the ashes, times five hundred. Their glossy green leaves stretched out and their deep red globe flowers bobbed above a carpet of papery mothwing shrouds, lying there like a child's discarded Halloween costume, or lovers' strewn clothes.

~~~

Yes, I really must temper my language.

It's all there in the photos attached to the official document for anyone who really wants to look. With any luck, that's the only place they'll be able to see them.

Looking at those globes, I think again of Quick's cricket-ball head. Maybe I should name the plant after him, something ending with *globosa terenciana*.

I suppose I should name it after me too: so *Luciana globosa terenciana*. In shape, the red flowers do resemble the yellow ones on a *Buddleia globosa*, the more commonplace buddleia's less invasive relative.

Are you happy with that, Lucy?

Hmmm. Not sure I am.

If my suspicions about these plants (?) are correct, maybe I'm not so happy to have my name attached to them.

29/04/22

When is a Plant Not a Plant?

I think I've killed them this time. It's been two weeks now, and they really, *really* are dead. The paraquat did the trick.

Are you happy with that, Lucy?

Yes, I know. It's banned in the EU. Not that this country takes any notice of that these days, but the government's hankering after the good old days of lax health and safety standards hasn't quite filtered through to reintroducing such things onto the market here. Good thing I smuggled some in when I returned from the Philippines. Clever of me, eh, Terence?

Well, I thought I was very clever until I went back home for the first time in days and read reports of other botanists first sourcing and transplanting, then taking similar measures against, these plants all over the world. My first reaction was to feel a bit put out that I hadn't been the first to discover this new plant, as I'd thought. I should have published and peer-reviewed my findings before I destroyed the plants. Not very rigorous scientific practice, Lucy! But I have been under a lot of strain with these plants (if they are plants). It might have affected my judgement. Maybe I was a little hasty. Or maybe…

Yes, I know this is going to sound insane, and I can imagine how Terence would react if I came up with a theory like this in his class. He'd give a smug little smirk and hold it up to the ridicule of the rest of the students.

Wouldn't you Terence? Well, you're not here now, are you? So you wouldn't understand what's happening to me, that I'm starting to think the plants (if they are plants) are playing tricks with my mind.

Then it hit me.

When it did, I knew I'd have to rush back to the polytunnel in the middle of the night.

Yes, I'd better do that—

Empty.

My first thought was that the application was so strong it didn't just kill the *Luciana* (I still think of them as that, whatever the other botanists might call it -- as if it's *my* discovery, my creation even, to my pride or perhaps shame...). Maybe the paraquat destroyed it utterly, so all the plants rapidly decomposed and disintegrated.

To nothing?

Well, why not? After all, I did use all the paraquat in the bottle. Well, not quite all, but over half.

But I didn't really believe this hypothesis.

I shone my torch around the polytunnel, my hands shaking, making the disc of light bounce and judder over the shining plastic, finally falling to the earth to illuminate the empty space. There was no trace, not even a fine powder to indicate the plants had once been there. Just bare soil.

I wondered if a gang of thieves came and dug up the crop. The plants might be extremely valuable to some collector or rival botanist, even dead! But there were no footprints in the soil, no marks at all apart from where I surmised the roots came free. The disturbance in the earth was minimal, suggesting it wasn't the result of hardened criminals hurriedly and messily digging over a plot to drag my *Luciana* from the ground, but of something gently, patiently easing the roots free from their earthly prison.

Maybe even something easing its own roots out.

But that's ridiculous, Lucy. Plants can't move. They're not animals.

Or maybe that's what they want me to think. Just like they wanted me to think they were dead. And I was certain they *were* dead! I cut layers and layers away from a random selection of the brown husks to check there was no green hidden underneath. And if they were animals, that would be bloody agony!

~~~

And yet ... they're gone, Lucy.

Maybe you didn't really want to kill them at all, your precious *Luciana*. Maybe you just told yourself they were dead to make yourself feel better about your recklessness in cultivating them.

Oh, stop this! They say talking to yourself is the first sign of madness. Who knows what that makes writing to yourself…? But is it any more insane than the other ideas I'm entertaining? Such as, if a plant could feign death, that would be the ultimate camouflage.

Not quite the ultimate.

Now, if an animal could pretend to be a plant…

I must stop thinking like this.

~~~

I'd shone the torch around the field looking out for signs of movement, perhaps thieves making off in a van full of dead plants. The shaft of light did pick out something moving. It looked at first like a human head bobbing in the beam, round and red like Terence Quick's but completely featureless. So the plants *did* escape!

Ridiculous, I told myself.

I thought the more likely explanation was that some seed escaped from the polytunnel when I opened the door and started a new infestation outside.

30/04/22

Well, I could deal with that tomorrow – there was still that almost half a bottle of paraquat left.

No, not now. There was still some paraquat remaining in the bottle. It's empty now. Because of what I saw outside the polytunnel.

I'm waiting for it to take effect so I won't have to live with the consequences of what I've done. I wave the torch around again. More of the bobbing heads appear to blush in its light. Hundreds of them. I don't know what frightens me more: the thought of them departing the polytunnel *en masse*, or the idea of them reproducing so quickly in such large numbers to replace the dead or missing ones. Or maybe it's the manner in which the male plant pollinates the female that leaves me sickened and desperate. As I watch and listen I imagine the creatures' glossy-green trunks swelling as they gestate. I hope the whispering sighs I hear come from the friction of leaf brushing against leaf, stem grinding, rubbing against stem, flower kissing red spherical flower, rather than from those obscenities expressing the pleasure of their writhing, with something approximating to actual vocal cords.

Now I'm the one blushing and gasping at the sight and the sounds, feeling faintly horribly aroused, as well as nauseous, even enviously thinking, *Well,* somebody's *getting it…* And thanks to my final libation in this lonely place, I've now guaranteed I'll die never once having experienced what they were enjoying, the joy of mutual carnality.

I think about this as I observe the cuckoo plants, no longer caring that I know what manner of beings they really are, much less that I'm observing their dalliance, not really blushing at all, altogether heedless of me, so passionately wrapped up in each other as they wantonly copulate on the bare, dirty earth.

It shouldn't be long now.

I hope the pain isn't too terrible.

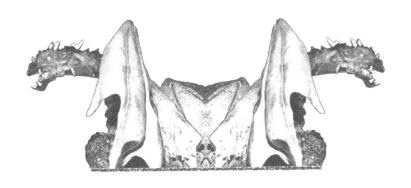

A SONG FOR CHRISTMAS

Ashe Woodward

"Where's my favourite one?" Sheila turns to me, beaming, as if I have a clue which of the thousands of tree ornaments she's talking about.

"Which one is that?" I ask, biting back any edge in my voice because it's Christmas.

"You know, the Victorian house you can stick a bulb into the back so the windows light up."

I look in the box, shifting balls and doodads out of the way and I think I know which one she means – it's the one that's lying broken in half at the bottom. "Why don't I pour us some eggnog?" I offer, hoping she'll forget about the little porcelain house that I take with me to the kitchen, one piece in each pocket.

"I think I hear music," she calls from the living room. I hear the front door open with its familiar squeak and the added jingle of a gaudy wreath Sheila picked out and hung there. "Oh gosh, Glen. It's carollers!"

Oh, God. Great. I never know what to do with these people. I reach for my wallet. Five or twenty? Ten would've been good enough but I can't ask them for change, can I? I take as much time as I can fixing the drinks: coconut rum, eggnog, ice, a dash of nutmeg on top. Just one of these and then a beer, I tell myself.

Sheila's at the door with a plaster-white smile. I hand her a glass. She's beaming along with the song, mouthing the words with them. Their costumes are great, though, exactly what you expect from puritan beggars, with those white bonnets and shawls on the women, the black hat and red ascot on the men. It is called an ascot, right? I can't be the only one that's uncomfortable: do I just stand here and smile, try not to make too much eye contact?

Their mouths hold too long around the words; the notes seem to go on forever. The smallest woman in front bounces joyfully along with the beat of the two-hundred-year-old melody. I try to catch the eye of the tall baritone in the back, maybe to get a knowing eyeball out of him, but no luck – he's fully committed to the part.

"We are not daily beggars
Who beg from door to door,
But we are neighbours' children,
Whom you have seen before."

"Thank you, folks, for opening your door this time of year to hear our humble choir. We accept donations for the children's hospital," announces the baritone. Of course.

"That was really something," I say. It's all I can manage as I hand him the twenty.

He holds eye contact with me for much longer than I feel is appropriate. "God bless and we wish you folks the happiest of holidays," he says, perfectly smoothly. Likely rehearsed. The tip of his hat is a lovely touch.

"Isn't that just the best? What a great thing to do for the neighbourhood," Sheila says.

I sip my coconut nog so I don't have to answer and we go back to the tree.

Sheila begins to hum the staccato rhythm in her off-tune way. I used to think her tone-deafness was cute but now I'm not so sure. How can you think that's the note?

"...and to you your wassail too, hmm, hmm, hmm." She turns to me and asks, "What does that even mean? Wassail."

"I think it's a drink," I hold out my glass in a salute or cheers.

"It is not," she flips the arm of my flannel shirt in her pitiful, flirtatious way.

"It is," I say, while slurping to drown out what she might say next. "Let's get this tree finished. Have you got an angel or a star for the top?"

"Love and joy come to you,
And to your wassail too."

~~~

"Look! It's snowing, Glen. Isn't it beautiful? I love the first snow."

"It's not the first. We've had flurries since November."

"Oh, I know. But this one looks like it'll stick."

Yay. To the driveway. And I'll have to shovel it.

"God bless the Master of this house,
Likewise the Mistress too."

"Are you still humming that song?" I say through my teeth.

"Christmas music is full of ear worms, isn't it?"

"I guess," I say flatly. It's the first time I've lost my Christmas charm, and it takes all my reserve not to say more. Starting in late October all I dream about is strangling Mariah Carey right at the top of one of her high notes. In fact —

"What would you say is your favourite Christmas song?" Sheila asks me.

I close my eyes and take a deep breath. "I'm — I'm not sure. Maybe that Mariah Carey one that's always on the radio." I hope I disguised the sarcasm well enough. "How about you?" I ask in return, though wondering why I'm trying to continue this conversation.

"Oh gosh, me? How can I even choose? Well, I really like 'Away in a Manger' – if someone can really sing."

"Right. That does help."

Then Sheila turns to me with that special glow that she gets at Christmas, like we're in one of those unbearable TV movies. She grabs my arm and leans her head on me. We stare at the tree. "Isn't it just so warm and cosy?"

I politely excuse myself and walk away like I've gotta go to the can. Halfway there I think I'll take out the trash, cool down outside in the wintery air. I take the pieces of the broken tree decoration from my pockets and throw them in with the other trash. I breathe in the winter air, just for a moment, and let snowflakes wet my cracked lips. When I go back in the house, I hear humming again. This time it's "Joy to the World". Lord help me.

"The tree's done. Let's put the last one on together." Sheila's holding out a pinecone unevenly on its red string. I grab the other side of the string circle and we move slowly towards the obvious branch together. "There," she says. She reaches up to kiss my cheek but stops short. "You're so warm, Glen. Like burning up. Do you feel sick at all?"

I shake my head, trying to keep my cool with her. I know I can't say anything that'll ruin the moment. She puts the back of her hand to my forehead. I take her by the wrist and slowly move it down. "I'm fine," I say. Again my teeth come together as I push out the words. I'm trying so hard, but she looks... I don't know. Hurt? Scared? Kind of like a fat squirrel in the middle of the yard that freezes in place when I open the door. What's that emotion called?

We stare at each other for a moment, both of us trying to be calm and not start a fight on Christmas. "How about a gift?" I say, quick-thinking and scurrying upstairs. A necklace will stop all of this nonsense.

~~~

"Oh, Glen, it's beautiful. I love the stone in the middle," Sheila says. "Put it on me?" She turns, holds the front against her chest, and we're back to the Christmas feeling that started off the night. Before I know it, her arms are around my neck.

When she pulls away she clears her throat. "You are very warm though." She moves to sit on the couch and finally takes a sip of her eggnog. "Mmm."

"Should we light a fire?" I ask.

"I'm not sure. You really feel okay?" Her voice is quiet and sweet.

I don't answer, but only stand to throw on a log and light the ends of the twisted newspaper. Stooping down I watch with fascination as the featured faces in the local news become distorted, then crumple and burn. Sheila starts to hum again.

"Wow. It's really stuck in my head," she says and I'm thankful she's interrupted herself. There's a silence between us as we watch the fire. It crackles and the wood screams in high-pitched sizzles. "Hey, did you know the original Santa was a woman?" Sheila's never done well with silence. I can't believe I used to find it exciting.

"Really," I say, feigning interest.

"Santa is the female title for saint, like Santa Maria or Santa Barbara. San is for men, like San Francisco. So Santa must be a female. It's from Latin. I heard it on the radio."

"Hmm... fascinating." The fire roars and the heat matches what I'm feeling from aggravation, just under my skin.

"Honey?"

I spin on the balls of my feet to look at Sheila. She clicks her tongue on the roof of her mouth. "What?" I stare at her, waiting.

"Hmm," she says. She swirls around her glass so the ice cubes clink against each other. Then she looks at me and smiles, "Oh, nothing. Never mind." Her tone is sultry, deep. Not like Sheila at all. And in a shot, she downs her entire drink. I turn back to the fire and the crackle makes me childishly excited. I'm ready to sit and watch it take its course.

"Here we come a-carolling
Among the leaves so green."

Then I feel Sheila reach out to me. It's romantic, I suppose. For a moment, I ignore her, see where she wants to go. As she tickles my neck I get goosebumps, despite the fire in front of me. It's better if I just play along. "That's nice," I say.

"What is, Glen?"

Sheila is talking to me from the sofa.

"Oh God!" I quickly brush off my neck and stand. Something was there but I don't see anything on the floor around me. I flick my neck a couple more times. Maybe a piece of fluff, or a spider. Where is it now?

"What's wrong, honey?" Sheila is holding a stare as she unfolds her legs and walks towards me. I have nowhere to go with the fire mantle already pressing under my shoulder blades. She's going to kiss me. "Are you sure you're okay, Glen?" She puts her arms around me and her head onto my chest. I take a breath to clear the surge of adrenaline from the fright of whatever crawled on me. We stand, embracing in front of the fire. It's calm, it's warm.

"Love and joy come to you,
And to your wassail too."

I put my forehead to hers as she hums and I try my best to enjoy the moment. She smells like oranges – orange shampoo. My hand falls onto her cheek to give in to the Christmas fantasy. I tilt her face up, my hand in her hair now. I look deeply into her eyes and feel my fingertips tickled. I jerk my hand away without thinking.

"Glen, seriously. What's wrong?"

A small droplet lands on the floor. I see it, and crouch down to look.

A worm.

"Oh. Must just be something we brought in with the tree," I say. I pick up and examine the stringy beige body before I toss it promptly into the fire.

"Oh Glen, that's so awful!" Sheila whines as it roasts.

I turn to her and shrug, wiping my hands on my pants and taking a long look around to be sure there are no more. I give my neck a few extra swipes. I look back at Sheila.

"I think they're cute," she says, staring at several of the same worms sitting on her arm, all the way up to her neck. They're stuck to her purple sweater, curling and writhing in place.

"Holy shit, Sheila. *What the hell?*" I go to brush them off of her but she moves back.

"No, you're not going to toss them in the fire."

"They're worms! What are you doing?"

"They're more than worms. Can't you hear them?" She bends her head over her arm, closes her eyes and smiles.

"But we are neighbours' children, whom you have seen before," she sings. "Can't you hear it? They're amazing."

I stand back as she sings to the worms on her arm. More and more of the beige strands appear on her and work their way up to her dark hair. From the back of her head they inch to the front of her bangs, then over top to blend in with the same beige colour of her face. She lets them stick there while she holds up more that are gathering on her arms, in her hands, on her fingertips.

"Sheila, come on. Is this a joke? Take them outside. What are you doing?" I'm trying to move further away, past the mantle to the window. But that's where the tree is. That has to be where they came from, right?

"Sing with me, Glen. Sing with *us.*"

I start to answer but I immediately throw my hands over my mouth. There's one on her lip, dangling. And then I hear them. They really are softly wailing. *That damn song!*

"And all your kin and kinfolk,
That dwell both far and near."

The worms have mostly covered Sheila's body. Some are dropping to the floor in soft small thuds. There are too many to even grab, to throw into the fire now. I have to get them off of Sheila but, *God!* I don't want to touch them or her. I just want to keep them off of me. I take another big step back and I'm at the window. She's walking so slowly towards me, careful to not squish the crawling worms beneath her slippers.

I lean slightly forward to try to look into her eyes – brown irises but the whites have become a foggy mucous. Maggots are hatching, emerging from her nose, her mouth, sliding from tear ducts. They keep coming from every orifice, it seems, and crawling across her skin.

My throat bubbles up before I can look away. I have to get out but there's only one route I can take. I drop down and crawl beneath the tree to get to the front door. The wreath jingles as I run outside into the snow and brush myself off. There doesn't seem to be anything on me. *Thank God.* I scramble on the porch and run to the front of the house. I throw the garage door up and find the axe, still dripping of sap and melted snow from cutting the tree earlier that day. I tap the side of it with my other hand. I get myself pumped. Ready.

~~~

I quietly push open the internal door from the garage to sneak back into the house. My eyes are wide open – but I'm determined to keep my mouth closed, despite my heavy breathing. I look from the hallway into the living room. Sheila's not there. I'm as silent as possible but I still can't hear where she is. With my axe held up, I walk in further, ready to be surprised. But it's complete silence in the house. *Oh, now she's quiet.*

I let the axe fall to my side as I stand beside the fire. The rug is now completely clear of the beige mealworms, if that's what they are. The fire crackles and the furnace clicks off. I move to the tree and look through the window to see if I can see Sheila outside. No one is around on the snowy streets, just those carollers walking up and down neighbours' driveways.

Then Sheila calls from upstairs. "Glen, where did you go?" Her voice so sweet.

I return to the hallway, raise the axe, remembering how to swing a bat. I don't quite know what I'll do but I'm not going to get those things all over me too. I see the bottom of her pants through the banister spindles; she's changed into pyjamas.

"I just wanted to be more comfortable. Now we can cuddle and maybe listen to some music by the fire." She takes her steps slowly and the back ends of her slippers slap the stairs as she comes down. "Oh, put that away, silly," she says to me.

She reaches the bottom step and turns. I look first to her eyes – they are clear of the maggots. But her skin moves unnaturally and twists into a mosaic of faint darker lines. The worms are woven tight, over her face and hands. Her snowman-print top shifts and stirs with the thousands of the little lives that must be beneath it.

"*Oh, Sheila,*" I say. The mask of wrinkled squirming bodies covering her face gives her the look of a sick old hag.

She smiles dazedly. "Aren't they cute? Can't you hear them singing?"

I move back to the living room, careful to stay on the side kitchen side for easy escape back to the garage. Sheila follows me in.

"*Glen,*" they all say together. Sheila's voice is the strongest; the small voices are squeaking along with her. "*Sing with us.*"

"*Here we come a wand'ring*
So fair to be seen."

"Get out of my head," I grunt.

"Glen, look at me. It's Christmas," Sheila says. She looks at me intently and begins to unbutton her pyjama top. She slips it down around her elbows. The worms churn like small whirlpools of flesh, covering Sheila's breasts and abdomen. And there, at her centre, they are becoming smooth, evening out like a sheet. Sheila undoes the drawstring of her bottoms and walks out of them, towards me. As the worms join together all over Sheila's skin I can see her gaining strength, getting bigger, more powerful.

I'm still holding the axe at the ready. I can only hope it will be sufficient.

More worms work their way down her body, merging to fill in the space between her thighs. Her torso seems to melt, transforming into an elongated body. The worms encapsulate her arms creating one long fat tube that stretches down from her face – which is still hers, I think. I can see her clear eyes with their brown irises.

"Don't come any closer," I say, hearing the cliché and the desperation in my voice. The sight of that thing disgusts me. That long stretch of flesh lowers itself to the floor, slowly wriggles closer. I step back just as slowly, trying to focus on Sheila's face. *Sheila.*

From somewhere inside the giant worm – the collection of many worms, maggots and Sheila – there's singing. Sheila's face contorts, disappears, becoming one with the rest of the pink-beige mass. In front of me it waits with its wide-open maw…

Sing with us
You know you want to.
I'm holding the axe.
I do what I have to do.
Throw the stragglers in the fire.
Fix myself a drink.

The eggnog covers the ice and rum. I notice on the side of the carton that it's been expired for a week.

"No wonder," I say to myself, and knock it back in one.
I turn on the radio.
"And God bless you and send you a Happy New Year,
And God send you a Happy New Year."

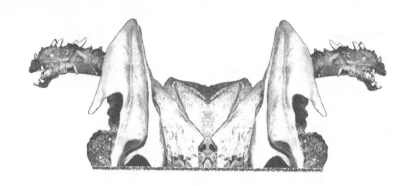

DREAM A LITTLE DREAM OF
ME AND MY SHADOW

Adrian Cole

Dawn squeezed sepia light through the city skyline. Police Chief Rizzie Carter was slumped behind the wheel of his wagon, his collection of chins crowding his chest, the price he paid for overindulging in fast food. I approached the car from the shadows – and he swung an arm up remarkably fast. Instead of staring at the expected fat burger I was eye to eye with a 44 Magnum, although the hand holding it shook.

"Nervous tonight, Chief," I observed.

He lowered the gun. "You got my message, Nick. Get in."

I slid inside, trying to ignore the reek of onions and relish and other dubious ingredients of his last repast. We headed into the city's dark maw. I had a feeling we'd become the fast food, about to be masticated by night's teeth, though I didn't comment – Rizzie's glum mood didn't need deepening.

"Got a weird one?" I asked. Whenever he dragged me from the excitement of my insalubrious office and its towering stack of paperwork there was usually something freaky going on in his world. His message had been brief, the tone suggestive of things he'd rather shove back into the gloomier bolt holes of New York.

"Remember that guy who sucked the ideas outta people's minds? A writer, weird pulp crap."

"Randall Stockhart. Sure." I'd called him the Scene Stealer. His trick had been to get inside his victims' heads (he specialised in fiction writers) and help himself to their big ideas then write them before they did – and clean up. I'd put a stop to it.

"We got another one. Only this one don't suck stuff out, he – or it – puts stuff in. Bad stuff, nightmares."

We reached the crime scene. Several cops were hanging around outside the taped-off basement apartment. All of the drapes and blinds in surrounding window were tightly drawn. There were no curious faces, which was unusual. This was the rough end of town; the local denizens didn't scare easy. Normally. Today was something else as I found out descending the cramped steps with Rizzie to the apartment, and I got why he had the shakes. The stale smell in his car was perfume to the stink I got as he tugged open the apartment door. It was like being punched by a sewage sandbag.

I fished a bandanna out of a pocket and tied it over my mouth and nose. It helped but my olfactory nerves were never going to be quite the same again. Rizzie seemed to cope though his face had kinda curdled. He flicked a switch and the place was thrown into a garish cemetery glow.

There were three bodies. One was slumped in a chair, the other two were on a couch. Their mouths were open obscenely wide, like a constrictor's. Their eyes bulged the size of apples, their nostrils flared wide. Viscous muck oozed thickly from mouth, nose and ears, coating the entire top half of the bodies. It gleamed like rancid cream. Whatever it was, it was thick as lava, and it seemed to steam.

Rizzie gave me that "now I've seen it all" look.

I shrugged. I'd seen worse but this was pretty bad. Outside, in the marginally saner world, I asked, "Who found them?"

Rizzie pointed to a café across the street. "He's in there. A couple of my guys are struggling to cheer him up." As we entered a thin silent ghost of a man in a greasy apron handed me and Rizzie hot coffee and pointed to the back of the shop. A nervous guy sat in a booth with three cops, his wide eyes staring about uneasily. It looked like he was about to run up the wall. He had an expression I'd last seen on the cover of a horror pulp.

Rizzie slid into the seat and the guy recoiled from whatever nastiness his mind had been gazing at. "Hey there, Marvin." Rizzie gripped the man's arm. "Can you tell Mr Stone here what you told me? What you saw through the window? It's okay, fella. It can't harm you now."

Turns out Marvin was a resident of the same apartment block of the three stiffs, a pal of them. He'd been about to visit the previous night, and as usual tapped on the window and peered into the lit room. His three buddies were there – but they had company. Marvin blurted out the details, punctuating his words with sudden sobs or deep breaths, like he was trying not to puke over the table.

"Thought it was a man at first, but it didn't move like a man. Arms and legs too long, real bony like a skeleton. Head was too big, with a mouth like a shark's. Had claws, too – I saw them dig into Hank's shoulders, one each side. Then it ... pulled Hank's head back – looked like it ripped open his face. It spat something white and slithering right into Hank's mouth making and his whole body rock, like if a huge hound was shaking it. I wanted to turn away, wanted to run, but couldn't. That thing did it to the others too. Poisoned them with spit. Now they're full of bad dreams."

The Chief took me aside. "He just repeats it over and over. Full of bad dreams. What the hell does it mean, Nick?"

I scratched my head but I couldn't worry anything loose.

At the door one of Rizzie's men called. "Chief, you better come."

We followed him out back of the apartment. A small yard led to a narrow path running alongside the river, which was as tarry and murky as ever. Dawn hadn't done anything to improve its look. A couple of the cops were pointing their guns at the shadows along the path. Something had given them the jitters judging from the way their hands were shaking.

"Don't know what the hell it is, Chief," said one of them. "But I swear to God it speaks."

A huge shape coalesced, hulking over us, dripping with river water, a monolith with arms and a head. Even in that gloom I recognised it.

"It asked for you," the cop told me, incredulously.

I pushed past and grinned at the unique visage of the Mire-Beast. He must have swum upriver and hauled himself ashore, a glistening amalgam of flesh and bone and vegetable, arms like gnarled roots, tree-trunk legs. Not the kind of thing you'd want to bump into in the dawn light – or any light for that matter.

"Nick," he said, the voice deep and rasping, a low growl of thunder. "You've seen inside the apartment?"

I nodded. "What do you know about those stiffs?"

"They're not dead."

"They sure look it," I said.

"They're in a kind of sleep. Dreaming the stuff the Seeder put into them."

"The Seeder?"

"A Dream Seeder. They've been stirred up like wasps from a nest, and they've broken through from the other side of the river, into our world."

I stared out across the Hudson to the blurred images of docks on the far shore.

"Not this river. The River Dreaming."

It was a new one on me.

"The cops need to get those men secured, Nick, and quickly. When they wake, and they will, they'll start harvesting and no one in the city will be safe. Right now those three are the only ones. If we don't act fast there'll be a swarm of them."

Rizzie Carter stood beside me. "You're talking to that ... thing," he said in a stage whisper that had me grinning.

"Sure. We're old pals. And he's one of us."

"Yeah? What does a thing like that *eat*?" I guess it was inevitable Rizzie'd be thinking of matters gastronomic.

"Don't ask. You heard Beastie boy here. We need to get those three guys into a lock-up. Fast."

"When they wake," the Mire-Beast added, "they'll be pissed as hell and stronger than bison. You'll need steel doors. Trust me."

Rizzie gaped. Then he shook himself and, muttering

something about bad dreams being infectious, gathered his men and got to work.

"I can't handle this alone," the Mire-Beast said. "I'll need you to come along – I'll explain as we go. Get tooled up then join me here and we'll go on a trip down the River Dreaming. For a little pest control."

I swore under my breath. This was going to seriously louse up my plans for the day. I was due to meet Ariadne for a quiet *tete-a-tete*. She would not be amused if I cried off. Daytime assignations weren't easy to arrange, given the demands of her work schedule.

"Problem?"

"Ariadne will have my hide—"

"She must come too. Besides, she'll enjoy the adventure."

I would have argued, but hell, the big guy was dead on the money. Give Ariadne an excuse to slip into her ninja gear, strap on her twin blades, and she'd be first in the queue.

~~~

He was right. I phoned Ariadne, expecting to get my ear chewed off but no, she was all for a bit of exercise.

"Randolph Coleman can hold the fort. He's the one man at HQ I can rely on." She'd handed over the reins to Randolph not long back and he was, by all accounts, a natural. Ariadne's cosmetic empire was blossoming, and better still, it gave her more time to herself. And me.

"And I can try out my new gear," she'd said.

"What's wrong with the old gear?" I'd grown very accustomed to her black ninja stuff. Turned out there was nothing wrong with the new outfit, either.

She rolled up in a car – if that's the right word – that would have had Batman drooling. Ostentatious? Hell yeah. A bright crimson, sleek as a Lamborghini, with shining chrome wheel hubs that dazzled the eye. It looked like it belonged in the air, zipping alongside a Stealth Fighter. My guts churned at the thought of getting into the thing. Luckily I didn't have to.

I turned my anxious bedazzled gaze to the shapely creature that emerged from the crimson missile. Now my eyes were really watering – Ariadne was clad entirely in matching red. A tight-fitting suit that must have made her eyes water, too. The familiar twin blades were strapped to her back. She wore a simple full-face mask through which her eyes sparkled with enthusiasm – and inevitably with a dash of mischief. She enjoyed making my pulse race, and in this case it wasn't so much racing as sprinting.

She'd parked the car where envious eyes would drink their fill, but if anyone attempted to touch it they would have a painful and debilitating experience. I hustled her off the street and down a side alley *en route* to the river and our rendezvous with the Mire-Beast. If anyone saw us they thought better of investigating. My guess was, in this part of town crimson leather and ninja blades were *de rigueur*.

"How is he?" she asked me, meaning David Goroth, the man who'd been morphed into the Mire-Beast by corrupt science. "Has he got used to his new shape?"

"I guess. He had a lousy time as a cop. Not a lot went right for him but he's clung on to his beliefs in what's right and what's evil. Being the Mire-Beast has given him a new purpose." I told her what Goroth had given me.

"So you trust him?" she said. "This isn't a trap?"

"I can't say I haven't wondered. But he says we're the only ones who can help, and we can't risk that he's wrong."

It was near noon when we reached the riverbank, but the skies were heavy with cloud, daylight only seeping through reluctantly, washing the river and its environs with monochrome strokes. The drizzle didn't help. I was glad of my hat.

Ahead of us a shape detached itself from the gloom, morphing into a low boat, a kind of barge, snub-nosed and wide. It looked like it should have been heaped with coal or iron ore, but it was empty save for the Mire-Beast.

"Our carriage awaits," I told Ariadne.

"You sure know how to charm a girl," she said. "I should have worn my boiler suit."

The barge bumped up against the quay; Ariadne and I clambered aboard. The Mire-Beast pushed the barge off in silence and we drifted into the current. Abruptly a thick swirling fog unrolled from the Hudson's mouth, as if it had been specifically laid on for us.

"I should have brought an umbrella," said Ariadne.

"We're headed for the left bank," said the Mire-Beast. "Two things you need to know about the River Dreaming. One, you do *not* disembark until you reach your destination. Two, never get off the barge on the other bank. That's the Ruptured Realm. Strictly off limits."

Ariadne and I both thought better of asking why.

"I'll go on ahead," said the Mire-Beast before I got a chance to ply him with questions. He slipped into the scummy water and sank down with only a few fat bubbles to mark his passing. The barge moved on and my guess was the tiller was fixed. The fog closed in, thick and cold. I pulled out one of my Berettas. It was going to be that kind of trip.

"This light is freakish," Ariadne said. "Midday just became twilight."

"Yeah, and I don't care too much for the colour of the water. I've seen thinner Irish stew. And it's choppy, like out in the Bay."

Ariadne had slipped out one of her swords as a precautionary measure. I now had both my twin Berettas to hand. We looked around us. The barge moved on down the river. For sure, we had crossed into another realm. As we watched the swell, something broke surface. An arm, its hand flexing long clawed fingers, grasping at the air. It was an even more sickly hue than the river. Then dozens of similar limbs were breaking surface.

Within minutes the water to our right was thronging with groping arms, slick with river mud dredged up from the bottom. They made their way towards the barge like a huge flock of mutated periscopes. It was impossible to see who or what bodies were under the water in that churning muck. Several hands slapped against the side of the barge and held on like lampreys.

I turned to Ariadne. "Did this tub shift off its course?"

"Being dragged to the right. The off-limits side." Scores of the grotesque arms – a mass of writhing tentacles – attached themselves to the barge. There was no doubt they were hauling us across the river to the right bank. I fired several rounds at them and had the satisfaction of seeing some arms burst and their grip loosened. Ariadne leaned over the side and made scything sweeps with her blade, slicing through arm after arm like so much pastrami. The waters churned wildly and I glimpsed faces, long distorted visages, wide mouths howling in silence. Fish-eyes fixed on me, beacons straight out of hell.

"If these suckers get aboard—" I started to yell at Ariadne but she didn't need me to tell her. She redoubled her efforts, using both swords.

It was looking like we were about to concede Mafeking as the prow of the barge swung round hard to starboard, but huge hands reached over the prow. I was about to give them both barrels when the Mire-Beast returned. His vast bulk dragged itself aboard and he was back at the stern surprisingly quickly. He dragged on the tiller using his prodigious strength, and at once the barge veered back on course, surging forward.

"Nick!" he shouted, voice like a gale. "Grab the tiller! Head for the shore."

I did so as the Mire-Beast dived overboard again. Ariadne prepared to repel anything with ideas of boarding. There was an almighty swirling and boiling of the waters. Arms, ripped and torn, were flung upwards. Scores of them floated uselessly on the surface like driftwood. However many of the aquatic horrors there were, they were no match for the Mire-Beast. He was in his element, a Godzilla on steroids.

I steered the barge shoreward. A broken structure emerged from the fog: a crumbling landing stage. As I took us in the Mire-Beast hauled himself aboard again, ripping off the last gangling arms and tossing them aside like burst leeches.

"What the hell were those things?" I asked him as we tied up.

"They guard the Ruptured Realm's banks, collecting visitors for the Dream Seeders. Now follow me; I gotta show you guys something."

We left the barge and wormed our way through tall banks of reed-like growths, eight-foot waving stems with sickly yellow heads. They swung round in unison – making my skin crawl– though no breeze stirred them. I expected eyes to open and glare at us. The Mire-Beast pushed banks of the stuff aside so we were able to use the trail he was making. He'd obviously been here before, following a familiar but hidden path. He brought us to a roughly circular area in the centre of which was something that looked like a fat log. With one enormous hand he lifted it up, shaking it vigorously.

Something fell out: a jumble of bones and limbs.

"I tracked it," the Mire-Beast said. "It's the Dream Seeder that visited the apartment in your world and sewed those guys with nightmares. I had a time of it twisting its neck and snapping a few limbs. Tough bastard. But it's dead." To demonstrate, he picked the thing up by the said broken neck and let it dangle, a mutilated puppet on strings.

"Is that thing human?" Ariadne asked. She saw our expressions and shook her head. "Okay, stupid question. So what, exactly, is a Dream Seeder?"

"They're spawned by the Moon Mother, their queen, in a nest not far from here. Kind of like wasps or hornets. You understand, this isn't your world. Things here are very different. Occasionally these creatures are sent out to other places to begin colonisation. Randomly, usually."

"Usually?" I said.

"This queen has company. Maybe even suitors? Who knows? Creatures with their own agenda anyhow. They want to establish a foothold in your Manhattan. I've been keeping an eye on them. This mucky terrain is the ideal cover. Bogs and swamps and reed beds and all are my speciality, right? Anyway, I found the hive and we need to neutralise it before the swarm emerges. If they get into Manhattan, well ... you can fill in the rest."

"How big is this place?" I asked, trying to remain calm, but several invisible fingers were playing a concerto along my spine.

"You'll soon see."

Ariadne poked the dangling corpse. Its bones jangled and I swear the reeds closed in a foot or so. "You want us to zap this nest, right? Three of us against a swarm? Forgive me, but I associate the word 'swarm' with ... with vast numbers. Usually."

"Let's get there. I have a little something for the Moon Mother." He carried the broken Dream Seeder to the edge of the reeds and dumped it. From a small nearby mound he scooped up what looked like a sack, bulbous and bloated, apparently filled with liquid. "This world is full of natural resources. These bogs are rich in oils." He dropped the sack on the Dream Seeder. It ruptured, spilling a thick gleaming mess over the remains. Then he snapped off a thick reed stem and did something to it with his spatulate fingers. In moments he was holding a flare.

"Stand back," he said, and I swear there was a vaguely lunatic gleam in his eyes. Ariadne and I retreated obediently, watching as he dropped the burning reed onto the oil-soaked corpse's remains. They went up in a vivid *whoosh*. Flames roared and the surrounding reeds bent back as if a high wind had buffeted them. A filthy black cloud discharged itself into the sky. Flames crackled. The Mire-Beast waited briefly before stamping out the miniature inferno. Finally he dumped huge armfuls of soil and compressed vegetation over the ashes. "The queen will already have sensed her creature is dead. She'll maybe feel the heat of this too. So let's get moving."

Ariadne and I were glad to return to the barge and out of those damn reeds. I swear, if we'd stayed they'd have reconstituted us as compost. We untied the barge and the Mire-Beast used his massive hands to paddle us back into midstream. We seem to stay on the river for a long time, although my guess was we were in a different time stream. The monotony of the journey was broken by another looming shape ahead, a long stretch of convoluted stone, metal, and possibly roots, running right across the river, a twisted distorted bridge.

The huge construction, choked with thorns and briers and nasty spiked branches, made our route look impassable There was vague movement up there and I sensed a pungent kind of malevolence.

"Permanent war zone," said the Mire-Beast. "Bad enough having the Dream Seeders on the left bank, but on the right? Shores of hell, buddy. War on the bridge. Deadlocked for a long time. We don't go up there."

"Fine by me," I said as we passed under the cold shadows and the bone-grating sounds from overhead. Some way beyond the bridge, back in the fog, we veered left, easing into a narrow creek. The Mire-Beast secured the barge and we hopped on to another slippery trail. It glistened as if it had been made by an enormous mollusc. There were more reeds although their attention must have been fixed elsewhere.

We reached a bog, which extended on all sides. The Mire-

Beast dug his arms in the slime, rummaged about, and dredged up another big sac, a veined bladder. It vibrated like a water-filled balloon. More oil, I guessed. He slung it over his shoulder before wading across the bog. "It's not deep," he called, as if the words would fill us with renewed vigour and enthusiasm.

"After you, *mon brave*," said Ariadne, her eyes as mischievous as ever. "I'll be your shadow."

I had both my guns out. This was going to end, if not in tears, then in a lot of smoke. We followed the huge shape, the mire up over our shins. The swamp bed was slippery but solid and soon we reached drier ground, rocks and a few boulders. The Mire-Beast led us up an incline until we were on some sort of knoll. We kept low among the stunted vegetation. Beyond was a wide valley, dish-shaped, with a forested floor though the trees down there looked as if they'd been imported from a planet called Ythagogg, or some such. Any sensible gardener would have taken a napalm-sprayer to them.

Sunlight barely seeped through the dirty clouds. In the semi-darkness I made out towers and walls, the broken superstructure of a small city. It was being engulfed and chewed up by the forest. A few miles in, roughly the central area, a very big mound had been heaped up. I thought immediately of an ants' nest, though on a gargantuan scale. Either the ants who'd built it were the size of tanks, or there were several zillion of them.

I swore crudely and said, "What the hell is *that*?"

The Mire-Beast grunted. "The hive. The Moon Mother is holed up in there. This city is a crude duplicate of Manhattan and it's the home of the Dream Seeders. Last time I was here one of them tried to rip me open and stuff a few crazy dreams into my head." There was a deep-throated gurgle – Ariadne and I realised he was chuckling. Hell's teeth, was he *enjoying* this?

"I burned the critter and tossed out the dreams like a mess of bugs," he said. "But not before I got a few pictures from them. Visions. The Dream Seeders are all linked to their queen's mind, so I got to see her plans. Conquest and all that crap. Soon she's gonna perform a ritual and summon the swarm to that citadel and then it'll be primed and loaded for action. We need to get in there, kick arse, and neutralise her majesty. A nice healthy inferno should do it."

"How exactly do we get in unannounced?" said Ariadne.

The Mire-Beast unslung the sac from his shoulder. "The magic potion," he said, with another low rumble of thunder that passed for laughter.

"You are kidding," I said. "No way am I going to drink that disgusting muck—"

"Not drink. It's poisonous! We just smear it all over, head to foot. The Dream Seeders hate the stuff. Won't come near us."

Ariadne said, "Fire burn and cauldron bubble."

The Mire-Beast waved a fistful of long reed stalks. "Cooking with gas. Ready to move? There's the place where we can get smeared." He pointed ahead.

I looked at Ariadne, who shrugged. "No time like the present. Hold on to your hat."

The far side of the knoll was steep and treacherous. We wormed our way to the edge of the city, to several tumbledown buildings half-hidden among the knotted trees and undergrowth. We ducked inside one, apparently unobserved. Then came the obnoxious task of coating ourselves with the Mire-Beast's oily concoction. I felt like a chicken being basted in preparation for a long spell in the oven, and tried, unsuccessfully, to banish the image. Dripping stickily, we waited until the Mire-Beast sensed things were astir deeper in the city.

After a while we moved through dimly lit narrow canyons of mouldering stone from which thick tongues of vegetation poked, in some places knotting across the path, swaying above us as if they'd trail down and scoop us up like insects. We sensed movements within walls – slithering, scuttling, shuffling. In one place a huge bulk pressed itself up against an inner wall in an effort to break out and probably attempt to digest us. The Mire-Beast used his prodigious strength to scrape away anything in our path that might have impeded us. Ariadne used her blades to slash at any errant fronds and creepers.

My energy was flagging by the time the Mire-Beast halted. He lifted his head, senses attuned to this weird wonderland, grunting as if he'd received a message. He led us out of the canyon to another great gash in the stone towards pure darkness. I was about to decline the plunge into that featureless abyss but the Mire-Beast turned and climbed up a stairway, his bulk squeezed between the walls so he had to alter his shape in order to pass, in the way that a massive slug would have done. The bulging sac he was now carrying was absorbed into him, but I had no time to gape at the bizarre transformation. Ariadne and I were barely slender enough to fit through the cleft in the stone. Claustrophobia threatened to pulp us as we climbed the broken stairs.

We emerged through a leaning doorway into a chamber with a low sagging ceiling. It stretched for some distance, propped up by numerous columns, pale as roots, and bizarrely it put me in mind of an underground car park. But there were no vehicles here; the place looked abandoned, which suited me fine. The Mire -Beast, who'd now assumed his original shape, inclusive of sac, plodded on, ducking low and weaving through more supporting columns. There were a number of large humped shapes lying in the deeper shadows, piles of bones wrapped in something pulpy – creatures long dead, entombed in this otherwise vacant area.

The Mire-Beast reached a parapet and knelt down to peer over it. Ariadne and I joined him. The view was spectacular though not as inviting as something observed from an alpine Swiss hotel. Across a fathomless void was the nest, mound, citadel, or whatever the Moon Mother ruled from. It rose like a mountain, composed not of stone and rubble but of twisted knotted vegetation – but I couldn't be sure. It emanated life, a skein of veins wrapping roots and branches, pulsating gently like an organ, though no organ in my world ever got that big. Below us were scores of thick strands crossing the void to the citadel, like cables supporting a suspension bridge. Maybe that's what they'd once been in this place, but mutated in an evolutionary cataclysm.

I said, "Don't tell me, we're going over those cables."

The Mire-Beast growled. "No. We're going *inside* one."

Ariadne's stare pinned me. Dammit, that girl wasn't fazed. "Come on, tough guy. Work to do."

The Mire-Beast led us down the outer wall, which was broken enough to allow us passage, and we clambered on to a cable. It's surface was translucent, like plastic, although plastic didn't usually have flecks and strains of what could've been blood riddling it. Ariadne obviously knew what the Mire-Beast had in mind: she used one of her blades to slice an opening in the fibrous cable, widening the slit until there was room for us to slip in. Inside, it was like a wide artery, sticky but otherwise empty. I didn't want to think about a sudden flow of blood, or whatever, along this conduit.

Above us, on the curved outside of the cable, something thumped down. I could see blurred appendages. Several more gripped the surface.

"Dream Seeders," said the Mire-Beast. "The summoning has started." As we moved on, the light above us turned to deeper shadow as more and more of the creatures joined what was becoming a procession towards the heart of the gargantuan nest. I thought of huge ants, and the kind of numbers you'd expect to see at a forest citadel. The cable shook and I held on to my sanity with great difficulty. Somehow we crossed that chasm. Our tube led us into the nest itself, anchored within it, with its end sealed. The things above us had disembarked and we remained unnoticed.

"Do the honours," I said to Ariadne. She didn't need telling twice, happily slashing a deep cut in the floor. The Mire-Beast shouldered his way out, followed by Ariadne, then me. We negotiated a narrow cleft, all the time listening for the Dream Seeders, and debouched onto a high ledge screened by dense shadows. There was light ahead in a cavern of cathedral dimensions.

I gaped at the numerous ledges around the cavern's perimeter, layer upon layer, all thronging with Dream Seeders. Stretched across the wide auditorium was a massive hummock, writhing as if composed of bloated maggots or grubs, or maybe energizing roots. On top, on a flattened area, a single monstrously grotesque shape lounged, its glittering wings catching light from phosphorescent secretions in the high ceiling. The Moon Mother.

The amassed Dream Seeders were also bathed in that bizarre light, daubing them with an iridescence that made them even more horrifying. Their oversize heads looked like something belonging on a great white shark. The creatures eyes bulged, globular crimson lanterns. Arms and legs were ridiculously elongated and ridged with spines, fit to rip a guy in two. The swarm was endless, its droning welling, deafening.

We remained unnoticed but my guts were churning. I figured it would be a good time to turn around and get the hell out of there. Surely the Mire-Beast hadn't anticipated anything as massed as this army.

"What's the plan?" Ariadne asked him. Even her eyes now had a nervous gleam. She's superhuman, but not that superhuman.

"Attack," shouted the Mire-Beast. He reached up and grabbed numerous strands hanging from above. They may have been rootlets, lengths of web, mutated lianas, whatever, but as far as the Mire-Beast was concerned they were secure. He tugged more of them, thrusting one each at Ariadne and me. I guessed his intent – he moved too quickly for any discussion. Gripping his strand, he swung out over the chamber. Tarzan would have approved.

Ariadne sheathed her swords and was quickly swinging outwards. I was about recoil but something flopped wetly on to the ledge behind me. It was all I needed to get me into pendulum mode. Things happened damn fast after that. The strands held and all of us crashed into the central hummock, the spongy surface softening our landing, although I sensed an immediate rush of something, as if a myriad of *things* were heading our way for an impromptu feast. The Mire-Beast led us upward making for the queen.

It was a dizzy climb, hampered by the creatures trying to grab, poke, or otherwise dislodge us. Ariadne busily chopped into them, both arms wheeling in that extraordinary fashion she's perfected, creating a mesh of steel. I used my fists and spared my bullets. I had a feeling I'd need them later. The things I hit pulped easily – it was like punching sacs of dough or bloated worms. Hanging on to the side of the hummock wasn't easy but it sloped gently enough for us not to topple off into the bottomless darkness below.

At the top the Mire-Beast hauled us up and we turned as one, facing the arthropod Moon Mother. The bulbous head was bloated, elephantine, the wasp-majesty's thorax black and shiny as polished metal, her abdomen fat enough to accommodate the three of us should she be disposed to ingest us. By the look of her aggressive stance her intent appeared to be exactly that. I trained my twin Berettas on her but I guessed bullets would simply whang off that armour like sand grains off a saucepan. Ariadne regarded me, suggesting that she, too, would have a problem inflicting any damage with her blades. Only the Mire-Beast remained calm.

He'd pulled a handful of long reed stalks from one of the sacs he carried and with a deft movement of his spatulate hands did something that ignited them. He plunged the burning stalks into another sac he had with him, this one full of fluid. At once he was holding a blazing firebrand. Its blast of heat sent me and Ariadne tumbling. The Mire-Beast immediately flung the incandescent missile at the queen, where it burst in a cloud of fiery globules spreading across that dipping head. The conflagration was almost blinding.

"Move!" the Mire-Beast roared above the deafening blasts of hot air. I watched, amazed, as he leapt forward and grabbed fistfuls of the furry abdomen, dragging himself upwards. "She'll fly to escape this. Can't let her douse the flames."

If I'd spent even a second thinking about all this madness I'd have scrambled the hell out of there, but the adrenaline was flowing and the wild ride was in full flight. Along with Ariadne I leapt up on to the queen's body. As soon as we'd gotten a grip, dangling like ornaments, the queen did exactly as expected: she flapped those wings before they caught fire, taking to the smoking air. Up we spiralled. I had a sense of sound and fury surrounding us, the combined outrage, the anger, of the Dream Seeders.

We burst through the matted growths of the ceiling, high over the citadel. We ducked to avoid the streaming flames from the queen's head. The air streamed by, either helping to ease the flames – or compounding their horrific work. The Mire-Beast, sitting astride her abdomen like a manic rodeo-rider, drove something into it, a fat weapon maybe – though nothing slowed the flight of the queen. Ariadne and I clung on desperately, our strength surely waning, our lungs in danger of filling with smoke. On and on, over the crumbling city we sped, at last into the night.

"Thought as much," shouted the Mire-Beast. "She's heading for the swamp. Hold on hard. It's gonna get real bumpy."

"He's insane," I cried as Ariadne rammed both swords into the queen's body and we each gripped a haft. I was praying for a soft landing. "And so are we for agreeing to come."

"Remind me, why was that?"

"We're indispensable, so he told me."

We crashed into a dark morass of muck and weed, great gouts bursting skywards, a sheet of mire spraying behind us. The queen intended to douse the fire. She ducked her head into the swamp. It hissed, steaming like a locomotive on hyper-drive. We leapt off, our falls broken by the wide pool, and wasted no time in struggling to firmer ground – a wide tussock of reed and snarled fallen branches, debris that had compacted into an island. On slightly more solid ground we looked back at the queen.

Her head rose from the mire, dripping waterfalls of sludge, clouds of steam still surrounding her thrashing body. Amazingly she was still alive though her head swung in blind confusion. If she located us the grand finale of our escapade would not be good.

"Nick!" shouted the Mire-Beast. He'd pulled a long wooden spoon from his pack.

I stared at it, bewildered. He was going to fight the queen with that?

"Your hat," he said, reaching.

Now, I have a real fondness for my slouch hat. It's been through a lot with me, and a lot's been through it. Remarkably, this little adventure had failed to dislodge it. No way was the Mire-Beast getting my hat.

"Give," said Ariadne. "I'll buy a dozen new ones."

Another frightful hiss from the queen, coupled with the flexing of her immense and obviously undamaged wings, prompted me to acquiesce. I handed over my hat. The Mire-Beast held it out like a bowl.

"I need blood," he said, as if asking for a glass of water. "Blood from both of you. Mine's no good – too green. You're the only ones I need for this – your blood isn't just red, it's very rare."

Ariadne and I acted on instinct. The bulk of the queen was sloshing through the mire towards us. Hell, what choice did we have? Ariadne bared an arm and nicked it, letting a trickle of blood drip into the hat. Me, likewise.

"That'll do nicely," said the Mire-Beast. He used the spoon to stir the contents of the hat, which were no longer a few droplets but had become, well, a hat full. He stirred away like a medieval harridan until white vapours rose from it.

The queen located us finally. Her charred head, still crackling with tiny fires, loomed like the crack of doom. The Mire-Beast swung the hat, releasing it so it curved away like a boomerang in a neat arc that hit the queen in her head. If she'd had human eyes the hat would have struck smack between them. The contents cascaded over her like red paint. We stood back as a series of frightful screams rent the air. Her entire body rocked as if an invisible hound the size of a small mountain was shaking her. She exploded. We ducked. It was as if she'd swallowed several barrels of dynamite that had gone off.

For a while it was raining gobbets of fleshy pulp and chunks of disintegrating Moon Mother.

"Time to get moving," said the Mire-Beast. "Her army will not be amused."

I felt my guts sinking down into my already sodden shoes. If that massed army back at the nest came after us we'd have no chance. The Mire-Beast seemed to read my mind. "We can outrun them for a while. They can't fly."

Heartened, Ariadne and I took to our heels, not that it was easy to get through the swamp. The Mire-Beast led us back to the River Dreaming where we found the creek and, wonderfully, the barge. We tumbled into it as he pushed us off.

"They're coming," he said. He was right – the ground was heaving to the sound of countless oncoming Dream Seeders, a great wave sweeping over the swamp. "I'll divert them. Try and get upstream to where we entered."

We used branches to pole ourselves into midstream as the Mire-Beast dived deep down into the river. "David Goroth has discovered his true calling," I said. But there was no time for chat, though. Behind us, on the banks, the Dream Seeders appeared to be deterred by the river, but they made their way along the shore trying to follow.

Luckily the tide was in our favour, moving us quickly. Soon the weird bridge loomed out of the fog. There were Dream Seeders up there too, but they were distracted – perhaps creatures from the forbidden zone on the far bank, or whatever. We punted under the bridge and away upstream, leaving the screams and terrifying snarls of battle behind.

At the landing stage we secured the barge and disembarked. The mist parted to reveal familiar buildings. Behind us there came a sudden cessation of air currents, as if a huge door had closed. For now, the Dream Seeders weren't getting in.

Deep in a pocket of my soiled coat there was a buzzing. I pulled out my cell phone. Rizzie Carter's voice grated on my ear. "You there, Nick? Those three dead things just woke up. You were right, they needed containing. Get over to the precinct – fast! You gotta show me how to deal with them before they tear the place apart and escape into the city!"

I put my arm around Ariadne. "About that dinner date—"

She gave me her long-suffering look. "By the way, what blood type *are* you?"

"I don't want to know."

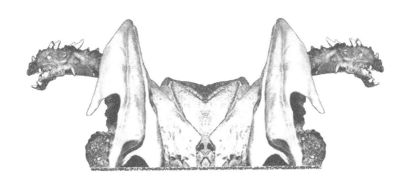

MEMORIES OF CLOVER

KT Wagner

Melisande drove by dozens of abandoned farms along the deserted road from the city to her childhood home. Most were once thriving honey operations. Good, she thought, and chewed her lip until it cracked and bled. Never much liked bees.

Seven years had passed since her last visit and she'd almost missed the turn-off into the farm. She pulled over to the side of the road and rested her forehead against the leather steering wheel of her Lexus. This close, the pull to return was unmistakable. It had been easier to ignore before.

Why had she allowed her younger sisters to talk her into checking on their father? It wasn't normally difficult to deflect their whining. They knew he cared more about the bees than his remaining daughters. She'd sworn on her older sister Deborah's grave that she would never return; yet here she was.

She lifted her head to stare past the silver hood of the car. Heat shimmered above the sun-baked ground. Summer-spent spirea billowed over the edges of the cracked pavement. The sepia-toned remnants of blossoms gave way to brown tangled scrub. On the other side of the ditch the remnant of a fence was visible.

As a child she'd perched on the splintered rails alongside her four sisters. They'd watch their father tend the hives. All of them wanted to help him but he mostly chose Deborah. Melisande had the honour to assist him a handful of times. The youngest sisters, never.

Back then, despite all, her father was Melisande's hero.

Once, she'd accompanied him and Deborah and several hives on a night-time excursion to an apple orchard across the county. Bees were dying and no one knew why. Farmers were desperate to rent pollinators and their father was happy to oblige.

If she had to put her finger on it, that's when he began to change. When he became obsessed.

She searched for the black and gold "Honey for Sale" sign. There was no trace of it. Did it fall down or had he removed it after Deborah died?

A gust rippled the hedgerow, chased by a dark undulating shadow. She cringed, then laughed at her fanciful imagination. Two worn ruts formed a rough driveway through a gap in the orchard. Rotting early apples littered the depressions. Puddles hid the depth of the potholes. She'd had the impression of drought and the rainwater seemed out of place.

The farmhouse lay beyond, out of sight of the road. Stupid to think she could simply drive up to the door, quickly check the old man still breathed, and then drive away. Not wanting to risk getting stuck on the track she decided to abandon her car. A sudden swirl of hot wind slammed the driver-side door out of her hand. She glanced around, half-expecting her father to emerge from the shadows of the orchard. He didn't.

She should have turned him in to authorities years ago. It didn't make sense that she hadn't done so. She prided herself on her ethical no nonsense logical approach to life and business. Her father didn't deserve to be an exception to that ethic.

Thick and flavoured with clover, the air pressed down on her.

Just get it over with. Squaring her shoulders, her heels clicked with authority as she crossed the forgotten road. She paused and tapped a manicured fingernail against the lock button on her key fob. The beep echoed oddly. The surrounding silence was puzzling. The soundtrack of any farm – the inescapable whine and buzz of insects – was missing, and on this farm it had been louder than most.

She scanned for the familiar hives. They were tucked within

the orchard, just as she remembered them, but the white boxes were cleaner and new looking. A contrast to the surrounding neglect. A movement caught her attention. Something leaked out of a hive, like a stain, then disappeared in a shiver. It reappeared on a nearby hive.

Sweat dampened her armpits, slithered down her spine. Her heels sank into the dirt of the farm's driveway. "Son of a bitch!" She jumped onto higher ground and yanked off her pumps. Pantyhose followed. Both were ruined.

The sensation of skin against earth was alarmingly pleasant. Almost a decade of monthly pedicures hadn't softened her thick calloused soles. She wiggled her toes, squishing mud between them as she strode through the orchard. Mud splattered her tailored skirt.

She ducked too late and a jutting branch snagged her hair. The pins securing her bun pulled free and honey-brown curls tumbled past her shoulders. She started to twist her hair back up and thought better of it.

That time her father stopped paying his bills she'd hired a private security company to send a man to check on him, but a shotgun was waved at him. It was prudent to remain recognisable at a distance.

~~~

The farmhouse was as she remembered. Same neglected sidings, bleached bone-grey by the sun, the same crumbling clay-tile roof, but it appeared abandoned now, in a way she couldn't define.

A dark splotch roiled just behind the faded-blue blossoms of a hydrangea bush. She recoiled, thinking it might be a web. After a moment, she gingerly spread its branches apart. They snapped and cracked. Pollen dusted the back of her hands. She ran fingers through her hair. Her imagination hadn't acted up like this since childhood – or perhaps her vision was failing. Her father's proximity infected her, and she hadn't even seen him yet. He had to be here somewhere.

Her nose tickled and she sneezed.

She trudged up the porch steps. The wooden treads creaked and the house sighed. The third shingle to the left of the door was loose, as she knew it would be. She curled fingers underneath to retrieve the key but the shingle held fast. With her other fist she pounded the wall above it.

Pain exploded through her fingers. She gasped and yanked her hand back. The dying bees had abandoned their stingers and entrails, which dripped from her swelling knuckles. As if shooting marbles, she flicked away the venom sacs, muttering, "Welcome home to me."

A clatter at her feet. The keys had dropped onto the porch.

~~~

Inside the house she yelled his name. "Beckett." Everyone called him Beckett, and he insisted his daughters follow suit.

"But you're our father," they'd argued.

"Not so much as you might think," he'd replied, but never explained no matter how often they'd asked.

Melisande called out repeatedly, her voice rising in pitch.

The house was tidy in a way that suggested the occupant had left for an extended vacation. She checked the fridge. A few jars of condiments and a pitcher of water. Nothing else. A ray of sunshine reflected off the kitchen table's chrome edge and the dust motes stirred by her passing. A light greenish film coated the Formica. She ran a fingertip across its surface and examined the sticky residue. Pollen.

Upstairs, the beds were made, the laundry hamper empty. In the barracks-like bedroom she'd shared with her sisters, a row of five neatly made beds remained. Agriculture posters were still pinned to the walls, their edges curled and brown. A rag doll reclined against a pillow. She couldn't recall which sister it belonged to, just that it wasn't her. She'd never played with toys.

In the bathroom, a tap dripped silently onto the rust stain circling the sink's drain. She twisted the tap on full and held her throbbing hand in the cool water. The stings burned more than they should have, and the water didn't help. Through the tarnish and grime of the mirror her eyes appeared larger and darker than normal. She looked like Deborah. Nausea threatened the back of her throat.

In the hall she leaned against the wall and shut her eyes. Beckett's letter had seemed urgent, but she'd put off her sisters' demands that she check on their father for over a month.

~~~

"He's old. He will have changed", they had promised, though they couldn't really know. Silly creatures, her surviving sisters.

"Why don't one of you go, then?" she'd responded.

But something else was also calling her back to the farm despite everything. It had made her skin itch, her attention wander, difficult to concentrate on her work. She hadn't mentioned this to her sisters, not even Beatrice, the next oldest. Perhaps she should have; Beatrice seemed to have matured since Deborah's death.

Beckett's brand of fanaticism rarely faded with age, Melisande knew, but in the end she had agreed to make a brief visit. It's more for me than him, she had convinced herself. For her own peace of mind she needed to finally do what she hadn't the strength to do seven years earlier. And she needed to know if he'd stopped experimenting.

~~~

Melisande opened her eyes. Perhaps he'd finally realised the futility of his quest and couldn't live with the failure, much the way she and her sisters couldn't live with him and his fantasies.

She sniffed the air. No taint of rot. If he'd chosen to end it she wouldn't find him in the house. Pulling back the yellowed curtain covering the window at the end of the hall, she peered through the warped glass at the barn. Her gut twisted. Run. Back to the car. Back to the city. She pressed a hand against her abdomen and forced herself to really look.

The barn's stone foundation appeared recently re-mortared, the boards above a deep red of freshly applied stain. Mammoth sunflowers bloomed along its south wall. In contrast, the fields beyond were brown. As far back as she could remember, they'd always been a sea of yellow and orange – and bees – in late August.

She could see the barn door trembling. Not tapping slowly as it did in a breeze but vibrating rapidly against its latch. Her chest tightened. She'd hoped to avoid the barn but unless Beckett lay dead in a field he could only be in there. She dropped the curtain and dust billowed.

~~~

As a child, the barn was strictly off limits. Mother's rule. Beckett argued. Mother held firm. Melisande never witnessed Mother stand up to him over anything else. In those days he spent his days in the fields and his evenings in the barn. Mother kept her daughters away, hovered over them, and avoided answering questions about their father. Only after Mother's passing had Melisande learned how much he obsessed over finding a cure for what ailed the bees.

Once, as children, she and Deborah snuck out in the middle of the night. Being smaller, Melisande climbed the pile of egg crates stacked under a high barn window. She had scrubbed at the dirty windowpane to peer inside but lost her footing. Deborah broke her fall but Melisande still took the worst of it. Their father had rushed out, his attention entirely on Deborah even though she'd only sustained a few bruises.

For years after, whenever Melisande's subconscious tried to revisit that glimpse of the inside of the barn that night, the gruesome memory of her shin bone poking through bloodied skin intruded. She told herself it was the trauma of the injury blocking her thoughts, filling her head with dread, but deep down she knew better.

Beckett liked to pretend the laws of nature didn't exist. Ignorant. Uneducated. Superstitious. He never had any hope of achieving his goal with that attitude. None. She knew better. She was right to leave, to study science. Her diplomas hung in her office, a reassuring reminder of reality. In the city she was respected. She had responsibilities. Her life was normal, fulfilling.

Beckett and the farm made her feel both suffocated and duty-bound at the same stroke, and horrible in every sense. She should've had him committed after Deborah had died, but her sisters had convinced her otherwise. He can't harm anyone except himself out at the farm, they'd pleaded.

Melisande never told her sisters that she had to fight an inexplicable urge to return to the farm, but that need made no sense, yet it lurked within her at all times.

~~~

She sucked on her aching knuckles and stepped inside the barn. The cavernous interior was fuzzy, like a wax-coated photograph.

Waiting for her eyes to adjust to the gloom she sniffed the air and called Beckett's name.

There was no scent of death, and no sign of life, either.

The stings in her hand flared. Beckett kept salve in the desk drawer, she remembered. She'd fetch it, take a quick look around the barn, then leave and call the security company.

She fumbled for a light switch in the dim but something brushed her face, her hands. She swatted at it and her mouth went dry. Spider web. She swallowed a shriek and tried to laugh at herself. Years of expensive therapy hadn't cured even this little phobia. She hated spiders. Like an ancestral memory, the terror of being caught in a web, the paralysing injection, the horror of being eaten alive... Nonsensical, but just the mention of the crawling monstrosities would leave her shaking and gasping for breath.

The gauzy stickiness clung to her hair, her hands, her arms, her face. She breathed deeply, as she'd been taught, trying to picture her inner strength and draw on her rational scientific mind. It didn't work. She hopped and flailed, hands now slick with sweat. Choking back bile, tears hot on her face, she finally managed to pluck at the wispy strands. They disintegrated and melted on her skin.

She ran further into the barn in her panic. The sudden bite of disinfectant seared the inside of her nose and shocked her into stillness. The scene in front of her merged seamlessly with other long-buried memories – she and Deborah had passed many hours here after Mother died. She'd forgotten that, until this moment.

The two long tables in the middle of the space were littered with short wooden planks bristling with pins and insect specimens. She recalled how satisfying it had felt to skewer and tape the little bodies into position. Gleaming metal trolleys had lined the barn's perimeter, the equipment on top draped in burlap, the exact way Beckett had always insisted on between use.

The returning memories were disconcerting and she needed to examine each thought dispassionately, figure out what they meant.

She saw the familiar carved oak of Beckett's desk. It wasn't in its usual place but now lurked in the shadows of a corner that used to be storage space. The air curdled around her and gooseflesh pebbled her arms. The hair on the back of her neck lifted. Her throat felt clogged. She clawed at her neck. Black spots swirled across her vision. Then the atmosphere popped. The room brightened. She sucked in deep breaths, almost giddy with relief.

A hooded figure was huddled behind the desk, wrapped in her mother's winter shawl. "Melisande, my dear, I feared you weren't coming. Here, take a seat." A corner of the fabric flapped toward a straight-backed wooden chair. It was Beckett but his words were strangely garbled. Maybe, she should have felt relief that he was alive, but she was disappointed.

He continued to speak in a slow hypnotic tone. She didn't want to step towards him, but the compulsions seeded in her childhood pulled her into the chair where she slumped, feeling younger, almost a child again; a strange sensation for a woman soon to turn thirty. It reminded her of something Deborah said before she died. The exact words were just out of reach. If she'd known her father would have this effect on her, would she have fought harder to avoid visiting him. She reached for her cell phone but couldn't recall where she'd put it.

"If our bees are to survive, you must stay this time." Beckett rumbled. "You are ready. You have been for a while. You can feel it."

Had she actually believed in his work? Surely not. She shivered and shook her head. "I don't belong here. I belong back in the city." Gathering strength, she attempted to stand. Fists clenched, she was halfway out of her chair when the wet smacking sounds began, like heavy raindrops striking a windshield. Her limbs felt light but her body heavy. Movement was becoming awkward and painful. She dropped back into her seat.

Turning away from the hunched figure of Beckett was all but impossible, the pull too strong, and nausea roared through her. He'd disappear if she blinked, she hoped. Melisande blinked rapidly. Nothing changed.

Tiny strands of membrane were clinging to her hands, her

forearms, and her skin burned with an itch that radiated from her bones. Her heart hammered hard against her ribs. A buzzing filled her head, and the room began to dim. She twisted slowly to the right and then the left, both to keep Beckett in her sight and to catch a glimpse of what was happening behind her, but she could only move a few inches. She deliberately bit her tongue. The explosion of pain dimmed her vision but cleared her mind a little.

The sounds grew. Melisande managed to tilt her face slightly, towards the high narrow windows. Like an unfinished jigsaw puzzle they darkened the glass in blotches, filling in a small piece at a time. The edges of the pieces squirmed and spun.

Bees. Thousands of them hurled their bodies against the glass.

The urge to admit them warred with that to run away. She staggered upright, tried to take a tottering step, and flopped back onto the chair, almost missing the seat's edge.

"Melisande!" Beckett's voice rang out, strong and clear. "Don't fight it. You are destined for this, the same as Deborah was. Deny and you'll die like her."

"This must be some kind of trick—" she was sobbing now "—another one of your awful experiments. I'm not Deborah. I don't believe in you."

Beckett became agitated, his cowl slipped. Melisande's stared at him, saw him a hundred times.

Then she screamed, a terrible sound that filled her, surrounded her, to coalesce with the memory of Deborah's own screams. Melisande buried her face in her hands. She felt soft bristles sprouting on her cheeks as well as her palms. Revulsion rippled through her. She wanted to run away, to escape her fate. Instead, she moaned at a sudden, terrifying realisation: this same fate awaited Beatrice if she died.

The urgency to flee dissipated, evolving seamlessly into a need to fly.

The drones outside the window crooned. She knew their invitation would fill the orchard and fields with a song from a long-rejected past. They sang of the chase, of how much stronger she was, stronger than Deborah. Melisande unfurled and rose. Her mind attempted hold onto the images of her life in the city, but they fell away as she forgot them.

Beckett spread his wings in welcome. She exhaled, expelling her human self, and stepped into his embrace. He wrapped his wings around her. The past and present merged. This was her time, her destiny, and now her life.

Her arms were thin, many jointed. She spread gnarled fingers wide and clasped both sides of his head. A gentle caress at first, before she twisted it off. But the satisfaction was brief.

The swarm surrounded her. She beckoned and it followed.

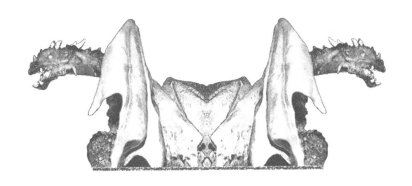

SUN, SAND, STONE

Marion Pitman

When I got on the plane, stupidly, I felt like I was escaping danger; the tension in my spine began to relax. It seemed like a good idea at the time.

~~~

At the bunfight after the funeral, over sausage rolls and samosas in the rather fusty function room of The White Horse, Dan's cousin asked me if I was going to stay in Yorkshire.

"I don't think so," I said, "there are too many memories."

"Will you go back to London?"

"I don't know."

"Will you go on working?"

What a tactless bloody question. Be firm. "Yes, of course."

For heaven's sake, woman, I thought, he's only been dead three weeks. Give me a chance to think. The accident was such a shock I hadn't yet got used to the idea he was gone. I abandoned my vol-au-vent and went to the bar for another glass of red. My friend Vicky had promised to take me home if I were too rat-arsed to remember where I lived.

But the woman had made me think – did I even want to stay here *now*, going back to a horribly empty house, wrestling with lawyers and banks and probate... I remembered what a nightmare it was when my mother died. Some things would have to hang fire while I waited for paperwork, anyway. I could take a week off, go somewhere a long way away, where I'd never been or thought of going with Dan.

Dan liked a holiday to be strenuous and not too warm. Doing nothing in the sun was not on his agenda. I do enjoy skiing and walking up glaciers and what have you, but sometimes I would have liked a change. A week's getaway, somewhere warm…

The funeral had been weird, half in sharp detailed focus, half a complete blur. There was a woman at the back of the church, in black, who cried through the whole service, and I wondered if she were Dan's lover. You can hardly ask, though, can you? I looked for her at the end but she'd gone. It must be pretty bloody for her; I wish we could have talked.

~~~

I suppose I thought of Greece because I'd been researching for the statue. It seemed nice and hot and sufficiently far away. So, I booked a trip to a Greek island. I wish I could remember the name of it. It was so beautiful – all the classic things: cloudless blue sky, blue sea, white buildings. I stayed in a small hotel where several more of the guests were English, so we chatted but I didn't tell them anything about myself, except in the vaguest terms. I didn't want to be me for a while; I wanted to leave all that behind, bereavement, grief, paperwork, having constantly to explain to people what had happened – God I hated that bit.

~~~

It was a commission for – a college? I'm not sure now. The stress of bereavement can do weird things to the brain, apparently.

A granite statue of Medusa, six feet high. I must have been bloody mad to agree, but they were offering a *lot* of money… And I was enjoying it, enjoying her… There's something about working with stone. People say the form is already in there. The sculptor's job is to release it, to cut away the parts that don't fit. You feel as if you're working with it, not on it, as if it's your partner. And when it's really difficult, it's exhilarating.

~~~

I got a booking surprisingly easily, but then the school holidays were over, so I suppose it was quiet.

~~~

It shouldn't have been possible. The damn thing was on a substantial base, and it wasn't top-heavy.

I was working on the snakes. It was a pig to work but immensely satisfying. She was beginning to appear, to show me what she looked like. So I was two foot off the floor, concentrating on serpentine curves, and Dan walked in.

"I need to talk to you," he said.

Well, it was damned inconvenient but I climbed down and took off my mask and goggles. There was a look in his eyes I couldn't fathom. And he told me he'd met someone else, that he wanted a divorce. I couldn't believe it. That he'd have an affair didn't completely faze me; we'd both had little adventures now and then, but – a divorce? Twenty years is a long time. You've got used to each other, you know? And all the paperwork, and the money arguments, and who gets the house … and I was fond of him, anyway.

Then he started, about how distant I was, how self-absorbed, how self-sufficient. "You don't need me," he said. "I need to be needed."

I just said, "What?" I couldn't take it in. And he started shouting and I don't like shouting, so I moved away, and he moved towards me– And she fell. I swear to God it wasn't possible, but Medusa fell on him.

I screamed, and made a futile grab – even if I had caught her I couldn't have held her.

He must have died instantly, they said. I suppose I was in shock, I went completely numb, walked out of the room, phoned the police, and waited, sitting on the hall chair. I suppose I let them in. It's a blank for a while after that.

~~~

They seem to accept that I couldn't have pushed her over.

~~~

When I was a child I had a recurring dream, where I was walking, and then running, down a shadowy road, and something was behind me – and the one thing I mustn't do was turn round and look at it. If I did that– I don't know what would have happened; it was something too dreadful to name or imagine. And the urge to turn was almost unbearable. I would wake with my heart pounding, far too terrified to attempt to go back to sleep. I don't know what brought it on. Perhaps it was reading the *Rime of the Ancient Mariner*.

After ... the accident ... I started to have the dream again, except that now I was walking on a daylit road with white buildings on either side, and I couldn't run no matter how hard I tried. The effort needed not to turn my head was unspeakable. When I woke from it I would get up and make tea and sit with the light on.

It wasn't death, to see the thing. It was much worse than that.

~~~

Dan's sister came and helped me with the funeral arrangements; I couldn't focus for long.

I locked the studio door without touching anything. I couldn't even think about it. I suppose the stone was still lying on the floor, but in my mind she's upright and leaning forward... Whenever I closed my eyes... I suppose it's a sort of PTSD. The doctor gave me sleeping pills. I think. Something, anyway. It made everything even more disconnected but I did manage to sleep.

The funeral was mostly a blur, as I say. It turned out he had a family plot in a cemetery in Chesterfield – I forget why – and Martina, his sister, insisted he be buried there, which was fair enough I suppose. We had a service in the local Methodist chapel, where Martina knew the minister, and then a few of us went to the cemetery, and the rest to the White Lion. It seemed wrong, somehow, to go to a pub after a Methodist service, but I think Martina knows the landlord of the White Lion as well.

~~~

So I flew out, three days after the burial. I'd never been to a burial before. Crematoria are all a bit anodyne and the chapel's never big enough, and they're on such a tight schedule it can feel like a bit of a production line. A burial's different: you're all out in the wind, you can't hear the words properly, there's this hole in the ground... We were all expected to throw in a handful of earth but I couldn't bring myself to do it.

That night I had the dream again. I got up and watched a film and drank white wine. The terror of the dream was still there when the sun came up.

~~~

I took a sedative for the flight. I hate flying. But when I arrived it was such a relief, hot and sunny and no-one knew who I was, or what had happened. The first night I slept like a log; if I dreamed I had no memory of it.

There was a terrace to sit on, and the food was good, and my appetite started to come back. I think a couple of blokes tried to chat me up, but I didn't respond and they went away. After a couple of days, I thought maybe I would do something besides eat and drink and sit in the sun. I went for a walk, looked at shops, and stopped for a drink at a bar on the beach. No-one spoke to me, it was wonderful.

~~~

When we were first married, Dan always said he liked my being independent, having my own work. And I thought it was a good thing that we were together because we wanted to be, not because we needed to be. People don't always say what they mean, do they. Or mean what they say.

~~~

The next day I went to the bar on the beach again but this time, as I was lying back with my eyes shut, someone said, "Hallo."

I thought, how do they know I'm English? and opened my eyes, and saw him. I say "him" although one doesn't want to make assumptions. He was tall, but not too tall, quite dark skinned, with a mass of wavy black hair. He was dressed in jeans and a cotton shirt, with a small gold chain round his neck, and large film-star sunglasses. And he was staggeringly beautiful. Beauty is impossible to describe, and is never quite the same for everyone. I can only say that his features were exactly what I found beautiful – and there was a kind of vibrancy about him. It wasn't sexual – I didn't fancy him. I just wanted to sit and look at him.

He spoke good English. He told me where he came from but I can't remember. He said to call him Leon.

He was very easy to talk to, he didn't say much but he seemed sympathetic. I found myself talking far too much, about my life, about my work, about Dan. About whether I could go back to work, or would it be too traumatic. About whether Dan's life insurance would allow me to stop working, at least for a while. Leon smiled and patted my hand. He asked me how I felt about Dan, how angry was I that he had had an affair and asked for a divorce.

I had to think about that. Strangely, that hadn't been in my thoughts at all. Was I angry? I didn't know. Dan's death had blotted out my reaction to what he had said just before he died. So I thought about it, and yes, I was angry. Furiously angry. And as I thought about it I felt a cold shiver down my back, as if – as if the thing that followed me in the dream were standing behind me. And then I felt a terrible grief, as if the numbness I'd been wrapped in had completely melted, and all the grief had suddenly consumed me. I sat, shaking, unable to move or speak. There were no tears, it was too deep for weeping. I was cold, breathless, almost feeling that I was dead as well as Dan ... or instead...

At length it passed, and I was slightly surprised to find the sun still shining on the beach, and Leon still sitting opposite me. He said, "I'm sorry. It's bad, isn't it."

I nodded. I still couldn't speak. The world seemed empty. I couldn't even mourn Dan properly because he had been about to leave me. And I loved him. I had got so used to him... Does it sound mad that I'd forgotten that I loved him? And now I remembered and it was unbearable. I felt the darkness at my back again, and my shoulders tensed. I glanced at Leon. I said, "Is there anyone behind me?"

He shook his head but said, "I understand what you're feeling."

He couldn't, I thought, but somehow I wasn't offended, I knew he meant it as sympathy. And perhaps, I thought, he'd been in a similar situation. Surely he was too young, but I couldn't judge his age: anything from twenty five to fifty.

He said, "You feel as if something is following you, yes?"

"Uh – yes. How do you know?"

"It's something many people feel."

"Really?"

"Oh yes. Here, at any rate. There is a darkness behind you, a coldness, despite the sun."

That was it, darkness, coldness, and I must not turn round, must not see it. I looked at Leon, his shades were very dark and I couldn't see his eyes, but I felt them looking at me. The menace at my back was suddenly too much for me.

"I must go back to the hotel," I said and stood up. He said nothing, just smiled, and I walked back to the hotel. I had dinner in my room, with a bottle of wine and some anodyne TV. That night I had the dream again, and woke gasping for breath just as I began to turn my head.

~~~

I wish I could stop seeing that moment when she toppled forward. I didn't push her – I couldn't have – but I feel guilty. I feel I released her from the stone and that's why she fell. Ridiculous, isn't it?

~~~

Two days later I walked to the beach again. I sat outside the same bar, with coffee. I stared at the calm sea; the coffee went cold. I didn't want to admit to myself that I was hoping to see Leon again. As I was about to give up, he appeared.

He brought me a drink – I don't know what it was but it was lovely – and sat down and sipped his own drink in silence. An oddly shaped writhing shadow flickered briefly across the table. I glanced up quickly; there was nothing behind Leon but the sea and the horizon. He saw me looking, and smiled. I turned my head and again saw something sinuous flicker to one side; I concluded it must be the sun in my eyes.

He said, "I'd like to show you something."

I was suspicious – etchings? His tattoos? "Show me what?" I said.

He laughed. "A statue. A carving. You will appreciate it."

"Where is it?"

"In the centre of the island. There was a village there, on the hillside, and there was a landslide, and the people moved away. But the buildings are still there, and the statue."

"A landslide? When was this?"

"Oh, many years ago. Long before I remember."

"Then how do you know what happened?"

He laughed again. "You are suspicious. People talk about it. The story is handed down. But in any case, what does it matter? The village is there, buildings and no people. Does it matter why they left?"

"Well… I don't know. I suppose not, if it's that long ago, whatever drove them away isn't likely to be there now." Why had I said that?

Leon smiled gently. "Exactly. So, will you come?"

I suppose I had intended to all along; it was just habit that made me wary. The way I had been feeling it didn't seem to matter if I was eaten by wolves, or whatever I was thinking of.

I had thought Leon might have a car but he took it for granted we would walk. I suppose it was a couple of miles before the ground began to rise. I looked up, and Leon smiled. "We don't have to get to the top. It isn't so far."

We still climbed a long way up a rocky path. I was glad I had flat-soled shoes on. There were bunches of vivid greenery scattered among the rocks. The rocks made me think of work, of Medusa. But these stones were not partners, not co-operative. They just stood there, as if in judgment.

The sun was baking my neck. I envied Leon his shades; my own seemed scarcely adequate to the blaze of light. I was sweating and breathless before we reached the outskirts of the abandoned village.

It was a strange sight. The sun was blinding on the white walls of houses and what must have been shops and tavernas and a church, but the roofs were gone, the windows were gone. Inside buildings I saw pieces of broken furniture or china. It was a very eerie feeling, walking through this place where people had lived and worked and loved and died, that was now utterly silent.

The streets were empty and clean, except for a few plants glowing in the light, but here and there were stone columns, some a couple of feet high, some up to five feet or more. They were worn and crumbling. They looked much older than the houses: moss and lichen grew on them – though nowhere else.

Leon led me through a maze of alleys till I lost all sense of direction, and we came into an open square. Around the square were the blazing white fronts of houses and shops, a wellhead, and more of the stone columns, apparently placed at random. In the centre was a statue – a statue of a woman, taller than me, facing away from us. I walked round and looked at her face: broad, blank-eyed and beautiful. Her body barely concealed in drapery, and her hair – her hair a mass of serpents, staring and writhing.

I had to look hard to be sure they were not moving.

It was beautiful, so beautiful. It was white marble, veined with a faint blue, and it was far more lifelike than my statue would have been if I had finished it. I would certainly never finish it now. I stood and gazed. I heard a hissing sound. Something seemed to move in the corner of my eye. I felt I must stop looking, must turn away. I turned.

Leon was standing beside me. There was something different about him – his hair. It was moving, though there was not a breath of wind. I was suddenly sure he wasn't a man at all. His hair was alive, rising; it was black and gold but it wasn't hair. It was snakes, gold snakes and black, and they were looking at me with little cold eyes—

Leon took off his sunglasses. His face behind them was not the same, but he was still beautiful. His eyes were gold – shining. I looked into them and could not look away. I felt the stone of the courtyard through the thin soles of my sandals. I felt the sun hot on my head and back and arms. I felt a thin cold air from somewhere. I could not move my eyes – or close my eyes. I could not move my head, or my feet, or my arms. The thin cold air spread through me, from my heart to my feet, although the sun was still hot.

I cannot close my eyes.

I cannot move.

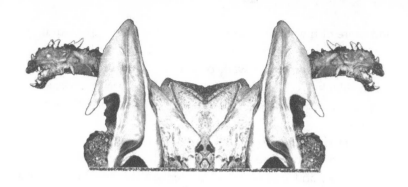

REDWATER

Simon Bestwick

Mist trailed over the wetland, twining through the reeds and cutting visibility to almost nil, even with the searchlight in the boat's bows. Normally I'd set off later to avoid the dawn fog, but since we were entering the Floodland's restricted area the mist helped us dodge the patrols.

The searchlight picked up hummocks of land – high ground or accumulated silt bound together by scrub grass – and scattered sections of broken walls, some still containing a door or window frame. A few buildings in the Floodland were more or less whole, but most had collapsed when the water undermined their foundations.

"Do you think—" began Tanner.

"Shh—" I whispered back.

Morg kept the *Jane's* speed to a crawl; he knew the channels and obstacles as well as anyone, but the banks and shoals could shift, especially after a storm – and I hadn't a second boat.

"All good up ahead, Bodie?" I whispered.

"Clear, boss."

I already regretted bringing Bodie along. He was a good lad, and I'd need a replacement for old Morg soon, but bringing a third crewman to balance our numbers with those of our passengers hadn't made me feel any safer. It just gave me one more thing to worry about.

"Fence up ahead," Bodie called.

"'Kay," I said. "Cut speed, Morg."

He throttled back until the *Jane* barely moved on the current. I peered over the side, holding the gaff pole at the ready.

The fence was twenty feet high, made of coated wire stretched between concrete posts. There was a lot of Floodland and river to patrol, and the river cops couldn't be everywhere at once. Fortunately they didn't know about the gap between two of the posts, where the wire had been cut away just wide enough to admit the *Jane*.

Submerged obstacles scraped against her sides as we neared the gap. Tanner gripped the rail with one hand, while Miss Zoll and our third passenger – a bald thick-set man she called Kolya, who so far hadn't uttered a single word – remained motionless and impassive.

Kolya had cold pale eyes and a gun under his jacket. Miss Zoll was similarly armed, probably. Tanner certainly had a gun; but at that moment he held nothing deadlier than a smartphone on which he was tracking a GPS signal. Once we were through the fence I asked, "Which way now?"

He pointed.

I gave Morg the bearing and he spun the wheel.

~~~

I make my living from the Floodland – setting nets and traps for fish, frogs, shrimp or crayfish – but I transport cargo, too. The river and its tributaries – the old ones and the ones that were born in the flood – are the main means of transport around here, now, having made the roads so unpredictable. I don't enquire too closely as to what I'm carrying. It's better if you can claim ignorance when you're pulled up by the river police, and better not to be nosy with some customers.

Occasionally I bring people into the Floodland, too – scientists taking water samples or out-of-towners wanting to gawk at it, which passes for tourism round here. I'll even take you into the restricted area, but only if you pay *really* well; it's a death-trap for any skipper who doesn't know it well. It's the former heart of the old town, where the ruins lie thickest. People have died here.

They brought in bodies for weeks afterwards. And more yet were never found at all.

The people who work the Floodland have a name for the restricted area, where so many died, and while technically inaccurate, it seems to fit.

They call it the Redwater.

~~~

We reached the half-sunken launch an hour later, steering through the reed beds and negotiating a maze of ruins clogged with silt. By now the mist was clearing so we could see some landmarks. A few seemed faintly familiar. An old distant familiarity – it had been over thirty years, after all – but familiar, nonetheless. The house where I'd grown up in – or whatever remained of it – lay in the heart of the Redwater. I suspect I could have found my way there easily although I never had. And I wouldn't today, either, because we'd reached our destination.

There had been a crossroads here once, now beneath the water, where a B-road met the A-road to the city. The launch was near here, at a relatively undamaged building – an old Gothic Revival church – and lay canted on its side, half-submerged in the churchyard, which was a relief; I hadn't fancied donning my scuba gear on this particular outing. Anyway, it was comparatively high ground here so the water was chest high at the deepest. Gravestones poked out of the water around the launch. Beyond it, the church's main entrance was clearly visible.

"All right," said Tanner. "Bring us alongside."

I shook my head. "Not happening."

He moved closer to me. "You're being paid to do a job, little man."

I had a short-barrelled revolver in my coat pocket and even with it I'd have little chance against Tanner, and Kolya, if it came to that. I ignored him and turned to Miss Zoll. "We can't bring the *Jane* that close, ma'am. There'll be gravestones and debris under the surface. Rip our guts out."

Kolya glanced at Miss Zoll before turning his wary gaze to me. She nodded. "Very well, Captain. How do we proceed?"

"Nothing complicated," I said. "Couple of us go over in the dinghy. Any idea whereabouts your merchandise would be stowed?" Miss Zoll hadn't specified the details of her "merchandise" and I hadn't enquired, for the obvious reason that if she approached me to help her retrieve it then it clearly couldn't be legal.

"It's a small package." She held her hands about eight inches apart. "Easily thrown overboard in an emergency and retrieved later." She gave a small cold smile. "The GPS is quite precise." I'd placed her accent as Eastern European; given Kolya's presence I was guessing Russian. A *bratva* queen-pin of some kind.

I considered what she'd told me. "And it'd be the Captain who made that call."

"Precisely."

"Most likely the wheelhouse, then."

I fetched a pair of binoculars while Morg dropped anchor and Bodie pumped up the dinghy. From what I could see the launch seemed more or less intact; a few windows had been blown in and there was minor but largely cosmetic damage to the side of the hull. The gravestones had probably caught her on the other side and torn the hull open.

Bodie put the dinghy over the side and climbed aboard. Tanner pocketed the smartphone and made to follow but Miss Zoll shook her head. "Not you, Mr Tanner. Give the phone to Kolya."

Tanner obeyed, scowling. I had no idea what he was, or even what he thought he was. Too much a pretty boy to be an actual hard man; I guessed him to be some sort of petty swindler with a halfway posh background that Miss Zoll had hired to help with local recruiting. Kolya grinned at him – showing half-a-dozen missing front teeth – and climbed down into the dinghy. The inflatable sagged under his weight but stayed afloat, and Bodie rowed them over to the launch.

They were alongside in a couple of minutes; Bodie tied the dinghy to the launch's prow and Kolya hopped aboard with surprising agility for his bulk. He crouched and peered through a shattered cabin window. I saw him frown – puzzled, if anything – then straighten, looking grimly up in our direction.

"Something's wrong," Miss Zoll said.

For answer, Kolya reached into the cabin and pulled out

something which he tossed into the water. Bodie gave a cry of disgust and recoiled, almost tipping the dinghy over.

"What the fuck?" demanded Tanner.

A human arm – sporting a selection of tattoos – bobbed in the water, severed mid-bicep. It had been sheared through, as if guillotined; but I knew it hadn't been severed by a blade. I was a fisherman, after all. Even if I'd never seen damage on such a scale, I recognised teeth marks when I saw them.

By now the morning sun had burned off the worst of the mist although a thin haze still hung in places; one such drifted over the former churchyard, between the protruding stones. I saw something in the water, between the headstones, something low and broad and humped. A monument, perhaps? No, it glistened, and then there was a pale flicker – two pale flickers – in the front of that humped shape, and I realised they were eyes.

"Bodie!" I shouted. "Cut loose! Get out of there!"

Both he and Kolya looked my way. Kolya reached under his jacket, obviously recognising danger in my voice but not knowing what – maybe suspecting treachery on my part. Tanner certainly did because in an instant I was slammed against the guardrail with cold metal pressed under the hinge of my jaw. "Stay where you are," shouted Tanner – I assumed he was talking to Bodie rather than me. Or perhaps he'd seen the hump as well, and was addressing that. In either case, he might as well have saved his breath.

Bodie hacked at the line and motioned frantically to Kolya, who clambered over the cabin towards the dinghy. Those pale eyes flickered again; then the thing flattened out in the water and shot forward, a low shiny blur that arrowed towards the dinghy with the speed and accuracy of a missile.

"Bo—" I began to shout but Tanner shoved the gun harder into my throat.

The thing in the water struck the dinghy a moment later and the inflatable burst like a balloon, with an explosive bang and a wet cascade of water. Bodie fell backwards, his mouth an O. He resurfaced, spluttering, and the thing sped past him. It looked as if it might be about to swim away but instead it veered back. Bodie kicked towards the launch, reaching out.

Kolya, crouched in the launch's bow, grabbed the railing with one hand and extended the other, but the thing hit Bodie before their fingers could touch. Bodie screamed and was dragged under. Kolya recoiled, shouting in Russian. The creature swam away leaving Bodie to thrash and scream in the reddening water. One arm was gone, ending in scarlet flesh and white bone.

The thing darted in again. This time it broke the surface just before it struck. At first the creature put me in mind of a gigantic pike – it had the same green-gold dappled colouration – but its pointed cone of a head was a cross between a crocodile's and a shark's, with teeth like bone chisels. The humped back was lined with a crest of spines.

The jaws snapped shut on Bodie's head with a crunch and a spray of blood. Then it plunged beneath the murky water, taking Bodie with it, leaving only a red stain on the water.

Kolya pulled a Skorpion machine-pistol from under his jacket and aimed at the water. Tanner, meanwhile, was off-guard, the barrel of his identical weapon no longer at my throat. I knocked his gun arm aside and hit him hard under the ribs driving the air from his lungs, then butted him in the face. He fell back onto the deck and I kicked his Skorpion away and stepped back, looking first at Miss Zoll, then across the water.

Kolya was watching the murky surface. Miss Zoll, a hand thrust in her coat pocket, looked a little pale but otherwise not unduly concerned – at least not about me. "Mr Tanner," she said as he scrambled to his feet, fists clenched. "Enough. Captain?"

"Fine."

Tanner retrieved his gun, half-raised it. "Mr Tanner," Miss Zoll repeated and he angrily put it away. "Captain," she said, "can you tell us what that was?"

I shook my head. The rest of me was shaking, too. "Never seen anything like it."

"I heard stories." Morg came out of the wheelhouse and stared at the fading red mark on the water. "People coming deep into the Floodland, into the Redwater, and not coming back. But —" He shrugged and stopped; he wasn't a big speaker.

"Fisherman's tales," Miss Zoll said, almost to herself.

"Bullshit," added Tanner.

Miss Zoll nodded towards the water between us and launch. "That was not 'bullshit'."

"A fish?" said Tanner at last.

"Big fucker," said Morg.

The waters were quiet now. Kolya stood waiting on the launch, gazing towards us. "We need to get him back," I said. "And then clear out."

"Agreed," said Miss Zoll. "How?"

"Get the spare out," I told Morg. "We'll use the outboard this time."

"You're fucking joking," said Morg.

"Morg," I said, "the dinghy."

Miss Zoll called to Kolya in (I presumed) Russian. The big man nodded, stowed his Skorpion, and reached into the cabin again. He shouted something; at first I thought he'd been attacked but then he stood up on the cabin roof, his arm dripping wet, clutching a plastic-wrapped package. He drew his weapon and scanned the water.

"Morg?" I said. "When you're done, get the rifle. Miss Zoll, can you operate the anchor?"

She nodded.

"Good. You'll need to raise it the second we're back on board."

"What about me?" said Tanner.

I didn't look at him. "Stay put, and don't touch anything."

~~~

We waited a few seconds after lowering the second dinghy, watching the water for any sign of movement, but all was still. I climbed down into the little boat and tried not to think about Bodie. He'd been a good lad, whom I'd liked and trusted, and I was going to have to tell his mother something of what had happened, but that would have to wait until we were clear of the Redwater.

The water lapped at the *Jane*'s sides, flat and undisturbed. The creature had broken the surface before attacking Bodie the second time; I hoped that was its habit, that there'd be a warning if it came at me. But I remembered, too, how fast it moved.

"All right," I told Morg. "Cover me, right?"

"Got it." He rested his elbows on the rail, tucking the stock of his Second World War M1 carbine into his shoulder. On the launch, Kolya swept the Skorpion back and forth through a 180-degree arc over the water.

The outboard motor caught on the first pull of the cord and I steered the dinghy away from the *Jane*. It was a clear run up until the last few yards where I entered the cemetery proper. I cut the speed right down to weave through the gravestones, and there were still moments when underwater objects snagged the hull, making my breath catch. I hadn't Bodie's touch with small boats in tight corners. I had done, once, but as my granny used to say, *old age cometh not alone, mate*. I forced myself to concentrate on the water ahead of me and not look around, but I kept imagining that humped shape, ready to strike. But Morg knew what he was doing, and I guessed it wouldn't be Kolya's first rodeo with the machine-pistol, either.

I was so intent on those last few yards of water I forgot about the launch and nearly ran into it, pulling round and killing the engine in the nick of time. I looked up at Kolya. "Come on if you're coming, big fella."

He bared his few teeth in that unnerving grin and climbed nimbly down. The dinghy sagged under his weight but quickly steadied. As before, to my relief, the engine caught on the first try, and I began steering it back through the gravestones. We were almost clear of them when Morg shouted: "'Ware to your left!"

It was maybe twenty feet from the dinghy. I made out the spotted green colouring and the cold bloodless eyes in the long head, its membranes flickering white across them when it blinked. Behind the head rose the hump of its spiney back. The bulk just behind its head resembled nothing so much as heavy shoulders.

Kolya took aim at the creature. It moved forward as we were passing the edge of the cemetery, flattening out and driving towards us. Both Kolya and Morg fired but the creature was too fast – their bullets only hit the surface, kicking up spouts of water. But it submerged and swam off. I glimpsed a long torpedo-like body, a pale underbelly.

I opened the throttle fully, wanting to get back to the *Jane*; but even as I did I realised I'd made a mistake: we weren't quite clear of the graves. There was a screeching rip as a stone caught the underside of the dinghy and we started to list. Kolya yelped and swayed sideways, then shifted his weight to the other side of the dinghy to steady it. The dinghy had multiple compartments – hopefully the tear had damaged only one of them.

By now we were clear of the stones and barrelling towards the *Jane*. Morg was firing again, over to our right where that now-familiar shape was speeding towards us. Kolya fired two short bursts at it as well. More bullets punched into the water just off our starboard bow as Tanner opened fire with his own Skorpion. I couldn't decide if he was trying to settle accounts with me – or just a very bad shot.

I kept my eyes and the dinghy's bow on the *Jane*, not daring to look elsewhere. When we came alongside Kolya pulled out the package – Miss Zoll's "merchandise" – and threw it up over the rail onto the *Jane*'s deck, before raking the water with the Skorpion as I scrambled up the rope ladder.

Morg was reloading the M1 when I got over the rail and I grabbed it off him. "Kolya! Move your arse."

He nodded and began climbing. He was halfway up when the creature burst out of the water beneath him. It was the clearest view I'd had of it yet: its thick cigar-shaped body was ten or twelve feet long, with large fins running down the sides, and a thick-ribbed tail. As it rose, the jaws of that monstrous head yawned open, and its side fins split away from the body. No, not fins, I realised, but two long finned arms that till now had blended seamlessly into its sides. A webbed claw with taloned fingers grasped the crown of Kolya's head, wrenching it backwards. Bone snapped and Kolya tumbled back into the water. The beast's other claw lunged up and grasped the boat's railing. The creature hauled itself up, its great fanged mouth grinning at us. I backpedalled and fell, sprawling on the deck, the M1 clattering away from me. Someone was screaming – I turned my head to see that it was Tanner. Morg was yelping "Fuck me! Fuck me!" over and again – understandable if unhelpful – while more usefully scrambling for the rifle I'd dropped.

Miss Zoll didn't look happy about events at all and for the first time her composure looked frayed, but at the same time she was a long way from outright panic. In fact she'd drawn a large sleek automatic from her coat pocket and aimed it at the creature. It was a heavy-calibre weapon, I noticed, bucking in her hands as she fired. Two shots hit the monstrosity, one punched a hole in its shoulder, splattering blood, the other caromed off its skull, exposing bone. The creature swivelled towards her and roared – a noise somewhere between a bullfrog's croak, amplified about a thousand times, and a maniac's laugh. It dragged itself further up the side of the boat, baring its pale abdomen. Two more rounds from Miss Zoll's gun thudded into its white paunch but it hardly seemed to notice.

At least its lower half was still fishlike, I thought; that would surely give us an advantage with it out of the water. As if to spite me, its lower body divided. One part swung over the rail and a webbed long-clawed foot slammed down on the *Jane*'s deck. Like the arms, the legs obviously knitted together when in the water.

Tanner was still screaming when the boat lurched, the deck tilting, when the monster heaved itself aboard. It was more than twice the height of any of us. Knives for fingers, chisels for teeth, I couldn't exactly blame Tanner for his panic.

It was more-or-less humanoid in shape, now, other than its height, its head, its hunched spined back, its clawed hands and feet. Three or four slits pulsated on either side of its head, like a shark's gills. It looked little more than annoyed, to say the least, at the damage we were trying to inflict on it. The creature shifted its gaze to Morg, who lay frozen on the deck, his fingers not quite touching the M1.

"Oh fuck," Morg said, very clearly.

It took a step towards Morg, and that was when Miss Zoll shot it in the throat. It actually seemed to feel that one; it reared back, gargling and roaring in pain. Perhaps there was a weak spot, after all.

Morg finally moved and lunged, catching hold of the M1, coming up on one knee as the creature twisted towards Miss Zoll. He aimed at its neck and might have got it too if Tanner hadn't broken into a wild run for the hatch leading below decks. The creature whirled at Tanner, who screamed again and fired his gun.

Panicking, he emptied the entire magazine into the creature in a single burst – or, at least, he tried to. Unfortunately, he was no expert marksman and the bullets sprayed wildly all across the deck. I dived and sprawled full-length to avoid them, as did Miss Zoll, but Morg wasn't so lucky. He was hit twice in the back and tumbled forward, dropping the M1.

The monster had taken at least half-a-dozen hits, even if none seemed particularly damaging. The *Jane* juddered as the creature loped across the deck, planks splintering under its webbed feet, and bore down on Tanner. He yelled just once before the mighty jaws snapped shut. The monster reared and shook Tanner like a rat, severing his body at the waist. The lower part of Tanner flew over the railing and disappeared under the muddy water.

By then I'd reached Morg. From the wounds in his back and the amount of the blood pooling around him I knew already that there was nothing to be done. If the creature hadn't have done the job I'd have killed Tanner myself. But it had and so I knelt in Morg's blood, shouldered the M1 and screamed, "Hey, you ugly fucking cunt!"

It swivelled towards me, its head down. I'd guessed correctly about its throat because it was clearly lowering its heavy bone-armoured skull to shield that weak spot. I shifted my aim; I was a decent shot and the range was close, but it was a moving target and the *Jane* was still shuddering. But near enough was good enough. I fired, the bullet scoring a line along its ugly snout before ploughing into an eye. The monster bellowed and – just as I'd hoped – flung its head back trying to escape the pain.

Baring its pale and already bleeding throat.

I emptied the rest of the M1's fifteen-round magazine so rapidly it sounded like a continuous burst. Bullet holes appeared in its throat, quickly merging into a large single ragged wound. Thick dark blood jetted over the deck. The creature swayed, its legs bowing. It bellowed again, but this cry was weaker. Its eyes flickered white, then stayed white, and it toppled backwards over the rail and into the water. A fountain of brown-red blood and water rained down on us.

Morg was barely alive, whispering, "Oh fuck. Oh fuck."

I took his hand. "Morg." I couldn't think of anything else to say.

"Oh fuck," he said and died.

~~~

I covered Morg with an old lifejacket and sat back on my heels feeling more alone and lost than I could recall since the aftermath of the flood, all those years ago.

"I'm sorry about your friend," said Miss Zoll. "Both your friends."

I nodded but didn't say the same to Miss Zoll. Tanner and Kolya hadn't been her friends; at best they had been employees and I doubted she'd mourned a death in a very long time, if ever. I stood and looked over the boat's rail. The pike-creature lay face-down in the blood-coloured water; it gave a last twitch and was still. "Well," I said. "You got what you came for. Right?"

There was a pause, and then she shrugged. "Yes. I did."

I gestured towards the huge carcass. "You could probably get a small fortune from any museum for that thing, too."

"I don't think so, Captain. This is more than enough."

"Fine by me." I briefly considered trying to take the corpse in tow for myself, but it would be hard enough sneaking our way back without lugging it behind us. Besides, I didn't want to overtax the *Jane* after the battering she'd just received. Half the deck was smashed and she was listing badly. It looked like Miss Zoll was going to have to sully her hands, pumping out water during the homeward trip. "We'll get going, then."

I reloaded the M1, surprised at how steady my hands were, and walked into the wheelhouse. Turning my back on Miss Zoll didn't worry me, not yet. She needed me to get her out of the Floodland. Back on dry land might be a different matter.

The *Jane* had drifted slightly after Miss Zoll had pulled up the anchor earlier, as instructed. It was just a matter now of getting the old girl started and steering her home. The motor coughed into life, to my relief; my big worry was that the engine might have been damaged in the recent free-for-all. I coaxed the boat forward, brought her round—

—and in our path: a line of low spiny humps with white

blinking eyes.

~~~

Whether it was the sound of the fight, the blood in the water, or knowledge of their fellow creature's death, a whole pack of the pike-things came running – or swimming, rather – towards us. From what I could see, most of them were built along the same lines as the creature we'd just killed. Some were a little smaller, but even so just one of the fuckers had damn near wrecked the *Jane* without even trying.

When the first of them arrowed towards the *Jane*'s side I brought the boat round as fast as I could. There was a judder and a howl as the creature's momentum carried it head-first into the boat's propellers. The engine spluttered and I feared we were about to lose power, but she quickly regained her old rhythm.

Having swung the boat around, I realised they hadn't approached from just one angle. A ring of the humped spined and white-eyed shapes surrounded us. There were a few of them in the cemetery too, dotted among the headstones.

Tanner's machine-pistol was fired, then again, and again, then stuttered to a halt.

"Everything all right, Miss Zoll?" I asked.

There was a clatter of metal, the snap of a bolt being pulled back. "That rather depends on you, Captain."

There was a tremor in her voice – and who could blame her? We were surrounded by water infested with monsters. I knew that trying to ram our way through them would be pointless. There were too many and before we'd gone any distance they'd board the *Jane,* tear her apart. We might as well try to ram our way through the side of the church—

"Grab onto something," I shouted and opened the throttle. I felt a pang as the boat shot forward but there was no choice. I'd build a new *Jane* – boats could be replaced. People couldn't, especially not me.

"What the hell are you doing?" Yes, Miss Zoll's composure was gone.

"Hold on," I shouted, and powered the *Jane* headlong over the graveyard boundary towards the open church doors. One of the beasts darted out of our way. Another tore at the hull with its talons. Submerged headstones added to the boat's damage.

"Sorry Mum," I said, before we smashed into the church's entrance.

~~~

I remember the rain, the flood warnings, but we'd had them before. Even the police going from door to door, telling us to evacuate, wasn't new. But the heavy rain was, the water sloshing round the car wheels, sheeting up on either side of the vehicle, Mum muttering to herself before smiling, far too brightly, and telling me everything was fine. Even at that age I knew it wasn't.

It was fortunate that the road ran alongside a railway embankment. When the surge came the worst of it poured into the cutting, filling it like a canal. But it flooded the road too, and the car's engine, killing it. The water rose and the pushed our car along like a toy. I remember Mum crying in fear just before we ploughed into a high wall. The wall held.

Mum popped the sunroof and climbed out onto the roof. She held me steady so I could reach the top of the wall. She was about to follow me up just as another surge hit, sweeping both her and the car away. They were there one minute, and then they were gone. I glimpsed the car's upturned wheels before it sank. I never saw my mother, alive or dead, again.

Later on the road bridge collapsed where it crossed the railway tracks, taking the old station building with it. The storm began slackening off after an hour, enough so they could send rescue helicopters. I was found about five minutes before I'd have passed out from the cold and slipped off the wall into the flood.

They never discovered my mother's body; or, if they did, she became one of hundreds of anonymous corpses in a mass grave. All I had to remember was her name.

~~~

"Captain. Captain!"

I could feel blood running down my face. Miss Zoll was shaking me, then stood and fired out of the cabin's door. Something roared, choked, fell silent.

The *Jane*'s motor was still running but she was wedged fast in the church's doorway. Wood creaked and cracked as the hull began to give. I grabbed the M1, the emergency flare-pistol and a torch. The boat's windows were already broken; I smashed out the remaining glass with the rifle butt and scrambled onto the bow. "Come on!"

"What the hell are you doing?" she shouted, then, *"What?"* as I jumped into the water inside the church.

It was barely waist deep – the floor was higher than ground level outside. The place stank of decaying vegetation, and the air was stale, dank and cold. I switched on the torch. Rotting pews broke the water's surface but I saw nothing else. I waded down the aisle. Cursing, Miss Zoll floundered after me.

The creatures' bellows, the sounds of splintering wood, rang and echoed behind us. Our movement felt maddeningly slow, the sludgy water fighting us every step. I climbed into the chancel, which was just about clear of the water, and headed for a door off to one side, hoping I remembered the church's layout correctly. The door was grey-green and slippery with moss and mould and fell apart as I yanked at it. Beyond, as I'd hoped, was a flight of stone stairs. Miss Zoll fell against me, almost knocking us both down. She looked bedraggled, her expensive clothes soaked, her hair a wet tangled mess, but she'd regained her old composure. She clutched her heavy automatic pistol.

Behind us, the creatures were howling as they tore the last remnants of the *Jane* apart. "This way," I told Miss Zoll, and we started up the stairs.

~~~

"This?" she said. "This is your great idea?"

The belfry was devoid of bats, at least. The wooden louvres that had screened it were long gone, leaving four stone columns and the parapets connecting them. It was a skeletal structure, and when I looked at the vaulted stone ceiling overhead it seemed disturbingly flimsy.

I stared towards the old railway cutting and laughed, weakly. "I can see my house from here."

"What?"

"Doesn't matter."

The church bell was still in place, now green with Verdigris. I rapped on it and dull growls echoed up from below in answer.

"They know we're here," she said.

Obviously, I thought but said, "Can't get up the stairs, though. Too bulky."

"A stalemate. So what now, Captain? Wait for the floodwaters to drain away in a hundred years?"

"No." I sat on the parapet, leaning against one of the columns. "A bit faster than that."

Miss Zoll lit a cigarette and offered me one. I hadn't smoked in years but decided I'd be lucky if I lived long enough to worry about any ill effects. I drew on the cigarette and coughed, but took another drag all the same.

"Well?" she said.

"Simple enough." I held out the flare-pistol. "This."

She frowned. "Who'll see a flare out here?"

"The river police."

"The river—" I thought she was about to lose her composure again. "The police? Are you insane?"

"They're the only people who patrol the Floodland," I said. "Especially these restricted areas. They might even send a chopper." That image brought back a few memories.

"And this?" She took the package – her "merchandise" – from her pocket before stowing it again.

"Won't come up. We're on a sightseeing trip that went wrong, if anyone asks. Out-of-towner with more money than sense, wanting to see the restricted area."

"We are *not* going to the police."

"Then we're back to waiting for the waters to go down on their own."

She glared at me. I waited. "All right," she said at last. "Do it."

I leant out of the window, aiming upwards. A webbed claw swept towards my face just as I fired the flare-pistol. I staggered back almost sliding through the hole in the floor below the bell.

Miss Zoll shot at the creature hanging from the stone column, trying to haul itself through. She hit it in the throat and it fell away. I crawled quickly to the parapet to retrieve the M1, and peered over the side. Three or four of them clung to the side of the tower, long claws digging into the stonework, crawling up.

"Shit," said Miss Zoll, looking over another parapet; I guessed she'd seen the same sight there. "So much for their not being able to follow us. How are you for ammunition?"

"One full magazine in the rifle, and a .38 snub-nose with five rounds."

She muttered in Russian and crossed herself, then gestured with her pistol. "I have five shots here, seven in a spare magazine. Also—" there was a click and a five-inch steel blade flashed in her free hand "—I have this."

I had a knife in my boot but I couldn't see what use it'd be. At least not until a creature rose into view – and Miss Zoll spun and slashed it across the eye.

~~~

After that it's a blur; only fragments remain, such as how, at point-blank range, you could inflict a killing wound on one of the creatures more easily by ramming your gun directly into its throat and firing. Sometimes, anyway.

I remember my rifle emptying and lashing my knife to its barrel to make a crude bayonet. I remember Miss Zoll covered in blood, her eyes no longer human, as though one of the monsters had flayed her and wore her skin. I probably looked the same.

After a while I decided the river police hadn't seen the flare, that no help was coming; that there was an endless supply of the monsters; that all that now remained was whether we died by their hands or our own.

Then I remember the beating of rotors, the searchlight's blaze, the crack of machinegun fire, and how, for the second time in my life, a police helicopter was the most beautiful sight I'd seen.

~~~

I was arrested, of course, but the charges evaporated. When I emerged from the lock-up, Miss Zoll was waiting.

"Thank you," I said.

She shrugged. "The least I could do. Come."

We drank coffee in a pavement café. We were in the city, miles from the river and the Floodland. Clean, hygienic, all mod cons. I couldn't wait to leave.

"I've transferred funds into your account," she told me. "It's compensation for your friends' families. And enough for you to get started again, however you wish."

"I'm grateful."

Another shrug. "Call it a bonus." She finished her coffee and rose. "Goodbye then, Captain."

"Goodbye, Miss Zoll."

I wondered if she'd tell me her real name; perhaps she would have if I'd asked. Maybe she'd have told me what the "merchandise" was, that Morg and Bodie had died for. But I didn't ask.

She studied me. "You're going back there, aren't you? To the Floodland?"

It was my turn to shrug. "It's who I am."

She smiled a little sadly. "Then I suspect you've only delayed the inevitable."

I watched her walk away, finished my coffee, and went in search of a ride home. I had a new boat to buy. And the Redwater called.

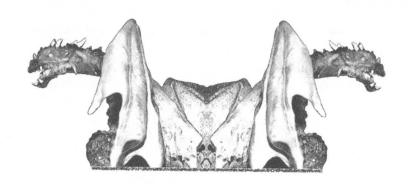

DREAMCATCHER

Pauline E Dungate

Ashley dumped the bag containing her meagre belongings onto the bed and scanned the room that was likely to be her home for some time. It wasn't high class but she'd slept in far worse. The walls were a plain off-white and from the smell, recently painted over. In an area above the bed it was possible to make out the underlying graffiti bleeding through. A brown stain was spreading across the ceiling above a narrow, grimy window framed by sun-faded curtains.

The furnishings were basic. One single bed with a lumpy looking mattress and a cheap table and chair. In the corner was a built-in cupboard but on opening it Ashley discovered that much of the storage space was taken up by a washbasin unit. As a plus, she couldn't see any spiders lurking in the corners. She really didn't like spiders, though she stopped short of admitting to a phobia.

"Bathroom's at the end of the hall." She'd almost forgotten that the hostel warden was standing behind her in the passage. Ms "call me Glenys" Williams went on: "A meal is served at six-thirty prompt and curfew is nine."

Ashley refrained from saying anything. She'd had the orientation lecture and she couldn't afford to be thrown out for offending the warden. She merely said, "Thank you," and waited for what she considered the shortest appropriate time be shutting the door.

She sat on the bed and clasped her hands behind her neck, letting her hair fall over her face. This wasn't where she'd expected to end up but at least she wasn't on the street. She'd get two meals a day and a small allowance to help her look for a job. Not that anyone would want her. She hadn't even got a decent set of clothes suitable for interviews, though Matthew, her probation officer, had said that could be sorted.

There was a tap at the door, a nervous sound. Not Glenys then. She would've thumped and pushed it open with brash confidence. Ashley had noticed that the locks opened easily from the outside, given something as simple as a coin. They gave a false security. She stared at the door for a moment before opening it. A degree of politeness wouldn't hurt.

On the other side was a skinny blonde of about thirty, her shoulder length hair ragged as if she'd cut it herself. The uncertainty in her stance made Ashley think that she looked like a typical victim. She held out the linens draped across her arms and said, "Glenys said to bring you these. You get your own next time,"

"What time is it?" Ashley asked. "I don't have a watch."

"I can get you one. It'll cost."

"Don't worry." Ashley took the bundle. The sheets had the stiffness of freshly washed cloth. They were well used but at least any stains would be clean. There was also a pillowcase and two towels in the pile. Glenys had explained that all – she called them guests – were expected to keep their rooms clean and do their own laundry. There was apparently a machine in the basement.

"I'll give you a knock when they start serving, shall I?" the woman said.

"Yes, you do that." Ashley turned away, pushing the door closed with her heel. She didn't want to get friendly with anyone else here. She didn't intend staying any longer than she had to. The hostel gave her the "permanent" address she needed. She spent a few minutes making up her bed and putting her few possessions out of sight. Orientating herself was her next priority. It wasn't so much finding where everything was but looking for exits. She was much happier if she knew all the ways to get out of the building.

<center>~~~</center>

There was a kind of communal room on the ground floor, next to the place where food was served. It was furnished with a scatter of mismatched sofas and chairs that had likely been donated at various times. A decent-sized flat-screen TV was pinned to one wall. It wasn't switched on. There were already three women in the room. One rocked a small baby in a battered pram. It appeared to have a wheel missing. She looked up as Ashley entered the room.

"It's all right," she said. "He's very quiet."

Wandering over, Ashley peered into the pram and realised that the occupant was a life-sized doll.

One of the other women waved her over. "You the new guest?"

"Guess so."

"I'm Bettina, this is Naydeen. Baby-mother is Hannah. You met Dolores yet?

"I don't know."

"Skinny blonde, pretends to be helpful. Just keep things out of sight when she's around. What's your sin?"

Ashley perched on the edge of one of the chairs. There was no point in being secretive here. Most of the "guests" were probably in the same situation she was, and there was probably an active gossip line. "Getting caught," she said, sighed and added, "three months shoplifting. Yours?"

Bettina gave her a broad grin. "Assault."

Ashley had the creepy feeling that she'd been dumped into the dire sit-com scenario and all these people were clichés. Bettina was the bully, Naydeen the fawning sidekick, Hannah the crazy, and Dolores the victim in need of protection. That would make Ashley the hero. She smiled. That would never happen.

More people began to drift in before a bell signalled that food was ready. There was a mixture of ages and ethnicities. The only thing they had in common was that there was nowhere else for them to go. Ashley escaped as soon as she had emptied her plates, taking them back to the service hatch. She'd noticed a shelf of scruffy paperbacks in the communal lounge and intended to grab one and retreat to her room. Keeping a low profile was her immediate intention.

~~~

Ashley locked the door and pulled the wooden box out of its carrying bag. Her grandmother had told her it was for sewing but to Ashley it was her treasure box, the place where she kept the few things that were important to her, all she had left of her childhood. She'd almost lost it when her grandmother died. She'd stashed it in the attic – the safest place she could think of – before she'd gone on the road gigging with a folk-rock band round all the summer festivals. They'd barely made enough to cover fuel, food and the occasional high, camping out most of the time. They'd been in a squat in Newcastle when the news had finally caught up with her. She'd had to hitch all the way back to London. When she arrived she found her mother and her latest druggie boyfriend chucking everything in a skip. After a furious row that left bitter feelings on both sides, Ashley managed to get into the house, the attic, and retrieve her box.

She had hidden it under the floor of a garden shed of the squat she'd been living in before she'd been arrested. She was lucky that the shed hadn't been demolished by the renovation company that had fenced off the row of houses since she'd been away.

She ran her fingers over the surface of the box. The polished wood with its inlaid design of an overflowing cornucopia had suffered. Despite being well wrapped in plastic, some dampness had got in leaving a bloom of mildew on the varnish. The lock had broken long ago and she had secured it with a couple of belts. Now, she undid these and lifted the lid, hardly daring to breath.

She smiled. The scrap of velvet cloth was dry and soft. Beneath, in crisp dry tissue paper was her prize. The dreamcatcher. The one her grandmother had made for her when she was six.

Ashley hadn't thought that spiders were scary. The ones in the garden sat plump and still in the centres of their webs. The odd one that got caught in the bath were comical as they scrabbled impotently against the smooth surface. Then her mother had dumped her at Grandma's. She'd sat at the bottom of the stairs surrounded by bulging plastic bags while the two women argued. Grandma's voice vibrated with anger, her mother's shrill with frustration. Then her mother had walked out slamming the door.

~~~

That night, the first of her abandonment, Ashley had slept on the sofa. Then, as her grandmother had turfed everything out of the tiny spare room and uncovered the framework of a bed, Ashley had begun to realise that her mother wasn't coming back for her.

As she lay staring at the ceiling watching the pattern of shadows the streetlight made as it passed through the branches of the tree outside, she realised that there was another type of spider. This sort had long thin legs which made them vibrate as they moved slowly through the patches of light. They were creeping up on her, resenting the intrusion of someone into their territory. Closing her eyes didn't make it any better. When she peeped she was sure there were more of them – and they were getting closer. Then one walked across her face. She screamed.

Grandma came rushing in giving her a hug. "Was it a bad dream?" she asked.

Ashley shook her head. "Spiders. They are coming to wrap me up and eat me."

Some grownups would have told her not to be silly. Not Grandma. She went away and came back with some little bags which had an interesting scent.

"Lavender," her grandmother said. "Creepy crawlies don't like it. We'll put them round the room. The spiders will stay away. Then tomorrow, we will make something to trap the nightmares."

It didn't help the six-year-old Ashley sleep. She sat up, her back pressed against the wall and watched. Just as she was beginning to think it might be safe to close her eyes the shadows above the window in the top corner of the room began to change. They coalesced into a darker more solid shape before stretching and moving down the wall. Two long thin legs probed ahead of it, other legs splaying out on either side.

Ashley stuffed the sheet in her mouth, trying not to cry out.

She didn't want to wake Grandma again. The huge spider crept down and disappeared into the blind spot at the end of the bed. She waited, scarcely daring to breath, hoping it had gone away, fearing it was now under the bed. She drew her knees up tight to her chest as the thin hairy legs edged over the end of the bed. They reared up, stretching towards her, the bulk of its body following. She could see its eyes, a whole row of them, black, shiny, staring at her. The mouth was wide and full of sharp pointed teeth. Just as she was sure it was about to pounce and eat her she smelt the lavender. It filled the room. The monster hesitated, then began to retreat back to where it had come from.

When she awoke, she was still scrunched up in the corner of the bed surrounded by a mist of lavender. She spotted one long-legged spider in the fold where the walls met the ceiling.

In the morning, Grandma had taken her to the park. "I want you to find some feathers," she said.

"What kind?"

"It doesn't matter as long as you like them."

Under a tree it looked as if a fox had caught a pigeon for its breakfast. Ashley kept away from the corpse but some distance away soft grey feathers, shot with purple and green, clung to the grass. Grandma produced scissors and cut long twigs from a willow, winding the flexible stems into her handbag.

"What do we want these for?" Ashley had asked.

"I'll show you this afternoon," she was told.

"What are you making?" Ashley asked as she settled down to watch.

Her grandmother had fetched her workbox and spread the contents over the floor. "It's a dreamcatcher. It will trap all the nasty dreams when we hang it over your bed."

"Is Mummy coming back?"

"I don't know, pigeon. She said some very rude words when she left."

"I heard."

Ashley chose the colour of the threads Grandma had woven across the circle she'd made from the willow, and the beads she'd threaded on them. The result looked like a surreal spider's web. She could imagine bad dreams getting tangled in it. The feathers she'd found dangled from the lower part of the circle.

"It's very pretty," she'd said, clapping her hands, eager to hang it up.

~~~

Ashley held up the dreamcatcher. The threads and beads of green, purple and yellow were still as bright as when it was first made. The colours on the feathers shone in the light from the window. She stared around the room wondering where, or if she should hang it. This was the kind of place where nightmares were likely to roam the corridors. She decided on a compromise. The cupboard unit had hanging space and a few rather warped metal coat-hangers. Bending some of the shape back into one of them she hung the dreamcatcher from the horizontal and closed it in the wardrobe, heeding what Bettina had said about keeping things out of sight.

She remembered the first night after Grandma had hung it over her bed. She believed her grandmother when she said it would trap bad dreams. It wasn't just the spider thing that came in the night. Living with Mummy had given her nightmares, too. Times when Mummy had drunk too much or taken too much "stuff". Mummy's friends frightened her as well, especially when they broke things and smacked Mummy. Those things came back in the night as well.

Ashley had snuggled down under her blanket and stared at the dreamcatcher, the feathers twisting slightly in an undetectable breeze. She'd glanced at the spider-shaped stain in the corner. "You can't get me now," she'd whispered to it.

A little noise had woken her. The spider monster was creeping down the wall again. Ashley very still. She had faith in her grandmother's magic. It crept closer. With no lavender to stop it, it heaved itself up onto the bed, front legs questing in her direction. She couldn't help it. A squeak escaped. The beast stopped, head swinging, eyes focusing in her direction. Ashley began to whisper, "You can't get me. You can't get me…"

It reared up on its other legs, the front pair stretched out. Then one touched the hanging dreamcatcher. In a moment, the monster was sucked into the web. Ashley there, hardly daring to breathe. It was gone. Just like that. The nightmare was trapped.

There were no bad dreams while the dreamcatcher hung over her bed.

~~~

Heading into the communal lounge, Ashley walked into chaos. Dolores was standing on a chair holding aloft in both hands what looked like a bundle of cloth. Hannah's pram was lying on its side and the woman was screaming "Give him back!" over and over as she tried to clamber onto the table next to Dolores. Naydeen's hands were linked around Hannah's waist restraining her but in danger of being hit by flailing arms. Bettina was standing, hands tucked into armpits, looking up at Dolores. She was speaking but her voice was too quiet for Ashley to hear. Glenys moved nervously around the group, hands flapping saying. "Calm down, calm down, all of you."

A number of other residents were edging out of the room or moving as far away as possible. Ashley asked one of them, "Does this happen often?"

"About once a week," she said and vanished down the corridor.

Ashley edged further into the room to watch.

Bettina raised her voice. "Give the fucking thing back, Dodo."

The tableau froze. Dolores grinned down at Bettina. "Make me."

"Are you sure you want me to do that?" Her tone was quieter but there was menace in it.

"You'll break your parole if you touch me."

"I won't soil my hands on you. You're nasty little thief."

"So whatcha gonna do?"

Bettina looked down. Ashley caught a smile as the woman said, "What's that?" and stooped as if to pick something up – and stumbled sideways into the legs of the chair. Her hand gripped the leg in an apparent attempt to steady herself. Ashley saw her jerk the chair; it toppled. She wouldn't swear to it, though, even if she had been sure.

As the chair tipped, Dolores jumped, more agilely that than Ashley would have expected. Hannah pounced, snatching the bundle from Dolores and clutched it to her chest, letting rip a mouthful of curses. The skinny blonde just laughed.

"It's not real," she said jeeringly, "it's just a fucking doll."

Glenys tried to take back control. "We don't use that kind of language here," she said.

"Don't fucking care. She pushed me over." Dolores pointed an accusing finger at Bettina who had righted the pram and was helping Hannah settle the doll back inside it.

"I over balanced," Bettina said.

"Bet there was nothing on the floor."

Bettina opened her hand slowly to reveal a coin nestling in a palm. The hint of a smile that touched her lips said, "Prove I didn't pick it up".

"Go to your room, Dolores," Glenys said. "Come back when you can behave yourself." To the others in the room she said, "I expect better from the rest of you."

Dolores sauntered towards the door brushing past Ashley. In the entrance she turned and raised the middle finger on each hand. Glenys bustled out behind her.

To Ashley, Bettina said, "Ignore Glenys. Everyone else does. She thinks she's in charge but in a crisis she's a bit of a wet blanket. Tries to treat us like naughty children and wonders why it doesn't work."

"A wet blanket might be some use in a fire." Ashley said.

"Yeah, right. The only reason why there's not complete anarchy is because she'll rat on us to our probation officers. Most of us are trying not to get sent back inside."

Ashley sat down next to Hannah, reassessing her opinion of these women. She still didn't want to make friends with them.

Hannah whispered to her, "I know he's just a doll. If they think I'm still crazy, they won't put me out on the street."

~~~

Ashley hadn't slept well the previous night. It hadn't just been the strange surroundings – she'd hadn't slept well in Drake Hall either. The dreamcatcher had been a good ruse of her grandmother. Six-year-old Ashley had needed the reassurance that it gave. As she got older it became a pretty ornament, but one she loved. That was why she had carefully wrapped it up and hidden it in the attic when she had gone on tour.

When she'd rescued it and taken it to the squat she'd hung it over her bed. Most of the others admired it. All except Eric. He wasn't just a dickhead – he was a malicious dickhead. He'd only remained in the squat because he was Sandy's boyfriend. And she had pleaded for him to stay as she "loved him". It was her brother's say-so who could live there. He was one of the band Ashley played with, which had got her the in when she had nowhere else to go.

Sandy was fascinated by the dreamcatcher. "Does it really stop nightmares?" She wanted to know.

"I believed it did," Ashley told her.

"Would it stop mine?"

"T don't know. Grandma said it only worked for the person it was made for."

"Can I try it?"

Reluctantly, Ashley had agreed, but only on a night when Eric wasn't there. He'd accuse Sandy of believing in superstitious nonsense. At minimum he'd humiliate her; if he was in a mood he'd slap her around despite being told that next time he hurt Sandy he was out. Problem was, she'd want to go with him, and her brother worried what would happen if she did.

The squat was a Victorian build scheduled for demolition before the temporary residents had arrived. Ashley didn't know how they'd got the water system working – and didn't ask – but there was no electricity. There were open fires in two of the rooms which gave some heat and light, but after dark there was mostly only flashlights and shadows.

Lower floor windows were boarded up but the upper ones glowed with the streetlights. Ashley had the smallest room so didn't have to share. It reminded her a little of her bedroom in her grandmother's house when she'd first arrived; streetlight, tree shadows and thread-legged spiders, but now no big hairy monster waiting to ooze out of the cracks.

Most residents retired with the sun. Ashley and Jaydan, her band mate, stayed in the kitchen – the only communal area – smoking skunk and sipping cider. The light came from a couple of candles, and with the back gardens surrounded by a wall it was unlikely anyone would notice the gleam of light through the cracks around the window boards. Most likely anyone living in the area knew they were there and ignored them, anyway, being more concerned with the winos using the end house in the block as a doss.

By agreement, last one in the kitchen made sure all the candles downstairs were snuffed out and the backdoor bolted. Ashley was wondering if she wanted to invite Jaydan to her room. Everyone was in except Eric who had gone to Telford, he'd said. Ashley drained her bottle and passed the joint to Jaydan who took a last long drag from it before pinching it out. The last few strands went into the jar by the camping gas stove.

"My room?" she said.

"Thought you'd never ask." Jaydan hooked an arm around her neck and pulled her into a kiss, the other hand kneading a buttock.

"Bolt the door," she said.

Before he could take a step it crashed open, the wood slamming back on the hinges. Ashley dropped to the floor covering her head with her hands. Her immediate thought was "Raid!".

As the ranting penetrated her mind she realised that it was Eric. She heard Jaydan say, "We didn't expect you back tonight," to be greeted by more profanity. Ashley stood up slowly and made little sense of what he was saying. Something had gone wrong with his meeting. He was pissed and annoyed and stomped through the kitchen banging into the door jamb on his way.

"Do you think Sandy can handle him?" Jaydan said.

"I'm not getting between them." Ashley waited just long enough to be sure Eric was clear of the stairs before rushing to her own room, all thoughts of anything but keeping out of his way gone from her mind. The fact that no one would protect Sandy was irrelevant. Pieces could be picked up the next day. She'd pulled blankets and pillow over her head to cut out the sounds that tended to penetrate the thin walls.

She was up and out at dawn. Yes, she was a coward and didn't want to face either Sandy or Eric, but it was also a good time to go down the market to spot dropped fruit and veg as the stall holders were setting up. It also meant she could get a good busking spot nearby. Usually Jaydan joined her part way through the morning. This day it had been much later. Since she was in the middle of a number she just glared at him. When there was a break he didn't give her a chance to comment, just said, "Eric's dead."

"You winding me up?"

"We spent the morning moving the body."

She glanced around. There was no one close enough to hear their conversation. When she didn't respond Jaydan said, "Can you come back and talk to Sandy? She's incoherent. Talking about monster spiders."

Ashley held out a hand, feeling the drops of the start of a shower. She put her guitar in its case, saying, "I won't make any money in the rain."

It took a while to walk the two miles back to the squat – buses cost money and Ashley hadn't made enough to allow herself that luxury. Sandy's brother and two others from the commune were in the kitchen. The air was already fugged with smells of dope. Ashley sank down onto a chair and took the joint that was handed to her.

"Jaydan says Eric was well loaded last night."

Ashley took a drag before replying. "Pissed and pissed. No way was I getting in his way."

"Wouldn't ask you to. We dumped him in the doss house. If anyone asks, you'd bolted up before he got here."

"She'll say nothing." He sounded very sure of that. "Sandy wants to talk to you."

"Hell. Okay. Where is she?"

"In your room."

No surprise there. Sandy had thought Ashley was her friend. The girl was huddled on the mattress. She had her knees drawn up, clutching them to her chest. There were new bruises and tear stains on her face. Her eyes were fixed on a spot near the ceiling. There was a long-legged spider hanging there. A breeze from the broken window caught it, sending it into a frantic spin. Beside Sandy was the dreamcatcher. One of the threads was broken.

"What happened?" Ashley had tried to make her tone sympathetic and wasn't sure she was managing it.

"He broke it. The nightmare got out. It ate him."

Ashley moved the dreamcatcher out if the way and sat down next to Sandy but didn't touch her. "Tell me."

"It was horrible."

Ashley waited. She didn't want Sandy to start crying again. She didn't know how she should react when people cried.

"He... He was drunk. He was angry. The meet had gone wrong. He...He..." Sandy gulped for air. "He fell asleep."

Not until he'd given you a good thumping, Ashley thought. "Did he just not wake up?"

Sandy shook her head. "I hurt too much to sleep. I tried to find the dreamcatcher and hang it up again. He'd pulled it down but I think it was an accident. The streetlight makes shadows. There was one on the dreamcatcher. It looked like a spider. There's always spiders. But it got bigger. It had long skinny legs and pulled itself out of the web. Then it crawled across the room. It climbed on the bed and Eric... It... It looked like it was wrapping him up in a web. And it stared at me. With all its eyes – and it smiled. I swear it smiled. And it bit Eric, it started to eat him."

"What did you do?"

"I hid under a blanket and closed my eyes. I was so scared. I was sure it was going to eat me next. When I woke up he was dead."

"It wasn't your fault. You had a nightmare."

"The dreamcatcher was supposed to stop them."

"It was broken." Ashley said.

When Sandy was calm enough to be shooed out of the room, back to her brother, Ashley looked at the dreamcatcher. The thread that had come loose was easily tied back into place. That evening she hung it back in place over her bed. She sat in the corner opposite the window, blanket around her shoulders and waited.

She'd dozed, jerked awake by a rustling. Something dark was oozing under the door. Two long thin legs, questing, then the inky patch of a body. It heaved its bulk up onto its other limbs. Ashley smiled. She wasn't six anymore. The tip of one leg touched a dangling feather and the monster was sucked into the web. Ashley stretched out on the mattress and slept.

Next day she'd wrapped the dreamcatcher in tissue paper and velvet and put it back on the box and hid it in the garden shed.

The residents of the squat had drifted away over the following few days. Ashley had been caught shoplifting – for lavender oil. It wasn't the first time and as she was regarded as having no fixed abode and she was remanded until the magistrate awarded her three months.

~~~

Over the last few days, little things disappeared from her room – the paperback she was reading, a few coins, half a bottle of shampoo. In themselves small but annoying to lose. She didn't have much and although she had a fair idea who was responsible, she couldn't prove it.

Thoughtfully, she fetched the dreamcatcher from the wardrobe and hooked its hanger onto the light fitting. Deliberately, she left the door ajar when she went to the bathroom, lingering in the shower. The little thief would have every opportunity to see it.

Ashley untied the broken thread before stowing the dreamcatcher in the wardrobe the next morning. She smiled when it had vanished by evening. She didn't report it; she might be many things but she wasn't a snitch.

"Sweet dreams," she said to Dolores when she passed her in the corridor later. The other woman scowled.

Ashley didn't know what to expect. She was guessing, and not everyone was afraid of spiders, not even big ones. Nevertheless she put drops of lavender oil around her bed – legitimately bought this time. The only sign of anything strange was at breakfast when Dolores cornered Glenys and demanded something to get rid of the spiders in her room.

It took two more nights before the rumpus erupted. Ashley was awoken by noise in the passageway outside her room. She opened the door a crack so to peer through, to see what was happening. Dolores was wielding a broom and striking it against the carpet and the walls. Her eyes were wide as she chanted, "Die, die, die…"

Bettina opened her door and yelled, "Shut the noise."

When Dolores ignored her, Bettina stepped up behind her and

snatched the broom from her hands. "What the fuck are you doing?"

Dolores froze, blinked twice and said, "Have they gone?"

"Have what gone?"

"The spiders. They are all over the place." She stared around, taking in floor, walls and ceiling. "Hundreds of them. Big ones."

"There are no spiders. Now go to bed. The rest of us are trying to sleep."

Dolores put on her victim-face but slunk back into her room. Ashley smiled and closed her door.

Rumours spread quickly. It took less than a day before all the residents knew about the incident. Opinions varied. She had got some bad skunk and hallucinations; nightmares from a guilty conscience; cracked.

That night, Ashley left her room and using a coin on the lock, let herself into Dolores's. The woman was sitting up in her bed, waving her hands around, slapping the bedclothes as if she was striking out at something crawling over her. Ashley couldn't see anything – it wasn't her nightmare.

Ashley crouched down beside the bed and grabbed Dolores's hands. She whispered, "It's going to get you. It will wrap you up and suck you dry."

Dolores stopped thrashing. "Make it stop."

"You have to promise."

"I'll promise. Make it go away." Dolores pulled her knees up to her chest as if something on the bed was creeping towards her.

"You promise not to steal from Ashley."

"I promise."

"You promise not to tease Hannah."

"I promise."

"What will happen if you break your promise?"

"I don't know."

"It will come back for you."

Dolores started kicking out with her legs.

Ashley took down the dreamcatcher from where it hung on the back of the door. "Remember," she said.

Back in her own room, Ashley mended the dreamcatcher and hung it over the bed. She had no idea whether Dolores would keep her promises, or even if she had realised that Ashley was in the room with her. She settled down, knowing that when she dozed her childhood nightmare would come oozing into the room and back into captivity.

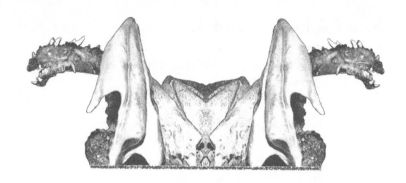

THE DAUGHTERS

Tim Jeffreys

So close to the open sea, the wind was biting and relentless. Kiara pulled up the hood of her jacket before pushing her hands deep into the side pockets. She had not seen the child since their first encounter that morning. She had called out to Kiara from inside the copse at one end of the park that Kiara had been using as a shortcut between the Seven Wives Inn and the police station in the centre of town. She wondered if the child had been watching her. If so, why had she waited so long to speak up?

"I know where they've put him."

The child, a girl of about twelve, dressed in a black hooded sweatshirt, had stood at an opening in the copse, the white oval of her face appearing to hover in a dark gap between the trees.

"What? What did you say?"

"I said I know where they've put him. Your boyfriend or whatever."

"My… My husband? Elliott?"

"I know where they've put him. They done the same to my big brother, Leo. But I went and got him back."

"Can you show me?"

It was proof of Kiara's desperation that she'd accepted the girl's statement without question. Clearly, after suffering the town's tight-lipped locals and evasive police officers for three days, she'd been willing to clutch at any straw. In truth, she would've gone along with anything that meant she could put off for one more day having to call Elliott's mother and tell her that her precious only son was missing. She had no doubt that Evangeline would somehow hold her responsible for his disappearance.

The girl tilted her head to the side. "Cost you."

"What? Are you fucking kidding me?"

"You want him back or not? Time's running out."

"Maybe I should just go to the police. I'm on my way to see them now, actually."

"Thought you'd done that already. Much help, were they?"

Kiera bit her bottom lip. "How much?"

"Two-fifty. Up front."

"Two—? Now?"

The girl shook her head. "Meet me at Begert Beach later. Five o'clock. You know where that is? Huh? *Don't be late.* Bring cash."

"I..."

Kiara had been distracted by an elderly man out walking his dog. He threw a suspicious glance at her and when she looked back the child had vanished into the trees.

~~~

On her way to the police station she'd taken a detour along the high street to find a cash machine. She wondered if the girl had only said two fifty because she knew that was the maximum that could be drawn from a cash machine on any one day. If it hadn't been a Sunday and the banks had been open, might she have asked for more?

Walking along the row of shops, Kiara noticed something she'd not seen before. There was a missing-person poster taped to a lamppost. It looked like it had been put up recently.

Simon Griffiths. Missing Since 27.09.19. Reward For Information.

Another one missing? And only a week ago? Why had the police not mentioned this to her? There was a phone number and a picture of a boy, around sixteen years old. When Kiara returned along the high street after yet another unproductive meeting with the local constabulary, a meeting during which the policeman she'd spoken with denied knowledge of another missing person, she was surprised to see that the poster had been removed.

Something seriously fucking strange was going on in this town, she was in no doubt about that.

Back at the inn, she'd looked for Begert Beach on the map Elliott had picked up when they arrived in Port Jared. It was close to the seafront ruins she and Elliott had walked around on their first evening here. Elliott had been excited to see those ruins. He'd even gone back alone to see them again the following morning, before Kiara woke up.

Once Kiara had pinpointed the beach on the map she didn't know what to do with the rest of the day. There seemed little point in going out and searching the streets as she had been doing for the past couple of days, showing Elliott's picture to the people she encountered. Remembering how the child had stressed that she shouldn't be late, and not knowing exactly how long it would take to get to Begert Beach, Kiara left the inn just after three. On her way out she stole a large knife from the inn's carvery, set out for that evening's meal, and made a hole in the lining of her jacket to hid it. It was a small solace to have that weight bouncing against her hip.

The beach was reached via a series of wooden steps leading down from the coastal path. It was an isolated stretch of sand, cut off from the rest of the bay by prominences of cliff at either end that reached out into the sea. When Kiara arrived, just after four o'clock, the beach was deserted. Despite the sun, the blustery sea wind soon chilled her. She paced from one end of the beach to the other to keep warm, sidestepping long tendrils of black seaweed strewn about the sand. The child arrived around forty minutes later. She carried a small backpack. Her face was expressionless.

She nodded at Kiara then said, "Got the money?"

Kiara took a breath. There was something she'd planned to say before handing the cash over, something she'd been rehearsing. "Listen, I want you to know who you're dealing with, right? I'm not some soft touch. I'm from Brixton. You know Brixton? In south London?" She jabbed one finger to her chest. "Born and raised. We don't take no shit where I'm from. If this turns out to be some kind of scam, I'll find you. I'll find you and I'll... I'll..."

The girl waved a hand impatiently. "Two-fifty, right? We agreed."

"I'm serious."

"You're wasting time."

Kiara reached into her jacket's inside pocket, took out the envelope of cash and handed it to the girl. She thought about sliding the knife out, as well, and threating the child with it. Show her she was serious. Instead she said, "I'll fuck you up. I will."

The girl only frowned, and threw Kiara a disdainful look. After a quick check of the money, she squirreled it away in her backpack.

"Gonna buy yourself some new creps?" Kiara said, gesturing at the once-white disintegrating Levi's the girl wore.

The girl narrowed her eyes. "You'd better be as tough as you reckon you are, lady. You'll need to be, where I'm taking you."

"Where *are* you taking me?"

"Come."

Kiera picked her way over the rocks in pursuit of the girl. "Hey, kid," she called. "You got a name?"

The girl's reply was snatched by the wind. It had sounded like "Laura" or "Lauren". Probably Lauren, Kiera thought. She looked like a Lauren.

Walking ahead of Kiara, the girl led the way towards the shoulder of cliff at the westerly end of the beach. On reaching the wall of stone, Lauren moved along it until the tide lapped at the soles of her old sneakers. She halted and turned to Kiara. "We have to go around," she said, pointing.

Kiara shielded the sun from her eyes with one hand. In the direction Lauren pointed, the cliff jutted out a few metres further into the sea. To get around it to the next part of the bay would mean going into the water.

"You're saying we have to swim?"

"We can wade. It's not that deep here. It's the only way to get into the tunnel without going through the ruins."

"Tunnel? What tunnel?"

"The tunnel where your husband is." The child looked up at Kiara. "Know how to pick a padlock?"

"What?"

"Do you know," Lauren said more slowly, "how to pick a padlock? You ever learn *that* in Brixton?"

"What do I need to pick a padlock for?"

Lauren sighed. "Watch," she said. From the pocket of her jeans she took a large padlock and held it up so Kiara could see it. From her other pocket she produced a handful of large paperclips. Unfolding one of the paperclips, she broke it in half so that she had two L-shaped wires which she presented to Kiara on her open palm.

"See?"

Using the two halves of the paperclip, Lauren demonstrated a number of times how to pick the padlock. Then she made Kiara try it. The icy wind had numbed Kiara's fingers and it took her a few tries before she got the padlock open.

"You're telling me someone's got Elliott locked up or something?" Kiara said.

"You'll see," Lauren said, taking the padlock from Kiara's hand and replacing it with the remaining paperclips. "Don't lose those or you're fucked."

"Be honest," Kiara said, shoving the paperclips into her jacket pocket. "What's this all about? Where're we going? You're screwing with me, right? You don't seriously think I'm going to wade out into the freezing cold fucking sea, do you?"

Lauren looked at her harshly before glancing up at the sky. Kiara followed her gaze. Clouds were moving in from the open sea. "Let's get going."

"Maybe I should just go back to the police. Tell them about this little scam of yours."

Lauren jerked her head around. "You *really* don't want to do that."

"Why? Are they in on this?"

"Everyone's in on this. The whole town's in on this."

Without further hesitation, and to Kiara's shock, Lauren began walking forward into the sea until she stood thigh-deep in the water.

"*Jesus*," Kiara said, suddenly realising that the child was deadly serious.

Lauren looked back at Kiara. "You coming or not?"

Kiara allowed herself a moment to look over the water. *Must be freezing.* Taking a deep breath, she cast away her reluctance.

At the shock of cold she cried out. She began at once to wade forward, following Lauren, half-carried by the pull of the retreating waves. She had to move cautiously, fighting the tide which threatened to throw her off balance and push her back towards the beach.

Lauren went ahead, quickly disappearing around the rocky verge at the cliff's end.

Once Kiara had made it around this verge herself, she saw what Lauren had meant by "tunnel". On this part of the bay there was no beach. The sea beat up against a flat wall of cliff. Cut into the rock was what looked like a man-made circular opening. About a third of this opening was submerged, which meant that the tunnel entrance, if that's what it was, swallowed tide water. Raising her eyes, Kiara saw that on the clifftop directly above stood those ancient ruins Elliott had led her around of their first evening in Port Jared. She lowered her eyes; the child was wading forward towards the circular opening. Glimpsing the darkness inside, Kiara shivered.

You better be as tough as you say you are, lady. You'll need to be, where I'm taking you.

While Kiara hesitated and allowed herself to be bullied by the sea, Lauren reached the mouth of the tunnel, climbed inside, turned, and stood making frantic gestures for Kiara to hurry whilst throwing wary glances up the wall of rock to where the ruins stood.

"Nah," Kiara said to herself, shaking her head. "Nah. This is crazy."

She glanced over her shoulder. Was it too late to go back? The sea answered: yes. The waves forced her inland, through the opening, and into the sunless confines of the tunnel where the child waited. There was a smell like dead things: thick, pungent.

Kiara wrapped her arms around herself, shivering, her teeth chattering. The seawater slapped around her knees. "What... What the fuck are we doing?"

"Getting your husband back."

"What the hell is this place?"

The girl – Lauren – appeared less sullen now that they'd reached the confines of the tunnel, as if she felt at home there in the dark. "This is where they put them. The men. For when the daughters come."

"*The daughters*? What are you on about?"

"Don't you know about the daughters of Port Jared? It's a legend. There's even a song." Lauren sang flatly under her breath:

"Beware, beware the daughters of Port Jared,
run ye home when their repellent caw be hear-ed.
With faces of women and the wings of the bir-ed,
they have come to fill their feathered gullets,
with husbands, sons and all afear-ed."

"What the fuck is that?"

"I told you."

Kiara remembered Elliott telling her something about Port Jared's local legend. He had shown her a picture, a pen-and-ink drawing of what looked like an eagle with the head and breasts of a woman. At the time she'd laughed. It was the kind of thing Elliott loved to talk about, the kind of thing she didn't pay much attention to when he did.

"That's just a story."

"Ha! What do you know? Come on."

Wading through the darkness inside the tunnel proved treacherous. A number of times Kiara almost stumbled and fell, her cries of alarm echoing in the dark throat. Staying close to the right-hand wall, she clutched at the thin, mossy edges of the brickwork. Behind her she could see the lighted arch of the tunnel entrance, but ahead was nothing but the dark. The water lapped at the walls on either side as it raced along, slapping and slurping and throwing back sinister echoes. The stink thickened. Kiara kept looking back to remind herself that the world of sunshine and sand she had vacated still remained, albeit shrinking further and further away as she followed the child deeper into the dark.

The water began to grow shallow. From being knee deep the water slowly reduced until she became aware of the noise she made as she waded – *splish, splosh! splish, splosh!* – and of her wet jeans clinging to her legs. She was shivering uncontrollably now.

A number of times she stumbled and almost keeled face-first into the shallow seawater. Her hand disturbed something as it moved along the tunnel wall, something that squirmed under her probing fingers. She could not prevent a small shriek of fright.

"Hush!" Lauren said from somewhere in the dark ahead of her. "For Christ's sake, you wanna get us caught?"

Stopping to recover herself, Kiara pictured the ruins. She remembered how much Elliott had wanted her to share in his enthusiasm as he'd led her around the ruins that first evening after the long drive from London; and how hard she'd tried to show an interest despite being hungry and tired and finding the ruins eerie, especially after Elliott pointed out what was left of a hollow stone tower inside which, he said, people had once been hung. When he'd suggested a holiday in Cornwall for their one-year anniversary, she'd known it would involve a tour or two around some crumbling castle. She'd always enjoyed the child-like glee Elliott had in visiting such places more than she actually enjoyed visiting them herself.

Could he really be down here?

After resting a moment against the wall, she turned her head in the darkness, her heart hammering as she listened for the sound of Lauren's footsteps in the shallow water.

I'm coming Elliott. I'm coming.

I won't leave you.

I'm your Brixton bride, remember? SW9 crew.

It's why your mother hates me.

It's why we're gonna get out of this.

Whoever did this didn't know who they were fucking with.

She tried to focus her mind, make some attempt to still the trembling in her limbs, ease her numbed and reluctant body from the wall, and continue forward. And she did.

"Where're we going? Hey, kid, you there? Where're we going?"

"Not far now."

~~~

Pale sunlight entered the tunnel through a shaft with a barred circular opening overhead. A large square cage was suspended from the bars, so that the light falling in spot-lit the captive within it. So mixed, so swift and powerful was the flood of emotion Kiara felt on seeing this, she had to support herself against the wall.

Who would do this? Who the hell would do this to another human being?

Steadying herself, she looked again. The shallow seawater flowed under and onwards, past the cage. Kiara looked to left and right and saw a further tunnel crossing this one, its two entrances in the wall on either side of the cage.

Without stepping into the dim light, Lauren circled the cage, as if inspecting it. The occupant was lying on his back in a cage barely large enough to accommodate him. His face was turned away from Kiara. One leg was hanging limply through the cage's bars. His head jerked up. At this, Lauren drew further back into the dark. The prisoner wasn't Elliott, and Kiara felt faintly relieved. It was a boy who looked to be in his teens. He stared into the darkness with fear and suspicion.

"Someone there?"

Slowly, the occupant reclaimed his leg from between the bars and drew both knees up to his chest. The cage tipped and swayed at his every movement. His eyes, alert and fearful, rolled from side to side, searching the dark.

"Go on, who is it? Who's there?"

There was something familiar about the boy's face. Kiara felt that she had seen him somewhere before but she couldn't recall where. "It's all right," Kiara answered, the soft lilt of her voice catching him unawares.

He froze with his head turned to one side. He looked for her in the darkness. His voice trembled when he said: "Who… Who's there?"

Kiara moved forward into the light, pushing the hood away from her face. She touched his hand through the bars. "Don't worry? We're gonna get you out of there? What's your name?"

Before the boy could answer, Lauren stepped forward and said in a hushed urgent voice: "*He's* not your husband?"

"Of course not. He's just a kid."

"Fuck! Leave him."

The captive had gathered himself onto his knees. He pressed

his face onto the bars of the cage. "Don't leave me for the daughters!"

"We can't just leave him," Kiara said.

"There isn't time. You want him or you want your husband? Pick one."

"Let me out. Please. Please! Pleeeeease!"

This last struck such a note of desperation that Kiara staggered backwards from the cage. Seeing her move into the darkness, the boy howled and shook the bars of his prison. But the rattling of his cage brought him attention from above. A voice bellowed down: "Shut it!"

The boy fell quiet, turning his face up to the light.

"Help," he pleaded. His plea was directed upwards at the shadow that had fallen across his circle of light.

Kiara's gaze too moved in that direction. She held her breath. Fearing attention from above, Kiara moved away from the cage. Her movements in the shallow water alerted the boy once more to her presence. He looked for her in the surrounding darkness, his eyes wide.

"Ghosts," he said. Raising his voice, he glanced upwards. "There's ghosts down here!"

"Shut it!" came the voice again. There was the sound of men laughing.

The boy lowered his head. He became still, holding himself and whimpering.

Appalled by her own impotence, Kiara moved to the mouth of the crossing tunnel, looking only to escape the scene. She was bewildered at finding this stranger in the cage, but as she came to the mouth of the second tunnel she understood at last what she had so far failed to realise.

Ahead of her, another cage was suspended beneath a shaft, covered with a barred skylight. Another prisoner lay inert within the bars. Beyond this cage, further along the tunnel, she saw another. And after this was another. And though she could see ahead no further than this she felt sure more would follow.

"Jesus fucking Christ! How many fucking people are down here?"

"Shush!" Lauren said.

Slowly, fearful, Kiara followed her into the one of the crossing tunnels. It would have been a mercy for Kiara if the second cage was occupied by her husband – but it wasn't. The man turned watery hopeless eyes towards them as they approached.

They kept to the shadows round the cage, not wanting to draw any attention from above. Kiara thought it would be easier on the prisoners if they were unable to see her and the girl. *Let them think we're ghosts*, she thought, knowing there could be no help from a wandering spirit. She did not want to give them false hope. She had not come for them. Besides, she could see by his condition that the man in that cage was not far from death.

They moved past his cage to the next one. This one housed a small figure, a young boy. He lay on his back, his wide staring eyes seeming to find her even in the darkness. He did not move or begin to shout, but his eyes were so alive and desperate Kiara could not look at him for more than a moment. She had a sense that he had been expecting someone, as though he had long lain in his cage certain that some help would come – but waiting, only waiting. It was all she could do to continue, to move past the cage of the trapped and helpless boy. She followed Lauren, wading through the shallow water.

"We have to do something!" Kiara hissed. "We can't just leave them! He's only a kid!"

"We can't," Lauren hissed back.

Coming upon the next cage, Kiara looked only long enough to ascertain that the captive was not Elliott. She felt her heart would break if she stared for too long, and she would be overwhelmed by her inability to help these people. Another cage, and still hadn't found Elliott. Kiara began to hope, with a sense of relief, that he was not down here. There had been a mistake. Elliott was not one of these prisoners.

At the following cage, a man lay curled within, his back to her. His arms were held over his head so that she could not see his hair, but still she recognised him. "Elliott!" she exclaimed. "It's you, at last, it's you!"

When Kiara said this she heard, behind her, quick retreating footsteps. Lauren was abandoning her. Spinning round, Kiara called in a clipped voice, "Wait! Wait!"

But the footsteps didn't slow. Lauren, her promise fulfilled, was getting the hell out of there. "Hurry, lady," Lauren called from further along the tunnel. "They come at dusk."

~~~

Elliott slumped against the bars of the cage. His lips were cracked with the salt water, his eyes red-rimmed. It hurt Kiara to see him in this state, thinking of the days he must have spent cooped-up down here. How scared he'd been. How he must have suffered.

When I find found out who's responsible, she thought, *there will be hell to pay, that's for sure.*

Kiara wished she had thought to bring a bottle of water, or some food. She'd extracted the knife from the lining of her jacket and handed it to Elliott, but he didn't look like he had the strength to do anything but hold it loosely. He watched Kiara in silence, through his grimy fringe, as she attempted to pick the padlock on his cage door. It was slow going because of her cold trembling hands, and she became agitated. Lines of sweat formed on her brow, stinging her eyes. She tried to remember the technique Lauren had demonstrated. Now and then she flicked a glance at the barred opening high above, wondering if the light coming through seemed dimmer.

They come at dusk, Lauren had said. What time would that be? Around eight? She checked her watch but she must have got it wet – it had stopped at a quarter to six and she was sure that it had to be later than that.

"Knew you'd find me," Elliott said in a clogged weary voice. "Knew you'd come."

"Have I ever let you down, babes?"

"I wanted one more look around the ruins —" he hesitated " — and someone put a sack over my head. I didn't see who. Hit me with something. When I came to I was in this place."

The paperclip Kiara was using to pick the padlock snapped in half. "Fuck!" She rummaged in her jacket pocket.

"They put us here for the daughters," Elliott said. "The daughters of Port Jared."

"There are no daughters. It's just a bullshit story."

"No … they're real. Why… Why would someone go to all this trouble if they weren't real? The daughters have to be appeased, to stop them attacking the town, that's what they said. That's why we are down here. Appeasement. Offerings. Just flesh. Fresh meat."

"No one's offering my babes to anything. I'm going to get you out."

"I think it might be too late, Kiara."

"Don't say that."

"You know I love you, right? I don't care what my mother says. It was always you I wanted. Always."

She sighed, wiping a sleeve across her brow. Tears stung her eyes. "Shut up. Don't say things like that. Not now."

He was about to say something more, but stopped. His turned his eyes toward the darkness further along the tunnel. Kiara also stopped picking at the lock and turned her head.

"Hear something?"

"I..."

There was a scream from somewhere further along the tunnel. Kiara told herself it was one of the prisoners seeing ghosts in the watery tunnel; she turned her attention back to the lock.

"Hurry," Elliott said. He sat up now, fretting inside the cramped space of his cage.

"It's not working. I can't—"

"Do something else. They're coming."

Kiara broke off from picking at the lock and took a step back. "Will you hush? I'm doing the best I—"

Then she saw his eyes widen. He gestured to the shaft above them. She had time to throw up her arms before feeling something strike from above. A leathery wing brushed against her face. Hands or feet – or claws – grabbed at her hair. Shrieking, she spun about in time to see something large and black moving next to the cage before vanishing into the dark. Elliott shrank against his prison bars, his sudden movement causing the cage to swing wildly.

Kiara scanned the surrounding darkness looking for whatever had attacked her, at the same time readying herself for a second assault.

"What *was* that?"

Elliott pressed his face against the bars and croaked: "Get out of here. Get out! There're more of them. There're—"

"No chance. I'm not going anywhere without you."

There was a screeching from above. To Kiara, what she saw arrowing out of the gloomy shaft defied explanation. It was some kind of patchwork monster: a woman's face, full of fury; beyond that, wings, a tail; legs ending in claws. She flung out an arm as the thing dived at her. Talons snatched at her face but she managed to sweep the creature away. It flew past her, screeching, then turned about and swooped at her again. Kiara swung a fist, striking the creature before it could complete its lunge, forcing it to draw back. She turned to the cage. Elliott's face was close to hers.

"What *is* that thing? What the hell is that?"

"One of them — the daughters—"

He offered back the knife but she shook her head. "You do it. I'll work on the lock."

He blinked at her. "Do what?"

"Fend it off. Keep it away from me!"

"I'm trapped."

"Do what you can."

Kiara took a deep breath, attempting to clear her mind, to think only of the padlock. She had dropped the paperclip she'd been using but a quick rummage in her pocket retrieved another. She glanced down at the water. Her movements had disturbed something, something that floated up momentarily to the surface. It looked like a bone – about the size of a human thigh.

Gotta do this. She thought. *Gotta keep calm*. She was calm.

A squawk from behind her. The cage shook as Elliott, finding a reserve of strength from somewhere, fought as best he could, his arm extended through the bars, slashing at the thing with the knife. Kiara waited for the shaking to stop, to continue with her picking.

Almost there. Large lock. Difficult. Heavy.

The creature attacked again. She tried to ignore the talons clutching at the back of her head, pulling at her hair. She pretended not to hear another scream from further along the tunnel. *Was something else coming? What was it this time? What horror?* Then, with this thought still in her mind, success: the padlock unlocked.

The flying thing that had attacked Kiara was obviously wounded. Elliott had slashed at it and it had fallen into the shallow water. It was a dark shape at the corner of Kiara's vision, twisting and struggling as it tried to take to the air before it became still and drifted away in the slow current. And that face she glimpsed, that horrible woman's face twisted in agony.

But Kiara now feared that another was approaching down the shaft – maybe many things. She urged Elliott to climb out of the cage, but when he did his legs failed and she had to catch him around the waist. With her free hand she took the knife from him.

"I'll never make it," he said.

"I'll carry you if I have to. Let's get out of here."

She let him stand by himself and they moved together, back the way Kiara had come, but Elliott stopped after only a few paces.

"Wait!" he breathed. He peered into the gloom above, trying to see past his hanging cage. His head tilted from side to side as if concentrating.

Kiara watched him. "What's the matter?"

"Something—?" he said, then sagged against the wall, almost losing his balance. "Watch out!"

There was a loud piercing shriek, and something heavy struck Kiara on the head, knocking her off her feet. She had time to see a pale vengeful face, a face that seemed to glow, descending upon her, its mouth open, full of pointed teeth. As Kiara struggled to stand a human skull pitched up to the surface, and she couldn't stop herself screaming.

Somehow she scrambled to her feet. The creature was approaching again. Gripping the knife in two hands, Kiara raised it above her head and slashed and chopped at the monster, across its body, using all her strength to throw it to the floor. She stamped hard on its head, then bent forward to slash with the knife until the monster was a mess of blood and feathers. Finally she speared it through the back. Its wings gave one final great flap and then fell still.

Finding that she couldn't retrieve the knife, so embedded in the creature's rib cage, she turned and caught hold of Elliott's hand. "Let's get the fuck out of here!"

Leading him, she retraced her route along the tunnel. He stumbled his first few steps then he was running with her. As they flew past the other cages Kiara had to divert her eyes. The prisoners cried out, pleaded to be set free. But there was no time to rescue them. The things were approaching along the tunnel, behind them. In her imaginations Kiara saw a whole army of twisted creatures, crawling and flapping towards them. She glanced back when Elliott stumbled to his knees, and although she could see nothing but a cage and the darkness beyond it, she sensed something monstrous was chasing them. Closing on them.

"Get up!" she screamed.

They reached the end of that tunnel. Kiara deliberated left and right then drew Elliott to the left. She thought she had spied the exit, a small pale spot against the surrounding darkness. Too, she felt the slight pull of the water around her ankles moving in that direction. They half-ran again.

Elliott was breathing hard, begging to rest, but she would not let him. She focused on the pale light ahead, which grew and grew in her vision, until last of the daylight enveloped them and they dropped from the dark world, and the sea was there to catch them, its current at once drawing them away from the tunnel entrance.

The moon sat low in the sky above the sea, a sallow yellow orb, big and full. Though the cold sea took her breath away, Kiara urged Elliott to find his feet, but he was struggling. She caught him around the shoulder, buoyed him on his back and kicked her legs to keep afloat. Then they half-walked, half-floated away from tunnel.

She looked back and saw – or thought she saw – a flock of what looked like massive birds swoop down from the clift top and into the tunnel's entrance, one after the other. She closed her eyes, thinking of those other prisoners – and that boy.

Just flesh. Fresh meat.

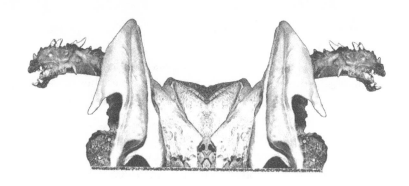

BLACK SPOTS

John Llewellyn Probert

"Here we are, sir."

"Thank you."

"As I mentioned downstairs, we've upgraded you. I actually think this is the nicest room in the hotel. It's certainly my favourite." The girl who had met him at reception stopped talking after that, leaving a yawning silence which Michael ached to fill, but couldn't find the words. In the end he left her to do it. "We don't do a lot of business midweek."

Her white blouse was a little too large and her black skirt a little too tight. Fingers interlocked and unlocked, unlocked and interlocked, repeatedly, maroon-varnished nails clacking against one another, all betraying her anxiousness to please.

"It's lovely. Thank you." With effort Michael summoned a smile. The girl's expression suggested she knew it wasn't genuine and immediately he felt guilty. It wasn't her fault, after all. He was about to say something more, something to paper over the cracks of his misstep, but the girl had already left, heels echoing on the grey-veined marble of the spiral steps that led back down to reception.

Should he go after her? No. That would look too strange. Maybe he could say something in passing when he went for dinner. If he went for dinner. He didn't eat much these days. He didn't feel the need.

When Michael had booked at the "Luxury Nine Bedroom Country House", as the website had described it, it hadn't been at all important which room he was given. Now, as he looked through the broad bay window, he wondered if maybe fate had stepped in to provide him with this one. He could see all he needed from here. There was the broad oval of grass encased by the driveway of yellow gravel, the patchwork of fields and hedgerows beyond and, half a mile away (he knew because he had measured it on maps), the glittering snake of the motorway.

The motorway where it had happened.

Michael would have used the word "beautiful" to describe the room if anyone had asked him. Curtains of a heavy burgundy velvet matched a carpet of such thick pile every footstep was noiseless. The rich furnishings were trimmed with matching scarlet and gold brocade. The bed was so large and doubtless so soft you could lose yourself in it with a friend for a weekend.

Yet to him the colours lacked vibrancy, the carpet could have been a threadbare mat, the curtains of the thinnest muslin. The bed was just a bed. It was symptomatic of how he had felt about everything since he had lost Julia a year ago. The vividness his life had once possessed had been taken from him, the picture switched from colour to black and white, the sound from stereo to mono, the intensity of everything turned right down, rendered to its most basic flat and functional level. Food was only to keep his body going. Sunshine was there to make it easier to see in the daytime. Most emotions were near impossible to express.

His psychiatrist had assured him this situation would pass.

"It will start to break up," Dr Wilmscote had said. "You'll have moments where you'll feel normal again, but when you do it's important to bear in mind that bleak periods will return, and that's entirely to be expected. In time the periods of low mood will get smaller until eventually, with any luck, they should disappear altogether."

With any luck.

A year later, luck still hadn't kicked in. Michael was starting to think it never would. He had told that to the doctor at his most recent follow-up appointment just over a week ago. She had gazed at him over her half-moon spectacles.

"What's really bothering you, Michael?"

Apart from the fact the woman I loved is dead, you mean. "I don't understand."

"You've been coming here for nearly a year, now. We've dealt with the grief reaction, we've tried medication." She leaned forward, her voice gentle. "I just feel there's something more, something you've yet to face, something inside you that needs to come out."

Only more tears. No, he thought, there were no more, there could not be any more. But then your body surprised you and there they were. In the middle of the night, when you were standing waiting for a train, sitting on the bus or at the cinema. Anywhere. Bloody things. Bloody stupid things that served no purpose at all.

The psychiatrist let the thought sink in before pressing further. "Have you ever been there?"

"Where?"

"The site of the accident?"

No he hadn't. The mere suggestion sent such a shockwave through him that he visibly twitched.

"I've really touched a nerve there, haven't I?"

Like it or not, she had. "No, I've never been there. I still don't know if I could face driving past it."

"Well considering your current clinical state I wouldn't want you driving yourself down that stretch of road either." She let that hang for a moment. "Maybe someone could take you?"

Michael shook his head. He'd embarrassed himself in front of too many friends already. They'd all been supportive and understanding for the first sixth months, but he could see it was starting to wear thin now. People could be amazingly compassionate and charitable, right up to the point where they realised your low mood was starting to rub off on them. Then they started to keep their distance. He couldn't blame them. In different circumstances he probably would have done the same thing.

"In that case I'm not sure what to suggest. It's not as if you can just walk around a stretch of motorway in the middle of the wilds of Somerset." She eyed him sharply. "And again, in your current clinical state I'm not sure it would be that good an idea anyway."

"I'm not suicidal." He didn't have the energy for it. Just like everything else. "So you don't need to worry about that."

From the way Dr Wilmscote's expression relaxed it was clear she had been worrying. She changed the subject to how his mood should eventually improve. He had been listening but what she said previously had set him thinking.

Visiting the place where it happened.

It couldn't make any difference.

Or is that you finding excuses because you're scared to go there?

Why scared?

You know why.

He did. Oh yes he did. It was the thing he hadn't told Dr Wilmscote about, or the police at the time, or anybody at all ever. The verdict had been accidental death while driving a motor vehicle. Death likely caused because the victim had been using a mobile phone at the time of the accident.

They knew she had been using a phone because Michael had told them so, and he knew because he was the one she had been talking to. He hadn't told them what she had said to him, though. Not all of it, anyway.

He had told the police that she had rung him at just after two in the morning.

"Oh, Jesus…"

She was missing him too much, she said.

"Oh Jesus Christ…"

Her meeting in Exeter had finished late and she'd tried sleeping in the hotel, but she just wanted to be back home with him.

"Jesus Christ, Michael, there's something…"

She was just going to come straight home. They had so much to do, what with planning the wedding and everything.

"…something crawling across the road…"

She didn't want him to be spooked by her coming through the front door at what would be close to three o'clock, so she thought she had better ring.

"It's not even crawling. It's more sliding as if it's… I don't know,

made of black oil or jelly or something."

And she would see him soon.

"Oh My God it's— Whatever it is, it's standing up! It's—"

He had begged her to put the phone down even before she had started going on about whatever it was she had seen, whatever it was that she claimed had crawled into the motorway lane in front of her.

Whatever it was that might have caused the accident.

And taken her from him.

That was what he was really hiding. The fact that he still believed it wasn't her phone conversation with him that had killed her. It was what she had seen in the road. And he had not told anyone. Because it was bad enough having a dead wife-to-be without everyone thinking she was a *mad* dead wife-to-be.

~~~

"This is private property, you know!"

Seven o'clock.

He had only intended to lie down for half an hour but it had stretched into three. He wasn't hungry but the room rate included dinner so he felt obliged to try it, even though he neglected to tell them what time he wanted to eat. He couldn't quite face a room filled with fellow diners right at the moment, anyway. Thank goodness for light summer evenings.

A walk would do him good, he thought, and might perhaps even help him work up an appetite. The hotel grounds were vast, yet somehow he'd ended up wandering off them and down a narrow path that led to a row of redbrick terraced houses. He had spotted the elderly lady glowering at him from the window of her brightly lit kitchen, but he hadn't expected her to come out and shout at him.

"I'm sorry. Is this not part of the hotel grounds?"

His apology did little to calm her down as she shuffled along the overgrown garden path. She stopped at the rusting gate that was all that now separated the two of them.

"It is not!" The words were weary, as if this had happened many times before.

"I'm sorry." It was always worth repeating. "I didn't see any signs."

The old lady coughed and for a moment he thought she was going to spit at his feet. She didn't, thankfully. "There aren't any. We keep telling them to put one up but nobody listens."

"In that case I'll go back the way I came." Michael turned, noticing a red glint through the trees as he did, the setting sun reflecting off something. Several somethings. Several moving somethings.

"Is that the motorway over there?"

"It is." She didn't move from the gate, presumably intending to see him off. "I hate it. Not as much as they do, mind. Bloody things."

"Who, the people who run the hotel?"

That yielded a tired laugh. "No, although I wouldn't be surprised if they did as well." She pointed at the distant road. "It's what's known as a 'black spot', you see."

That perked his interest. "You mean like an accident black spot?"

"Yes." That obviously wasn't all she meant. "In a way."

The words came out before he could stop them. "My girlfriend was killed there a year ago. That very spot. They said it was an accident."

"Well they would, wouldn't they?" Her tone softened as Michael's words sank in. "It's always been a bad place."

"You mean since the motorway was built?"

She shook her head. "Since before that. Way before. Always bad things happening there." She reached out a hand and Michael took it in his own. She had a surprisingly strong grip. "Are you a superstitious man?"

Michael hadn't considered himself to be any kind of a man for nearly a year now. "I'm open to possibilities."

"Now you sound like one of those bloody reporters, the ones we get round here from time to time when there's been another one and they've gone and dug up the same old stories about the history of that road. They never listen, though. In one ear and out the other, words on the printed page that are just tomorrow's fish and chip wrappings."

"Another what?"

She looked at him as if he was stupid. "Another accident.

Another little prank from those buggers who live beneath that road."

Michael felt all his senses come alive a little at that. "You mean there's a tunnel? Under that stretch of motorway?"

She nodded and coughed again. "They had to account for the lane when they built it. There's been a bridleway crossing that stretch of land for centuries, probably a cart track before that and before that..." she shrugged "...a path of some kind."

She was rambling and Michael needed to get her back to the modern day. "And you say there are people who live in this tunnel beneath the motorway? People who've been causing accidents?"

Again there was that look, the kind one might give to a small boy who has said something so inordinately stupid that the only reaction is to stare at him open-mouthed.

"No," she snorted. "Not people."

She left that comment hanging in the air for Michael to pursue if he wished.

"If not people ... what?"

The old lady rubbed her hands together. "It's getting cold. I'm going in. Make sure you follow the trail back. Wouldn't want you getting lost, not with it getting dark." She looked over to the motorway again. "Not with them living so close."

"Please," Michael said to the back of her rose-patterned cardigan. "Please tell me what you meant."

No answer.

"I need to know what killed her!"

Still no answer. She was at her back door now.

"Do they crawl?"

She stopped.

"Are they like black oil, or jelly?"

When she turned back to face him, Michael almost yelped at the look of horror on her face.

"You've seen one?"

He shook his head. "Julia did. Just before she died. She was on the phone to me. She said she could see something made of oil crawling across the road. Something that stood up and looked at her."

"And then?" The woman's voice was almost a croak.

"And then nothing. The phone call was over. Her life was over. And so was mine." Time for tears again, his cheeks soaked despite his having no memory of actually crying. "My boy, if that's why you're talking to me now then you have to get away. No good will come of you being here."

"Tell me who they are!" He was shouting now. "Tell me *what* they are. I have to know."

The old woman let out a sigh as she shuffled a little way back to the garden gate. "They have many names, but none describe them properly. Fairy folk, piskies, gremlins, demons. All terms that have been turned into cosy nonsense by television programmes. All made by people who have never suffered the misery of cowering in their beds at night while those things pick through whatever's outside the house, tinkering with car engines or pulling gardening equipment apart. I think it fascinates them."

"Fairy folk?" Michael tried to keep the disbelief out of his voice.

"Yes, fairy folk. The true fairy folk of the ancient myths and legends, the ones about blood and fear and panic and terror, the ones used to explain away the cow that has been gutted or the traveller found dead on a lonely road with the look of terror in his eyes. If he still had eyes." She paused to cough and draw breath. "Roads attract them. Nobody knows why. There are stories of crossroads, junctions, anywhere that roads join, being sacred places. And in times of old, sacred often meant sacrifices, sacrifices that needed to be made or the fairy folk would take what they wanted anyway."

"Take?"

"Some say they started by tripping unwary travellers on deserted stretches of road. A man with a sprained ankle could die out here in the middle of nowhere. Then they took to digging holes, little ones, to falter horses. When carriages came, so did rocks and boulders carefully placed to shatter a wheel or damage an axle."

"And now we have modern roads."

That yielded a vigorous nod. "And so they cause accidents, and because they don't like to move very far afield, those places become known as black spots. Accident black spots."

"Caused by creatures made of ... oil?"

She sniffed. "I don't know. They're creatures of darkness. Could be oil. Oil is ancient, it's primeval. It has power, the power of all the living creatures that have died to make it." She was turning away again now. "It's important to respect creatures with such power. Respect them, avoid them, leave them alone. I won't be telling you again. If I should need to, you'll already be gone."

Gone?

And so, suddenly, was the old lady, the back door clicking shut behind her, the kitchen light switched off leaving Michael bathed in the haze of the late summer evening.

It was easy finding his way back, which was strange because everything looked different, more immediate, more vivid, as if somehow the conversation he'd just had, perhaps the entire experience, had brought him to his senses, revivified them. The sound of twigs cracking beneath his shoes, of branches rustling, of the owl above and to his right, all seemed closer, more immediate.

Was this what Dr Wilmscote had been talking about? If so, it was amazing, like being on some kind of sense-enhancing drug. Everything had been brought back into focus, not gradually, but like the shutter of an old-fashioned camera snapping, turning the world around him from a vague haze into something he could once again touch, hear, sense, feel; but it had been such a long time that the sensations felt new, pure, almost as if he were reborn.

When he got to the hotel his senses were still ablaze, his fingertips tingling at the touch of a breeze, his ears attuned to the distant melody of the motorway traffic. Even the main door, creaking open as it did, seemed to add its own line of music to the symphony of nature that had accompanied him back.

~~~

The first course was a pâté that set his taste buds afire with its flavour. Subtle hints of orange and a variety of spices had been mixed in with the meat. Michael felt as if he could taste them all as they dissolved on his tongue. The ciabatta that accompanied it hinted of exotic lands, each bite taking him one step closer to the rustic kitchen where it had been prepared with loving care he could actually taste.

The main course wasn't as good. The vegetables had been overcooked, draining them of most of their taste and reducing them to chunks of fibrous roots and stems. The steak lay limpid on the plate, bearing not a trace of the appeal of the starter. The meat itself came apart easily between his teeth but all he felt in his mouth was a dull sense of texture, as if the food itself had been leached of whatever vitality and goodness it possessed before it had reached his plate. Even as he finished it, he had trouble remembering what the dessert was supposed to be.

By the time Michael retired to his room he felt the same as when he had left it earlier, exactly the same as he'd been feeling for the past year, aside from a scant couple of hours ago. That experience already felt a lifetime away, perhaps even something that had never actually happened at all.

You'll have moments where you'll feel normal again, but when you do it's important you bear in mind that the bleak periods will return.

Did it need to have happened so quickly? He opened the door into his room that held no beauty for him, so much so that he didn't even bother turning on the light. The curtains had not been closed; there was still enough light from the clear sky for him to see where the bed was. Instead of collapsing limply upon the covers, he skirted it and went to the window.

The thumbnail of a new moon was rising over to the right, and the stars were starting to come out, pinpricks of white against the darkly reddened horizon. Michael thought he could see some of those stars moving until he realised they had to be vehicles on the motorway. He strained to see the tunnel the old lady had told him about, but it was impossible in the soft darkness that now cloaked the landscape.

They live under the motorway.

The memory, the mere thought of what he had learned over at the cottage, sent a tiny thrill though him. It was nothing like what he had experienced on his walk but for a moment, as he sat down on the bed and his fingers came into contact with the rich fabric of its covers, he was able to appreciate just how soft, how silken, how … fine they were. As if the memory of something claimed to be primal had triggered something primal in him, washing away the anxieties, the neuroses, the misery that had been stifling his senses, laying them bare to experience the world as it was meant to be.

And then the feeling was gone.

He repeated the action in the hope it would work again, possibly even better this time. Moon, stars, motorway, landscape.

Nothing.

To have that briefest sensation of feeling, of knowing, snatched away from him once more was, if anything, worse than that awful gradual diminution of his ability to feel that had occurred over dinner. Once again there were tears. He switched the light on, drew the curtains, and looked at his watch, registering the time with a dulled sense of horror.

Nearly midnight.

He would never be able to sleep, not in this place, not now. In amongst all his buried, blunted, stifled feelings the sense of this new loss remained almost unbearable. Suddenly it was just all too much and, for the first time, he found himself considering suicide. But there was nothing to hand and the idea of asking whoever was on reception for something sharp or a bottle of pills seemed somehow both ridiculous and pointless.

He could leave the room, though.

Through his haze of misery one thought held. The old lady's talk of whoever or whatever lived beneath the motorway had revitalised him. Seeking out the tunnel where they were rumoured to live had provided him with the tiniest flash of what he had felt before. What if he actually went there?

At this hour?

Yes, why not? He wasn't going to get any sleep, and if he stayed here there was the chance he might hurt himself – his mind had already shown him that.

And if you find nothing?

Whether he found nothing or something, the prospect terrified him, but considering the way he felt now that strong sting of terror somewhere deep within was like a scalpel to his soul, painful but somehow therapeutic at the same time. Like an act of deliberate self-harm, but to the spirit rather than the body.

Let's go, then.

He was halfway down the spiral staircase when he realised he hadn't locked the door of his room, but it never occurred to him to go back.

~~~

Ever since the accident, Michael's attitude to having a mobile phone had been mixed. It may have been responsible for Julia's death (although he had always believed otherwise), but he had clung to the concept of owning one with the irrationality of the recently bereaved, hoping against hope that the next time it rang he might hear her voice once more. Now, in the pitch-dark country lane in which he found himself, he was grateful for having it with him. The screen guided him along the path with all the accuracy of the latest satellite technology, while the torch located in the obverse side ensured he didn't trip in one of the numerous potholes that peppered the dirt track.

Some say they started by tripping unwary travellers on deserted stretches of road.

He wasn't scared.

Not yet, anyway.

He couldn't quite describe how he felt, only that it was better than the creeping depression that once again had threatened to overwhelm him back in the room. Right now he felt alive, sharp with a keen sense of anticipation. Anticipation of what, he still wasn't sure, but just being out here in the wilds of the countryside, after dark, on what was probably a lunatic wild goose chase, gave him the kind of thrill he hadn't experienced in what felt like forever.

He was nearly there.

The wind began to pick up. Michael heard rather than felt it. The susurration of the overhanging tree branches was a little louder, a little more vigorous as they were pulled and pushed by unseen forces. The thick hedgerow to his right rustled as if short but bulky creatures were pushing through the deepest parts. Finally he felt it in his hair, a gentle plucking that became more insistent as the force of the breeze intensified.

Ahead of him loomed the open-mouthed blackness of the tunnel.

There was no traffic on the motorway now. When he had set off there had been the sound of the occasional car but Michael hadn't heard or seen a single vehicle since he had been walking, here, on the darkest part of the track. The only reason he could see the tunnel was because the hedgerows and trees had parted to unveil it for him. The motorway crash barriers that crowned the tunnel were a sharp silver-grey against the stars.

They've repaired them since Julia...

He hadn't realised he had stopped. The silence that surrounded him was almost tangible, created just for him. He reached out a hand as if to touch it, then snatched it away again, feeling foolish. Instead he just stood there, congratulating himself on proving there was a tunnel exactly where the phone's SatNav had said there would be one, all the time knowing he was delaying the inevitable.

Go in.

Michael looked again into the yawning darkness. In there? He leaned from side to side but still couldn't see any suggestion of an exit. Maybe they had bricked up the other end, in which case anything – or anyone – could be lurking in there, could have made it into a home.

That's what you want to find out, isn't it?

Like the parachuter about to leap from a plane, or the bungee jumper at the edge of a cliff, Michael suddenly felt the inexorable desire to turn round and go back. But at the same time he knew that nothing awaited him back at the hotel, an all-consuming nothing that he was convinced would never end.

He took a step forward.

And then another.

The tunnel loomed closer. The light from his phone now revealed the square opening made of rotting, cracked cement. Root tendrils and scraps of dried weed hung over the entrance. The ground within looked wet.

Now he was at the mouth, poised between a world he could understand and the bleak unknown. His phone allowed him a few feet of visibility within, allowing him to avoid the worst of the puddles.

How far should he go?

If temperature was to influence his decision, then this was already far enough. The interior of the tunnel was like ice. The air was bad, too – thick and cloying, a mixture of stale earth and animal leavings. He found it hard to believe anybody ever passed through here.

He shone the torch ahead. More of the same. The walls had been punctured here and there by the same creeping growths that had begun to invade the entrance, although these looked paler, thicker, more likely to reach up and wrap themselves around a wrist or an ankle and never let go.

Stop that.

He stamped his feet. Whatever he was hoping would happen, it needed to be soon otherwise he'd freeze to death in here. He felt an extra chill as he wondered if perhaps that was what they wanted. There was a sound to his left. Then, out of the corner of his eye he saw something moving quickly. From the place where it had been hiding, somewhere up the wall, it flopped down to the ground and scurried past him. Michael shone the torch at the rapidly receding shape.

A rat.

This was pointless. What the hell was he doing here? It was too cold to stay any longer anyway. Michael hugged himself as he stepped back out into the normal world. He kept walking until he was far enough away from the tunnel that he felt safe. Then he turned to look at it for the final time.

Something was climbing up the right-hand slope. Something man-sized and terribly thin. Michael resisted the urge to shine the light at it, instead relying on his night vision to make out the abnormally long and spindly limbs, the body that looked the same thickness. Did it even have a head? He had thought of it as man-shaped but it looked more insect than human. A huge black stick-insect whose body glistened like wet leather.

Or oil.

It didn't seem to have noticed him. It crawled up to the road, slipped beneath the crash barrier, and disappeared.

Michael had to follow. He tucked his phone away and began to climb, not caring that the hill was damp, that brambles tore at his skin and hair. He grasped the thickest vines, the most robust roots his hands could find, ignored how his feet squelched in the soft undergrowth, and levered himself up the slope.

By the time he reached the road he was muddy and sore and bleeding. He sat on the curved metal support of the crash barrier. The curling ridge of metal dug into the underside of his thighs as he panted for breath.

Michael stood up and dusted himself down, peeling away the biggest chunks of mud and wet grass. The road was empty. No sign of vehicles in either direction. There was no sign of the thing, either.

Had he imagined it?

No. He had suffered so much in the last year, but he knew what was real and what wasn't. It was here, somewhere. The thing that took Julia.

"Where are you?" Before he could stop himself he bellowed the words. They echoed off the tarmac, breaking the stillness of the night.

"I saw you climb the slope!" Could it understand him? No matter. The noise was enough to announce his presence. Surely it knew he was here?

It did.

There was a slithering sound from behind. Michael turned to look and there it was, low to the ground. It was exactly as he had seen it on the hill. Like a large black stick-insect, only the way it slithered suggested those limbs were more fluid than chitinous.

Could be oil. Oil is ancient, it's primeval. It has power.

It had no face, nor head to speak of. Instead, two tiny white dots glowed from its buried stump of a neck.

"Did you take her?"

The white dots swelled in size. An acknowledgement? A denial? It didn't matter. None of it mattered.

Michael took a step forward, no longer afraid, no longer imprisoned by the anxiety and misery that had kept him in chains for the last year. If things like this existed in the world then who knew what else was possible? There might even be an afterlife. He might see Julia again.

The creature's eyes swelled again, almost as if it could read his thoughts, almost as if it was agreeing with him.

By the time he realised those shining twin points of light were actually the headlights of the car headed straight for him, it was too late to do anything about it.

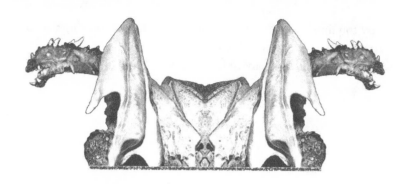

ECHOES OF DAYS PASSED

Mike Chinn

May 4th 1936
North Atlantic, somewhere south of Reykjavik

Bendix grabbed at the rigging as the deck heaved without warning. He clung on a moment, watching the grey sea. There was very little swell; in fact they might have been in the doldrums, the water was so placid. A dismal mist hung in the air reducing visibility to no more than a hundred yards. Bendix had no idea what had caused the small ageing fishing boat to pitch so badly and abruptly. There were no reefs out here – not unless they were ridiculously lost. The seabed should be at least two hundred feet below the keel.

The old boat calmed, sitting on the still water with all the grace of a sodden cardboard box. Bendix glanced over the side. It was like ink down there: nothing to see.

He made his way to the wheelhouse, sliding open the door and stepping inside. It wasn't much warmer, and instead of mist there was the fragrant murk of pipe smoke. Fisk was hunched over an array of electrical paraphernalia that had no place in a fishing boat's wheelhouse: two of the latest wireless receivers, a barograph, an innocent looking box which Bendix knew was fitted to hydrophones, and a set of cylinders and wires that included a continuous strip of graph paper along which three pens were dragging inky lines. One of the pens had just traced an enormous peak. Fisk was looking at it, the pipe clenched in his teeth twitching in time with the pens.

"That's not the target, is it?" said Bendix, peering over Fisk's shoulder.

Fisk stared hard at the trace. A column of smoke signals rose from his pipe. "No," he murmured thoughtfully. "That isn't due for at least thirteen or fourteen minutes."

Bendix pointed at the single peak, now halfway to being wound around the end cylinder. "Then what was it?"

Fisk shrugged. "Nothing, most likely. I'd just switched on the equipment – making sure it was warmed up in time. Just a random spike."

Bendix didn't like random things. That spike coincided with the boat's sudden wallow. "Not a whale?"

"Did you happen to see a whale while you were out on deck?" His tone told Bendix exactly what Fisk thought of that idea. Fisk held his hands wide apart. "Big thing. Exhales clouds of wet fishy breath. No, lieutenant, it's an artifact. Neither of the other detectors registered anything."

"Does ASDIC normally play up like that?"

Fisk shrugged again. "It's an improvement on the standard echo location system. More powerful, more sensitive. Problems are to be expected." He puffed out another cloud of smoke. "That's why we're here."

The lieutenant knew better than anyone why they were pretending to be fishermen out in the North Atlantic, miles from anywhere. Which reminded him. "Better check in with our opposite number."

He switched on one of the wireless sets and hit the transmit button. "Gemini Two calling Gemini One. Over." Bendix waited several seconds before trying again. "Gemini Two calling Gemini One. Do you read me? Over." There was nothing but a faint popping crackle. He would have checked the frequency but both radios had been pre-set and locked.

"What are they doing out there?" Bendix muttered. It was not like Captain Travers to leave wireless telegraphy unmanned.

"Come in Gemini One, this is Gemini Two. Are you receiving? Over." He glanced at his wristwatch: nine minutes or so before the target was in range. He needed Gemini One's confirmation that the sub was on its way – or a delay signal if something had come up. "Hello Gemini One, this is—"

The fishing boat lurched again. Bendix stumbled, almost falling over Fisk. He had time to note all three pens were thrashing across the moving paper, marking ever increasing spikes as the experimental ASDIC equipment responded to something.

The boat rolled. Bendix was thrown through the open wheelhouse door. He fetched up hard against the ship's rail, the breath driven out of him. He began to slide down the deck: the vessel's stern was going down. The sea – no longer calm – was foaming over the rail. They'd struck something and were sinking.

The bow rose. Bendix snatched for the side rail. He was no longer just sliding to stern – he was all but hanging. The trawler stood upright, sinking vertically into a sea that beat and thrashed against it. The water was seconds away from him. Bendix would have to try and swim free or be dragged down by the ship.

The wheelhouse was now above him. Bendix glanced up. Fisk was halfway out of the door, flapping like a beached fish. He looked as terrified as Bendix. The boat shook again. Bendix yelled in pain as his hands were almost torn free.

Above him, Fisk was struggling, trying to prise himself free of the wheelhouse. He slipped and tumbled into the churning water. His flailing body crashed into Bendix, almost knocking him free. Then Fisk was gone.

Bendix looked at the pounding swirl that was getting ever closer to him. He told himself there wasn't really something like a huge claw just below the surface, digging at the deck. That the trawler wasn't sinking – it was being dragged down. When the water was within a few feet of his dangling legs Bendix's pain-racked fingers lost their grip. He fell. Straight towards the maelstrom.

Just before he hit water a cavern lined with vast curved daggers rose out of the surf, engulfing him.

~~~

May 7th 1936
The Labrador Sea, somewhere east of Newfoundland.

Commander Brad Munrow leaned negligently against the bridge rail as the submarine cruiser USS Oswin floated in an Atlantic that was showing its good side. He was scanning the clear sky with his binoculars. The afternoon sun turned the ocean a deep blue. Tiny waves lapped the sub's four-hundred-foot-long hull.

Munrow tweaked the focus dial on his field glasses. A dot grew sharper. "Plane, captain. Far, two eight zero, elevation four, approaching."

Beside him, Captain David Bannon pushed back his cap and raised his own binoculars. "I see it, Brad. Better get the welcoming committee on deck." There was an edge to his voice.

Munrow couldn't tell if it was excitement or apprehension. "One welcoming committee coming up." The commander unsealed a watertight hatch and removed the talker phone handpiece secured inside. "Control, this is the bridge. Break out the gangplank, chief. Our visitor's here." He replaced the handset. "Any idea why the brass is paying us a visit?" The brief signal they'd received that morning hadn't been big on details.

Bannon lowered his binoculars. "This boat's been something of a pet project for Admiral Corrigan. I guess he wants to be sure I'm taking care of it."

A hatch opened on the rear deck and two sailors hauled a collapsible gangway out, manhandling it carefully into position. Bannon and Munrow stowed their binoculars and made their way down via external steps aft of the bridge.

The plane circled to land. Sunlight flashed off its silver fuselage as it came down on the sea. It was a Douglas Dolphin, a twin-engined Navy amphibian, big enough for a half-dozen passengers. Or in this case, a single admiral.

The plane taxied towards the sub, engines blipping. As it came alongside the pilot rode the port wing float up onto the slope of the Oswin's main hull where it broke through the surface of the ocean, like the body of a huge whale.

The plane's hatch opened and the head of Admiral Rory Corrigan – unmistakable with the almost white spade beard covering its lower half – rose through it. He waved.

"Better get the gangway out now, boys," Munrow said to the crewmen. "Don't want to get the admiral's feet wet."

The admiral hauled himself up out of the plane and onto the gangway with the spriteliness of a man half his age. As he reached the *Oswin's* hull officers and men snapped to attention. Slade piped Corrigan aboard. The admiral saluted briefly, turning to greet Captain Bannon. The two men shook hands, both grinning like old friends.

"Welcome aboard, admiral," the captain said. He had to raise his voice as the airplane's engines revved. The gangway was disconnected, the plane turned, and the wash from its engines sprayed everyone on deck with a mist of seawater.

"He's in a hurry!" Bannon yelled.

"Yeah, well I'm not officially here," Corrigan replied. "And he has to get my taxi back to Gander before it runs out of gas."

Bannon and Munrow shared a look. Yeah, thought the commander, the old man wants to play with the new toy.

Corrigan was taking in the *Oswin*. "Hard to imagine the Coast Guard has smaller cutters than this." His eyes fixed on the eight-inch twin-barrelled turret gun situated forward of the bridge. "And not so well armed."

"Few subs are, sir," said Bannon. "Shall we get below?"

"Of course. After you, captain."

Bannon led Admiral Corrigan inside the boat. Corrigan whistled as he passed through the command centre.

"It's one thing to look at the blueprints, quite another to see it in the flesh. Pretty sure you could fit the old subs I served on in '18 inside of this can and not even notice." He waved at the crewmen standing to attention. "At ease. This is no official visit so don't treat me any better than you would your captain." He winked at Bannon. "Well, maybe a little better."

"Officers' quarters are below, sir," said Munrow. "This way."

As Bannon ordered the *Oswin* to get under way Munrow led the admiral down to the lower deck. The quarters were snug, with ten tiny cabins arranged around the wardroom.

"We have eight serving officers in total," said Munrow. "They've been ordered to keep it down – your cabin is the most isolated so you shouldn't be too disturbed."

Corrigan looked inside the shoebox-sized room. He turned to Munrow with an easy smile. "Don't worry about me, son. This place is a palace compared to some of the sardine cans I've served on."

"If you say so, sir. Also, Captain Bannon wondered if the admiral would care for a tour of the boat…"

"You bet, commander, but I've had a tiring day. Maybe tomorrow?"

"Very well, sir. Is there anything else?"

"Thank you but you can quit worrying about this particular old man. And please tell Dave – Captain Bannon – the same, would you?"

"Whatever you say, admiral." Munrow saluted. "I'll see you tomorrow."

Corrigan returned the salute. "Look forward to it, son."

~~~

The admiral had seen pretty much every inch of the sub. Since Corrigan had been involved with the conception and design of the *Oswin* from the get-go, Captain Bannon let him have a full inspection. They wound up in the spare aft section, where auxiliary bunks had been fitted for another forty people, on top of the one hundred and eight crew. Bannon sometimes wondered just who the designers thought the sub would be taking on board. The *Oswin* wasn't a pleasure cruiser.

Admiral Corrigan leaned against an end bunk and took out a cigarette case. He offered a smoke to Bannon but the captain refused; instead he stuck a half-smoked cigar between his teeth but didn't light it.

Corrigan blew out a cloud of smoke. "Well, Dave, so far you haven't asked me why I'm here."

Bannon shrugged. "I figured you'd tell me if I needed to know. Wanting to be with your baby on her first voyage. Something like that."

Corrigan ran a hand down his beard. "Sure. And I'm glad to see she's performing so well."

"But…?"

The admiral smiled. "Am I that obvious?" He took a creased

scrap of paper from a shirt pocket. "We intercepted this signal five days ago. It was encoded, of course, but using an old cipher we've known for years."

"Where from?" Bannon was thinking Nazi Germany.

"Iceland. The British Royal Navy are carrying out a low-level exercise up there."

Bannon took out his stogie and examined the chewed wet end. "How does that concern us?"

"Our information is, they're using fishing boats and an old wartime sub to test some new echo location gear. And being damned hush-hush about it."

"And...?" Bannon slipped the cigar back in his mouth.

"This boat has the most advanced echo-location equipment our boys can come up with." Corrigan's voice dropped to a whisper. "If the Brits have made breakthroughs, we'd like to know about it."

"You want us to just sail up there and ask them?"

Corrigan stroked his beard, half-smiling. "Three days ago they went quiet. Sudden radio silence. The *Oswin* was already en route for the Arctic Circle and it seemed like an opportunity to pop by. See if they needed help."

Bannon did a quick calculation. "I reckon we're still over a day from Iceland. Their own boys will be out looking already."

Corrigan shook his head. "So far the Royal Navy have done nothing. Probably weighing their options, trying not to be noticed. If they send a bunch of ships out, the whole world will know."

"Sounds like half the world already knows."

"We got lucky. Our concern is that Germany might also get lucky.

Bannon glanced from the scrap in the admiral's hand to Corrigan's face. "What was their position when they went quiet?"

"I don't have an exact fix but I can narrow it down to twenty or thirty square miles."

"That's still a lot of water, admiral."

Corrigan grinned and crushed out his cigarette. "And this big new boat's the best thing to cover it, captain." He jammed the scrap back into his shirt. "The very best."

~~~

Admiral Corrigan slipped out of the officers' quarters. He made no sound, sure that safe in their own cabins, neither captain nor commander heard a thing. Carefully, the admiral climbed to the upper deck, not slipping on his shoes until he was immediately outside the command centre. He stepped inside.

Even though he'd kept abreast of the construction of the *SC-1* – to use her original designation – from the moment her keel had been laid he couldn't get used to how roomy it was. Centralising features normally found in the conning tower – like periscope and steering – alongside stations situated in the control room – such as diving and pressure – in the upper deck resulted in the kind of breathing space Corrigan and his shipmates could only have dreamed of back in the Great War. The boat's commander had pretty much everything he wanted in his sight and within reach of his voice. Even the radio room was close by, tucked in aft of the periscope.

For a moment, everyone on the night watch was oblivious to his presence. Then a guy in navy khaki – a CPO, Corrigan saw from his insignia – glanced up from a map laid across the chart table. Instantly he snapped to attention.

"Admiral on deck!"

As the crew came to their feet, Corrigan raised a hand. "Easy boys. As you were. I'm not here, remember?" He gave them all a wide friendly smile.

They settled back to their stations, murmuring among themselves. Corrigan strolled up to the chart table, trying not to look like he was studying the map, and spoke to the CPO. "Would it be possible for me to witness a dive? I'm curious as to how a boat this size handles underwater."

The chief, who looked to be around thirty but his cropped hair already showing signs of grey, frowned, uncertain. "I should clear that with the captain."

Corrigan's smile grew wider. "I doubt Dave – Captain Bannon – would object. Just a dip below the waves. Humour an old man, chief—?"

"Vallone, sir." He hesitated a moment before going to the talker phone. "Bridge, this is command centre. We're running a test dive in four minutes."

"Test dive in four, aye."

"Rig for dive."

As the admiral waited, all of the submarine's compartments reported back they were rigged for dive.

"Very well," acknowledged Vallone. "Clear the bridge."

"Bridge cleared." Seconds later a junior lieutenant dropped smartly down into the command centre, dogging the hatch above him, and took position at diving control.

"Very well. Dive, dive, dive."

Corrigan felt the unmistakable dip as the boat blew her buoyancy tanks. The sound of waves engulfing the hull echoed around him. It was a sound he sorely missed.

"Pressure in the boat," the lieutenant at diving control called. "Green board."

"Six-five feet," ordered Vallone. "Open bulkhead flappers and start ventilation."

One by one the compartments reported back that the ventilation had started.

"Final trim six-five feet," reported diving control.

"Very impressive, chief," said Corrigan. He moved to the port side, standing behind the hydrophone and echo location operators. Both men glanced around nervously but Corrigan simply gave them a smile and a wave. "Carry on, gentlemen."

The hydrophones operator slipped headphones over his ears, adjusting controls. The EL operator – another junior lieutenant – did nothing.

"You not going to switch anything on, lieutenant?"

The operator looked back up at Corrigan again. "EL is activated only when likely to be needed, sir. We're in open water. Apart from a chance whale, there's nothing out here for the gear to respond to."

"Hydrophones enough, eh?"

"If the 'phones pick anything up the captain would order EL to be activated. The equipment's still experimental…"

"Yes. And one of the *Oswin's* ongoing tasks is to test it, lieutenant. As a favour, just show me what it can do – but keep it simple, eh?"

The lieutenant shrugged, turned a control and two circular green screens began to glow. Tweaking another two knobs brought up two bright lines on each. As the equipment warmed a series of sinus waves began to march across the upper line on both screens.

"Like oscilloscopes," commented the admiral.

The lieutenant nodded, adjusting one screen so the image was sharper. "Pretty much, sir. The waves show each sound pulse as it's generated – this is the forward projector, this the aft. Any echoes coming back at us will be registered on the lower trace. Amplitude can be used to measure the range, while these—" he tapped a series of dials "—indicate heading and depth. They're linked to the hydrophones."

"What's the maximum range?"

"That's one of the things the *Oswin* aims to determine, admiral. Several thousand yards in theory."

"Better than the British ASDIC?"

"I wouldn't know, sir."

"Pretty powerful, though."

"We're advancing all the time, admiral."

The upper trace on one of the screens blipped, a ragged curve sliding right to left. There was a second. And a third.

Corrigan leaned forward. "What's that?"

The lieutenant shook his head, tweaking a couple of knobs. "You got me, admiral. It's big – far too big." He consulted the dials, shook his head again, and turned to the hydrophones operator. "What you make of it?"

"Could be a thermocline but it appears to be moving. And fast."

Corrigan was intrigued. He hadn't imagined he'd actually get a chance to witness the EL gear in proper use. "What's the heading?"

The lieutenant glanced at a dial. "Straight for us, sir."

"If that's a whale, it's one for the record books," muttered the 'phones operator.

"Another sub?" The ragged echo traces on screen were growing in amplitude. Corrigan could figure what that meant. "It's almost on us! What's the range?"

"Seconds away, sir. It's going to—!"

A hollow moan belled through the hull. Corrigan felt the impact through his feet. The sub rolled to starboard by a degree or so. It sounded as though something huge and soft was pressed against the pressure hull, squeezing its way aft.

It fell silent. The boat righted.

"Is it gone?" asked Corrigan.

The lieutenant checked everything. "Yes, it's— No, it's coming about!"

"That's no sub!" muttered the 'phones operator.

A moment later the boat rang as though struck by a titanic hammer. It shuddered again, heeling over to port as whatever was out there rubbed against it.

"What the hell's going on!"

Corrigan turned at the voice. Captain Bannon was partway into the command centre, still half-dressed, holding on to a bulkhead doorframe as the sub bucked and pitched.

Chief Vallone, one hand on the periscope, came to attention. "Apologies, captain, I—"

"Save it, chief." Admiral Corrigan pushed himself across a deck that was still a degree or two off level. "I take full responsibility, captain. I ordered a demonstration of the boat operating underwater."

Bannon said nothing, just pulled his cap on tight. He clearly had no intention of causing a scene in front of the crew. He jammed his cold stogie between clenched teeth.

"We'll talk about this later. Chief—!"

"Skipper!"

"Make all preparations for surfacing. Check for leaks – on the double."

Commander Munrow appeared at the bulkhead door, shrugging into his shirt. "What's going on? We at war—?" The surfacing alarm cut him off.

The captain put a hand on the steps leading up to the bridge, pausing with one foot on a rung. "Open the main induction once the decks are visible. Brad – fetch a searchlight. And perhaps you'd like to join us, admiral?"

Corrigan knew that wasn't a request. He followed up the

ladder, with Commander Munrow close behind.

Outside, it was still dark. Once all three were on the bridge Munrow plugged a large Klieg light into the sub's power supply, fitted it onto the guard rail, and flicked it on. A powerful beam swept the ocean.

The Atlantic was fitful, throwing black waves over the deck. Foam glowed in the searchlight. They heard nothing outside the sounds of the boat's diesel engines and the splash of waves.

"So what's the deal, admiral?" asked Bannon, softly.

"I just wanted to see how she operated." Corrigan didn't sound convincing, even to himself.

"No thoughts of trying to sneak up on the Royal Navy's operations unseen, I suppose."

"Captain, let me assure you —"

"Stow it, admiral. For now we have a boat to check over." His eyes followed the sweeping Klieg beam. "So what did we hit?"

Corrigan puffed out a breath that gleamed in the reflected searchlight. "Your boys seemed to think it hit *us*."

Bannon bit down on his cigar. "Whale?"

"Too big. Too manoeuvrable."

"Then what?"

"Captain." Munrow pointed. The searchlight had caught something ten degrees to starboard. It gleamed in the light, slipping below the restless waves. Phosphorescence glowed in its wake.

"Sure looks like a whale to me," muttered Bannon.

Munrow kept the searchlight on the water, panning back and forth. After several seconds something broke the surface again, about thirty feet from the submarine's starboard beam. Corrigan had to agree with Captain Bannon: it looked like a big whale arching through the swell.

Except, in the Klieg's harsh light its sides looked pale, oily – even scaled.

Whatever it was, it sank out of sight as it headed past the bridge. A huge fluke rose above the waves, poised for a moment, raining water.

"That can't be right," Corrigan said. Unless his eyes were getting old and unreliable, the fluke looked more like a fish's tail.

One that was something like twenty feet across. It smacked the water as it sank creating a wash which momentarily flooded the deck.

"Tell me you both saw that." The admiral looked at captain and commander: their expressions answered his question.

"That's one hell of an anchovy," breathed Munrow.

The sea erupted. Something breached. Something that reared over the bridge, staring down at them with cuttlefish eyes set in a skeletal face that was a perversion of human. A medusan nest of thick tendrils writhed from its skull. Its mouth gaped; fangs the size of Roman pillars gleamed in the searchlight. It raised pale scaley arms, reaching toward the bridge with harpoon-sized talons set in steam-shovel paws.

For a frozen instant no one and nothing moved. Then something buried deep inside Corrigan's mind began to wail. The huge thing sank by degrees, never taking its strange eyes off the sub, until it had vanished below the black water. Corrigan began to breathe again.

Commander Munrow laughed, a timid scared noise. "Always wanted to see a mermaid."

~~~

Back inside the command centre, Bannon stood at the chart table with Munrow and Corrigan. "Did we see that – or are we all crazy?"

Corrigan shook his head. "Both hydrophones and echo-location picked it up."

"They picked *something* up," agreed Bannon.

"You see anything else out there?" asked Munrow.

"God forbid there's another," Bannon sighed. "Chief … are we okay to get under way?"

"Damage control reports nothing beyond bruises and a picture of some guy's girl that fell off a bunk," called Vallone.

"Then proceed on original course."

"And hydrophones, keep listening out for … anything," added Munrow.

The EL operator tapped his rig. "Sir, I shut the dorsal projectors down when we surfaced, but we do have an experimental ventral array. It's not directional, but what it lacks in accuracy it more than makes up for in sheer volume. If you follow."

"Good idea, lieutenant," said Bannon. "You and 'phones keep a weather eye out."

Corrigan leaned forward. "Captain, I—"

"Later, admiral. You can explain when we get back at Norfolk."

"Captain," called hydrophones. "Something out there. Large. Moving fast."

Dammit! Bannon mouthed. "Very well. EL, can you get a fix?"

"Far as I can tell, it's directly below us, sir. Approximately five hundred feet – and rising."

"Very well. Chief, rig for impact."

Before Vallone could give the order the whole sub shuddered, rolling to port as it was struck from below. Bannon hung onto the chart table with both hands. "Get us out of here, chief, full speed!"

The *Oswin* yawed. Something had the boat by the bow. Bannon sure as hell wasn't about to call that *something* a mermaid. He pushed himself off the table. "Up periscope! Darken command centre."

As he grabbed the rising periscope the lights dimmed. Looking forward over the turret gun, his eyes adjusting, he tried to make out something – anything – in the darkness. There it was: a vast silhouette against a not quite black sky. Hulking over the sub's bow, holding onto it like it was some kid's toy in a bathtub.

He stepped back. "Down 'scope. Battle stations – gun action! Gun crew to fire control." He looked round at Munrow. "Man the bridge, commander. Time we gave our main guns a trial run."

"Aye, captain." Munrow began to climb the steps.

Corrigan looked at Bannon, almost pleading. "We need to stop them—" he murmured. "It."

Bannon gazed at the admiral's drawn face. His skin was pale as his beard. There was a fever in his pale eyes that the captain didn't like the look of. "Okay, admiral. You wanted to watch this tub in action, now's your chance."

They scaled the steps as fast as they could. Munrow was already on the bridge, Klieg light back on. The beam played over the towering, scaled creature, still grasping the sub's bow in its huge paws. Bannon grabbed the talker phone.

"Fire control. Target is – directly ahead. Bearing zero zero. Range one double-zero."

"Zero zero, one double-zero. Aye."

"Commencing firing."

Both barrels of the eight-inch guns fired, the report deafening. Almost instantly the shells impacted, hitting the creature square in the teeth. It bellowed – a roar even louder than the guns – and fell back into the ocean. Waves foamed across the bow.

"Cease firing. Manoeuvring, steer course two zero."

"Did we get it?" Admiral Corrigan stared at the white-tops.

"We hit it," said Bannon. As for whether it was enough, he had his doubts.

"Starboard!" A huge plume of water erupted amidships. It was back and clearly not dead. A skeletal head gazed down on the bridge, its face a mess. Chunks of flesh were blown away, turning its mouth into a bloody snarl, teeth on one side exposed in a rictus grin. The thick tendrils on its head writhed, some oozing a dark fluid. Its strange cuttlefish eyes glared with pain – or fury.

"Can't bring the deck gun to bear," muttered Bannon. It was too far aft.

Munrow stepped back from the searchlight. "The AA gun!"

"Brad!"

The commander was already half sliding down the stepladder. He reached the rear deck mounted anti-aircraft gun, swivelling to aim up at the colossal shape looming over the sub. Bannon played the searchlight over the thing giving Munrow something to aim at. The creature glistened, shades of blue and green, refracted light sparkling off its scales.

Munrow opened fire. The thing twitched and bellowed. Bannon could see the impact lines stitching across the scaled torso, but they were about as effective as pitching rocks at an elephant. It just got madder and reached forwards, flinching with every hit. An arm swept down, batting at the AA gun's barrel. Munrow was swatted aside, slipping on the wet deck. He vanished into the darkness.

"Brad!" Bannon started for the rear steps. Corrigan grabbed him by the arm.

"I'll get him! Command this boat, Dave!"

Before the captain could argue the admiral was making his way down to the deck, muttering incoherently as he descended.

The mer-thing had lost interest in the AA gun now it had fallen silent, its ruined face turned left and right as if it was looking for something. It sank, almost up to its oddly jointed arms, slapping at the sub's hull. Bannon winced at each blow. Too many of them and the *Oswin* would crack like a rotten log.

He called down the talker. "Manoeuvring, full astern."

The sub began to reverse, slipping by the looming thing. The creature seemed baffled at first, its shattered jaw hanging loose; then it surged forward with a deep rumble – that Bannon felt in his guts – crushing several feet of guardrail with a petulant swat.

On the rear deck, Corrigan was dragging Munrow's inert body back into the light; at least he hadn't gone overboard. The admiral shuffled clumsily, his head constantly swinging about to check on the half-submerged creature. It remained indifferent to both men, more interested in punching out the *Oswin*.

"Medical detail to the aft deck!" Bannon called down the talker. "On the double!"

Munrow was hidden from Bannon's sight now. At the foot of the ladder, the captain hoped, and alive. Corrigan reappeared, shuffling towards the AA gun. Bannon leaned from the bridge. "Admiral, get back up here!"

Corrigan shook his head. He was still talking to himself, his words difficult to make out above the waves, the creature's rumbling, the sub's engines. "...All along ... fooled us ... me ... this was ... ASDIC..." He was laughing. "ASDIC! Last laugh, though ... take ... we'll get ... I'll get..."

Bannon watched as Corrigan took up position with the AA gun, handling it with surprising ease. He fired, hitting the thing's injured head and left shoulder. It howled, leaving Bannon's ears ringing. The admiral fired again, keeping up a constant barrage. The creature was hurting. Its howls now ones of pain. Agony. It swiped at the sub, hit the sea instead, drenching Corrigan. It hit out again, this time heeling over – capsizing. But it righted itself, shaking its head, its tendrils hanging limp.

Corrigan never let up, hammering the thing with every shot. Stinging it, wearing it down. Until his ammo ran out.

The thing had been falling back, increasingly reluctant to stay in range of the reversing sub. Now it surged forward again, porpoising, its scaly fishlike lower parts slapping the water.

Several crewmen were on the rear deck now, armed with automatics and machine guns. As the thing rose out of the water they fired in unison but the creature didn't even notice. Its attention was focussed on Corrigan, still manning the empty AA gun. It slammed a huge-webbed paw down. The admiral paused in his constant incoherent speech long enough to laugh again. Then the paw raked the deck, crushing, tearing. When the creature fell back into the water, the deck was empty of both AA gun and Corrigan.

"Rory!"

Bannon had to restrain himself from racing down to the deck. He couldn't help the admiral – not now – and he had a submarine to look after.

Machine gun and small arms fire were almost continuous. The creature was holding position, probably hurting badly. It sank down into the waves until only its ruined head showed, keening a mournful whale-like song that reverberated through the water. Gradually, the *Oswin* increased the gap, Bannon keeping the searchlight trained on it all the time, waiting for the moment when it came at them again.

He had a sudden crazy idea and picked up the talker phone. "Torpedo tracking party, man your stations. Forward room, order of tubes is one, two, three, four."

"Forward room, aye."

"Forward room make ready forward tubes. Set depth one-zero feet."

The creature still wasn't moving. From what Bannon could make out it was treading water, watching the departing sub, contemplating its next move. Or was he giving a dumb monster too much credit?

"Forward room ready to fire."

"Very well." The thing was around two hundred feet away

now, around half the length of the sub, although it still stood out clearly in the searchlight beam. "EL, do you still have it on track?"

"Aye, captain – but I wouldn't bet my pay check on the positioning."

"We can see it, lieutenant. Do you have the amplitude up full?"

"It won't increase the accuracy —"

"Give it everything you got."

"Aye, skipper."

"Stop engines!"

The *Oswin* slowed. Above the slap of waves on the hull Bannon could hear the medical detail taking Munrow below, armed crewmen making their way forward around the sub's superstructure. The thing ahead moaned, its cries flat and muffled by the choppy sea.

"Come on you son-of-a-bitch," Bannon muttered.

Its head quirked. If it had ears, the captain imagined it alternating them, trying to zero in on a certain sound. It howled, surging forward like a swimmer pushing off a poolside.

"Got your attention! Forward room. Fire one! Fire two!" Bannon imagined he saw the wakes as the fish burst from their tubes.

The creature plunged below the sea. In the searchlight the captain could just make out the bow-wave as it surged towards the sub.

The sea drummed. A second later it geysered up in an explosion of foam. The creature's head and shoulders surfaced a moment afterwards. It was screaming. Water and blood poured off it.

"Fire three. Fire four!"

Both struck the thing square, ripping into it. Tearing it apart. What remained collapsed into the churning waves. There was no more eerie howls.

"That's for Rory Corrigan, you bastard," murmured Bannon.

~~~

Munrow stood, buttoning his shirt. Bannon was standing in the door of the tiny sickbay, arms folded, his expression leagues away.

"Doc says I'm fine, captain." He picked up his cap. "Few bruises. Nothing broken. Better shape than the sub, anyhow. We returning to Norfolk for repairs?"

Bannon nodded.

"Listen, I—" Munrow shuffled his cap in both hands. "I'm sorry about the admiral, sir. I guess you and he were old friends—"

"Thanks, Brad." The captain shook his head, back in the present. "Reckon he died saving the sub – or so the log will record."

They left the sickbay together, walking back towards the command centre. "Speaking of which, what *was* that?" wondered Munrow.

Bannon shrugged. "Sailors have been seeing mermaids for centuries – human sized ones. Maybe the longer they live, the bigger they get."

"Cheery thought. So why did it attack us?"

"Maybe it was the echo location gear. It seemed to pretty much ignore us when it wasn't switched on. I had EL turn the amplitude way up and even though it must have been hurting it came back at us." He dug around in a shirt pocket and produced his cold stogie, popping it between his teeth. "The admiral told me about a Royal Navy mission off the Iceland coast that suddenly went silent a few days ago. They were testing some new ASDIC equipment…" His voice tailed off.

"You think they ran into tall dark and ugly?"

"Something like that. I wouldn't like to think there was another one out there."

"Amen to that," said Munrow with conviction.

~~~

A hundred miles south of Reykjavik, settled on the continental shelf, a dozen opaque packets, each the size of a suitcase, waited in the cold nutritious waters. Nestled inside rocky clefts and held in place by thin tendrils growing from their corners, each held a small dark shape. Occasionally, each would wriggle and thrash, testing the walls of their eggs with sharp claws.

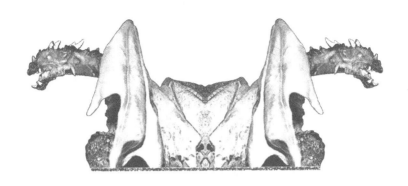

WHAT THE SNOW BRINGS

Ralph Robert Moore

By late afternoon they had made their way through two miles of heavy woods, knees tired from lifting up over obstacles in the path, elbows sore from pulling branches away from their faces, finally approaching a crest in the woods. Bending their backs, mouths hanging down, huffing, plodding forward to reach the summit, where in the noise of the forest they'd get a better orientation of their location. To decide in which direction they should set out tomorrow. Laura planting one foot in front of the other climbing up the crest. At mid-point, exhausted, turning around to look for reassurance from John, struggling on the trail below her. Above all else, they needed to locate a stream so they could replenish their water supply.

Off to the left, something flitted away from their presence behind branches and bushes.

Leaning forward, resting her palms on her thin knees, catching her breath, Laura looked up. "Was that a deer?"

Joachim, their guide, didn't look at her. "Could be anything. All sorts of things in the woods."

John sat down on the path, both hands rubbing his face. Almost immediately stood back up, swatting at his ass. Seat of his pants dark from the dampness of the trail. Had to be uncomfortable.

Started snowing.

Pretty in the moment, white flakes falling, top of their hair, noses, maybe beautiful as it accumulated, covering all the other colours in the world, but that coldness out in the open would slow them, numb them, freeze them.

Buttons getting buttoned, zippers yanked up, hats pulled out of knapsacks.

Cold throughout their morning's hike this far north, but now too cold. That extreme coldness that settles around the shoulders, inside the lungs, puffing out white vapor. The coldness that hurts.

John standing in front of Laura, rubbing his gloves up and down her arms. Jaw swinging over his shoulder towards Joachim. "Where can we safely set up camp?"

Joachim hesitated. "There's an old fort in the woods. It's not an ideal choice, but under the circumstances, it's probably our best option. We won't last long out here in the open."

~~~

By the time the three of them reach the fort, their black footprints in the snow trailing behind them, the sun was sinking, the ground, and the trees towering around them, were white. Snow blindness was getting into their eyes, making it even more difficult to see where they were walking.

The fort stood with tall wooden walls all around it, to protect it, but those walls had rotted to such a degree over the decades since the fort was last occupied it was easy, despite the reinforced gate being shut, to enter through a collapsed section of wall near the gate.

Inside, there were wooden stairs on either side of the gate, leading to the top of the wall, to the two guard posts, now not safe to climb, both stairs missing steps, and in the modest courtyard a small building to the left that might have been a commissary, sleeping quarters for the troops, an armoury, or all three; and an even smaller shack against the right wall that was probably the fort's outhouse.

Joachim led them across the accumulating snow of the courtyard to the larger slant-roofed building at the rear of the fort, kicking in its front door, snow blowing through onto the wood floor, Laura and then John following, Laura leaning against the door to push it shut against the cold winds. Joachim dragged a nearby chair to the door, waited for Laura to move out of the way, wedged the back of the chair's top under the brass doorknob, which must have been a luxury back then, this far north, to keep the door shut.

Silence in the black shadows of the old room, the three of them facing each other, camping gear strapped to their backs.

"I don't know how long this storm is going to last. There's a black iron stove in that corner. We can break up furniture, use it as fuel, use those buckets over there to gather snow, melt it on the stove, and we have drinking water."

John lowered his knees, dropped his backpack on the floor. "What do we do for food?"

"At the most, this storm will only last a few days. As long as we have a steady water supply we can survive. I know we're near the end of our rations, but I thought we'd be able to reach the ranger's station before nightfall, and replenish our supplies there. I didn't anticipate this storm. It wasn't on any of the computer projections I consulted before we set out. That's on me. But we don't need food. We'll be hungry, but we can survive. Once the storm lets up, we can make our way to the station, about a mile away."

Arms spreading out from his waist. "Why can't we do that right now?"

Joachim, lowering his knapsack. "We each need a breathing mask and filtered goggles, at this point in the storm's intensity, to survive out there long enough to reach the station. It's like swimming underwater. Can't do it if you don't have the right equipment." Pointed at his knapsack on the floor. "I'm the only one with that equipment. I can make it to the ranger's station, but even though it's a straight path on that road outside the fort, it would take hours in this blizzard. I can't leave the two of you alone that long. It would be a bad idea. We're very far north. There are things that only exist in the very far north. Respectfully, you don't have any experience on how to deal with them. Let me do my job of protecting you."

John and Joachim, working as a team, one man at either end, noisily dragged a table with deep knife gouges across its top over to the black iron stove, using upraised boots, their hands, to break up the table's boards, tossing the shards into the belly of the black iron stove. Joachim, on his knees, pressed some yellowed newspapers from fifty years ago under the chaotic angles of shattered wood, hovering the flame from his green cigarette lighter under the brittle newspaper columns, tiny yellow and red flame licking up at the old wood, smouldering it, smoke rising, active flames following, reaching up, wavering below the wood, blackening the shards, loud crackles in the quiet dark open space of the room, the bucket of snow on the stove plate starting to melt, shift, lose its cold whiteness, dissolving into translucence.

Lifting the hot pot off the stove, setting it on the floor. "Okay! We have drinking water."

John glanced at Joachim. "Why did they build a fort out in the middle of nowhere? What was it they had to protect themselves against?"

Joachim looked around at the walls. "That's a long story."

~~~

Joachim found an old lantern, carried it swinging below his hand by its thin wire hoop to the centre of the room, rotated the threaded side screw counter-clockwise to lower the wide white wick inside until it dipped into the kerosene, using his green cigarette lighter again, to light the top of the wick.

Lowered the curved glass bowl back in place.

The lowering magnified the small interior flame, throwing light outwards across their faces, projecting giant shadows of them onto the wooden walls.

"We should all sleep in the same room. To keep an eye on each other."

John watched the snow falling outside the front windows.

"As a guide, I've been in this position once or twice before. It can be an opportunity for us to talk about our lives. To share our experiences so far. Think of it as a long plane ride with a stranger."

"Just before the plane develops engine trouble and crashes down into the Atlantic Ocean."

Laura snorted, reaching to her left, squeezing her husband's bicep.

John opened his mouth. But then said nothing. Motionless for a moment. Twisted his head side to side, eyes alert, aiming his ears at the darkness around him.

Laura looked behind her right shoulder. Left shoulder. With her eyebrows and shoulders mimed, What are we hearing?

Joachim lowered his voice. Moving his face down closer to the lantern's illumination, so John and Laura could see his eyes. "It's very important we only whisper. Don't make any loud noises. Don't sneeze. Don't cough. Anything that would let them know where we are in the room." Leaning his face even further forward, yellow glow across his cheekbones. Voice barely audible, speaking slowly since his voice was so quiet. "That rustle all around us is the staring bugs."

Laura and John didn't speak.

Joachim quietly lifted the lantern off the floor, swinging its sway to the left, in this remote fort far north of everyone else in the world, so its light more fully illuminated the side wall. Black movements, scuttling sideways across the wall.

In the dimness John couldn't quite make out their shape. Only that they were bigger than cockroaches, with oversized doll's eyes.

Laura stared at them, right hand going up to her mouth. Keeping her voice low. "How many legs do they have?"

"I don't know. I've heard from other guides it varies, bug to bug. Anywhere from five to sixteen legs. They come out from their hidey holes this far north when it snows. They don't like the snow. When it does snow, this far north, they seek shelter in caves, or abandoned man-made structures, like this fort."

"Why are their eyes so big? They're insects. But their eyes are as big as fisheyes."

"I have my theories, but I don't know."

In the yellow shadows cast from the lantern, John watched as one of them, articulating joints rapidly picking its black abdomen up the wall, froze its motion, all its long legs still, big staring white eyes rolling around below its antennae, searching for the source of their voices.

The three of them sitting on the floor didn't speak.

After a moment, its multi-jointed legs articulated it higher up the wall.

"Why have I never heard of staring bugs before?"

Joachim kept his voice low. Talking out of the side of his mouth. "There's a lot in the world we're not aware of. There's just too much in this world to know everything."

More and more of the staring bugs crawled up onto the wall, in starts and stops.

"The way it works, the more it snows, the more bugs crowd inside."

"What happens if too many get in here?"

"They don't like each other. As long as they can keep some space between each other, it's okay."

John could see how the staring bugs had arranged themselves on the walls, evenly spread apart, like birds on a wire.

"But if they feel too crowded ... you don't want to be here when that happens."

The bugs on the walls kept scuttling on their long legs, sideways, up and down, repositioning themselves in relation to each other. "Why? What happens then?"

Joachim put his hand over his jaw. "For one thing, they start hissing at each other. Staring bugs have loud hisses, and those hisses are filled with rage."

More and more staring bugs scuttled up onto the walls, causing all the other staring bugs to rearrange where they clung across the wooden planks.

~~~

Since the snow had them trapped inside this fort for the next few days, they had to sleep at some point. John decided to take a nap first, while the danger was still at a low level. Laura held his hand while he gradually drifted away.

"It's clear he's very protective towards you."

Laura nodded, looking down, smiling to herself. "I grew up poor. Real poor. A sandwich was two slices of bread. But I was smart." Looked at Joachim. "That's not easy on a kid, when you know you're smarter than any of the other kids you play with, smarter than the adults you know. Even smarter than your parents. The only thing that gave me hope was reading books, because reading them, I found out there were other people out there, out far beyond this small town, even smarter than me. When you're a kid, you really need to know there are people smarter than you. Books can be a tremendous lifeline to a kid. Smart as I was, it didn't take me long to realise you needed a lot to succeed in the world, but above all else, you needed money."

Borrowed Joachim's green lighter to get a cigarette going. "I ran away from home when I was fourteen. Just left the kids my own age I was playing with, who were throwing mud at a tree, and walked the couple of miles it took to get to the highway. Thank God for highways. Despite what anyone thinks, they're really built for children. Stuck my thumb out. Once you stick your thumb out, especially as a kid, you better be ready.

"Got a bunch of rides that ended up in Dallas. Didn't pay for those rides with cash, because I didn't have any cash. But like I said, I got a bunch of rides to Dallas. And what really reassured me about the bigger world I was riding towards in different passenger seats was that despite all the horror stories you hear, almost all of the people who helped me get to Dallas were kind, supportive people. All of them gave me advice, many of them gave food, and some of them gave me folding money. The one or two creeps who weren't nice were easily foiled. They seemed to understand there was something wrong with them.

"Once I was in Dallas, I did whatever I needed to, to start accumulating money. Hooked up with someone I met in a McDonald's who had a car, and with her help I was able to sit in at college classes at SMU. Took a lot of notes.

"I eventually drifted into doing studio work for different local bands. After a few years I got some jobs as an audio engineer, which I absolutely loved, but the assignments, as they say, were few and far between. So I applied for a job as a medical claims adjudicator. Pay wasn't great, but at least it covered the rent on my tiny basement apartment, the windows above the sofa showing shoes walking by, the stove and sink three feet from my bed; utilities; and enough ramen, eggs, and vegetables to get me through each month. I didn't date. Most of the men I met were either stupid or married, or both, so I spent my evenings developing apps, just to have something to do in my cramped apartment. I didn't have a TV.

"My first app, Vegan Velocity, was based on a program I coded to produce recipes based on the foods you already had in your home. It actually wasn't that hard to write, because most purchasers who downloaded it didn't have that many food products on hand. Very few people bought it at first, but then it got some favourable reviews, my sales each day increased, and after a few months I was making as much money from app sales as I was from working eight hours a day at the third-party administrator processing medical claims.

"So I wrote a second app, Vegan Fellowship, meant to establish a network of vegans across the globe who could connect with each other, share recipes, food resources, philosophy, and also be a dating app for people who didn't exploit animal products, but it bombed. Less than a thousand downloads.

"My third app was Make Them Pay Medical and Dental Claims Submission Pro, which schooled people on how to submit denied medical and dental claims for appeal. It went big. Even bigger than Vegan Velocity. I quit my job at the third-party administrator. Got HBO. And Showtime. Ate filet mignon twice a week, serrated knife slicing through all that pink tenderness, and at the end of June bought a two-pound lobster, brought it home, lifted its claw-waving protest out of its brown paper bag, steamed it, cracked it open, pulling out the meat, dipping the red and white chunks in melted butter. I wasn't poor no more."

More staring bugs clambering up onto the walls, the dark mass of them scuttling across the wood, rearranging themselves.

New cigarette.

"So I was doing okay, financially. I actually opened a bank account." Smiling, laughing at herself, black hair to her shoulders, rolling her pretty blue eyes. "I was so tense, going into this official 'bank', the wide concrete entryway, the tall glass double doors, the carpeted hush inside, all these serious, educated people with eyeglasses inside it sitting behind desks, me feeling totally intimidated, wearing a new outfit I bought just for this visit, to give me some confidence, but I did it. And ... they were helpful. They weren't condescending, which was my biggest fear.

"So I was able to support myself, I was accumulating some money I could stockpile for the future, but I was lonely. Cooking-for-yourself-standing-in-silence-in-front-of-your-stove lonely, talk-ing-to-yourself-as-you-moved-around-your-cramped-apartment-straightening-a-picture-on-the-wall lonely. Participating in some online discussion groups, leaving comments on different discussion boards, and sometimes someone would reply, but once I turned off the computer, it was just me and my furniture.

"I finally dealt with my loneliness the way most people do, by getting a pet. I got a cat." Grins. "I know. Dear, sweet Rudo. Long-haired black cat that I absolutely loved. We'd curl up on the sofa together watching *True Blood* under a blue blanket; he'd sleep next to me in bed each night, paws stretched out to my upper arm, snoring.

"We moved into a new place, a two-storey house I bought, and he was brave. He explored the lower rooms, then started up the stairs to the second floor. I was so proud of his courage! The stairs were the type where half the flight goes straight up, then you have a square landing, then the second half of the flight headed in the opposite direction. He took about two steps up that second flight, suddenly stopping his black paws on the white carpet of the next step, turning his head around to make sure I was following him. The look he shot me with his small dark eyes over his shoulder was, I can do this, right? And I loved him for it."

"Do you still have him?"

Pretty dark-haired face, blue eyes, turning sad. "No. He died years ago." Thin shoulders lifting. "My old pal. He had cancer. Lost a lot of weight. That's hard to watch in your living room, bedroom, bathroom, kitchen, as it slowly takes everything away from him. As his face narrows, and his whiskers turn grey. Tremendous pain, and that pain would only get worse as the cancer progressed. I had to make a decision. I spoke with the vet, Rudo rubbing the sides of his face against my ankles while I was on the phone, oblivious to what I was discussing, me making arrangements to bring him in the next morning to be put to sleep. He didn't mind the ride to the vet. We'd made it before, and he always returned home afterwards to his safe little kingdom. This time, after he was put up on the metal examination table, he saw there was something new. The short, black-haired vet came back into the room with a syringe in his right hand. Once again, Rudo looked over his shoulder at me, and gave me that same trusting look. I can do this, right? And once again I smiled at him and nodded."

<div align="center">~~~</div>

As the evening darkened, it was Laura's turn to get some sleep, John's turn to guard.

Sitting on the floor across from Joachim, John's eyes looked alarmed at the number of staring bugs that had gathered on the walls, and halfway across the ceiling.

"Laura was telling me about her childhood, how she got out of her poverty."

"She's tough. A real fighter. When I met her, she was operating a rolling hot dog cart in a downtown square where many of the local companies let out at lunch time. She had a lot of spunk. Young women in skirts looking down on her, they work in an office, they would never have to demean themselves selling hot dogs; young guys in business suits who started each day at the gym, flirting with her, making childish innuendoes about the shape of hot dogs. But I have to say, she always kept her chin lifted. And that really impressed me. She used to run an app company, she did different apps for vegans, and people appealing medical claims, but eventually they became less popular. Other, similar, more powerfully financed apps came out, building on her ideas. She had a house, but she lost it. When I met her, she was pretty much at her low point. Living alone in a crummy little one-bedroom apartment, loading up hot dogs and buns and condiments each morning for her cart out in the parking lot. We got to talking in the downtown square once the lunch crowd drifted off, and … I just saw this was a woman with some substance to her. I could tell by her eyes she probably cried sometimes when she was alone, in her apartment, but she never cried or showed any sign of 'poor me' when she was out in public. I asked her out on a date. We've been going out ever since, and last month we moved in together. To my apartment.

She surprised me with this camping trip, having saved up the money from all the hot dogs she sold. So like her. To go out of her way for someone. That's one of the first things that attracted me to her. Everyone she meets, she finds something nice to say about them. To make them feel good about themselves."

"Are you thinking of marrying her?"

"I am! When we get back."

Joachim pulled his long brown hair away from his face, curling the hair behind his ears. "Is something wrong?"

"No. It's just—" Glance at Laura, to make sure she's still sleeping. "She always says I'm her rock. And I know she depends so much on my steadiness. Me being 'true blue'. Cooks breakfast for me every morning. Pulls my tie apart every evening when I get home, so I can relax in our private world. We were walking in the snow, I slipped, started to fall, and she yanked my hand up, to steady me, even though as a result she fell on her ass herself, really hurting her back. But. Last month I had to go out of town to a convention. It was the first time we had ever slept apart. And … I got really drunk. I just wanted to be free for an evening, be irresponsible, like I used to be? Anyway, while I was drunk, waiting for the elevator to take me back up to my room, I did something I shouldn't have."

Joachim's sad face. "Does she know about this? Did you tell her?"

John shook his head.

"Are you going to tell her?"

John hesitated. Big, friendly American face lowered. Shook his head.

~~~

The white winds blew left and right outside the windows, tossing more snow against the glass. A short distance from where John and Laura sat facing each other, Joachim lay sprawled on his back, snoring.

Laura raised her eyebrows. Apologetic. "Some vacation!"

John looked at her with love. Leaned forward, hand reaching, squeezed her thin knee. "I love it. Because you did this for me. That's what counts."

Her confident nod. "I know we're going to get out of this. It's just one more challenge in life."

"That's all it is."

"After we get back to Texas, I want to stop at the market on our way home from the airport, pick up a lot of ingredients, then that night after a couple of drinks, listening to our music, try a new Paul Prudhomme recipe."

John raised his right forefinger. Said nothing.

Politely confused look from Laura. God, she was beautiful, with her dark hair and her blue eyes.

He stood up from the floor, knees cracking. Walked quietly over to Joachim's knapsack on the floor, watching Joachim's face to make sure he was still sleeping.

Went down on his haunches as Laura watched, sitting up. Slowly unbuckled the green straps on the back of the knapsack. Glancing at Joachim's snoring face, dug his hands into the sack, fingers slowly pulling out its contents.

In a whisper. "What are you doing?"

Right forefinger raised.

As Laura watched, John pulled from the green knapsack Joachim's breathing mask and filtered goggles.

Crept on his shoes and hands back to where Laura was sitting on the floor.

Laying them out on the floor, leaning against her shoulder, whispering in her ear. "One of us has to get to that ranger station to let them know what's going on, and rescue us before this gets out of control. A few more hours, and the number of staring bugs scuttling in here to hide is going to reach the density where Joachim said things turn bad.

"With this mask and these goggles, you can do it. The ranger's station is only a mile away. And the route to get there is on a road. Not through the woods. I know you. You're strong. Determined. You'll make your way to the ranger's station, and bring them back here. I trust you. I owe you."

Laura's pretty face, puzzled. "You don't owe me anything."

"Put the equipment on, before he wakes up. Please."

Eventually, she did.

She tended to give into his requests.

She was born poor. Remember?

Standing up in the room with the breathing mask strapped across her mouth, the goggles strapped across her eyes, Joachim still snoring on the floor.

Laura at the front door. Lifts the black rubber mask from her mouth, goggles still in place over her eyes, to kiss John one more time on the lips.

The blast of cold air from the door being opened for her to leave wakes up Joachim.

And just like Rudo looked back heading up those white-carpeted stairs, needing reassurance from someone he trusted, Laura looked back heading out the door. I can do this, right?

After she was out in the white swirl of the fort's courtyard, John leaned his shoulder against the front door, pushing it closed, bolting it.

Whatever happens here, in this abandoned fort far away from everything in the distant north, at least she'll be safe.

Joachim rubbed his eyes, adjusting to being awake. "Why was the door open?"

John lit a cigarette, blowing grey smoke up at the increasing density of staring bugs on the walls, ceiling, like the spreading red bumps of measles. "I gave Laura your breathing mask and goggles. She can make it to the ranger's station, and at least she's safe."

Joachim lowered his face. "You had no right to do that!"

"Yeah, well, I'm sorry, but sometimes you just decide to do the right thing. So why are the staring bugs so afraid of the snow?"

Joachim shook his head at John's stupidity. "They're not afraid of the snow."

John snorted. "So why would they—"

"They're hiding inside from what the snow brings."

Outside the door, Laura's agonized scream.

Staring bugs frantically rearranging themselves across the walls, ceiling.

Another scream from outside.

Silence.

Staring bugs frantically rearranging themselves across the walls, ceiling.

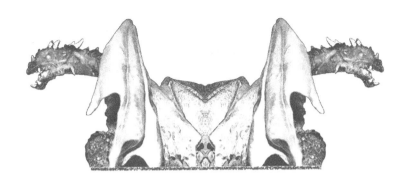

CONTRIBUTOR NOTES

Sarah Ash lives in Bath – and the local legend of The Beast of Bathwick has intrigued her for many years. She trained as a musician but writing fantasy fiction has allowed her to explore her fascination with the way mythology, folklore and history overlap and interact. Sarah's latest published novel is *Scent of Lilies*, a ghost story set in the ember years of the Byzantine empire. www.sarah-ash.com

Jenny Barber is the co-editor (with Jan Edwards) of *Wicked Women*, *The Alchemy Press Book of Urban Mythic volumes 1 & 2* and *The Alchemy Press Book of Ancient Wonders*. Her short fiction has been published in multiple anthologies and has garnered an honourable mention in Ellen Datlow's *The Best Horror of the Year Volume Eleven* for her story "Down Along the Backroads" from the first volume of *The Alchemy Press Book of Horrors*. www.jennybarber.co.uk or on Twitter as @jenqoe

Simon Bestwick lives on the Wirral and dreams of moving to Wales. He is the author of six novels, four full-length short story collections, and has been four times shortlisted for the British Fantasy Award. He is married to long-suffering fellow author Cate Gardner, and still hasn't kicked his addictions to Pepsi Max or semicolons. His short fiction has appeared in *Horrified* and *Railroad Tales* and his latest books are the novella *Devils Of London* and the novel *Black Mountain*. Simon posts new fiction every

month at https://www.patreon.com/SimonBestwick
http://simon-bestwick.blogspot.com/

Randy Broecker has been drawing the things he loves –
"Ghoulies and ghosties and long-leggedy beasties and things that
go bump in the night" – for well over forty years. His art has
appeared regularly in books and magazines worldwide,
including *Tales from the Magician's Skull, Phantasmagoria,* and most
recently in *New Supernatural Stories* by Lionel and Patricia
Fanthorpe, Aidan Chambers' collection *Dead Trouble & Other
Ghost Stories* and the anthology *Terrifying Tales to Tell at Night: 10
Scary Stories to Give You Nightmares*! edited by Stephen Jones. He
has been Artist Guest of Honor at The World Horror Convention,
and has also written and compiled the World Fantasy Award-
nominated art book, *Fantasy of the 20ᵗʰ Century: An Illustrated
History*. Although he has illustrated stories by the likes of Ramsey
Campbell, Brian Lumley, Manly Wade Wellman, Kim Newman,
Stephen King, and Neil Gaiman, amongst many others, he finds
himself returning time and again to the works of HP Lovecraft for
inspiration. Not surprisingly, his illustration in this volume is
from a favourite Lovecraft story, "The Dreams in the Witch
House", and is a portrait of Brown Jenkin – a rat-like creature
with an evilly human face and human hands. Randy lives in an
old house in Chicago, along with a monster or three.
http://www.randybroecker.com/portfolio_page/

Mike Chinn has published over seventy short stories and
scripted several comic strips. He has edited *Swords Against the
Millennium* and three volumes of *The Alchemy Press Book of Pulp
Heroes*. His first Damian Paladin collection, *The Paladin Mandates,*
was short-listed for the British Fantasy Award in 1999. A revised
and extended (by 10,000 words) *Paladin Mandates* was published
in 2020. A second Paladin collection, *Walkers in Shadow,* appeared
in 2017. Mike Chinn has two short story collections in print: *Give
Me These Moments Back* and *Radix Omnium Malum*. In 2018 his first
western, *Revenge is a Cold Pistol* was published. In addition, Chinn
sent Sherlock Holmes to the moon in *Vallis Timoris,* and is
currently reimaging Arch Whitehouse's classic 1930s pulp

adventure character *The Griffon*. Chinn notes that the submarine *USS Oswin* first sailed in the Damian Paladin story "Cradle of the Deep" in issue one of the reborn *Startling Stories* magazine. http://saladoth.blogspot.com/

Adrian Cole is a native of and lives in North Devon, England. His sword & planet trilogy *The Dream Lords* (1970s) was followed by more than two dozen novels and numerous short stories. He has written science fiction, heroic fantasy, sword & sorcery, horror, pulp fiction, Mythos, and young adult novels. His stories have appeared in the *Year's Best Fantasy* and *Year's Best Fantasy and Horror* anthologies. His *Nick Nightmare Investigates*, the first arc of stories about the hard-boiled occult private eye, won the 2015 British Fantasy Award for Best Collection. The second volume, *Nightmare Cocktails*, is now available. Other works include the three volume Voidal sword & sorcery saga and *Elak, King of Atlantis*. Adrian has contributed to *Weird Tales Story* (recently revised and updated) and *REH Changed My Life.*

Peter Coleborn created the award-winning Alchemy Press in the late 1990s and has since (co-)published a range of anthologies and collections. He has edited various publications for the British Fantasy Society (including *Winter Chills/Chills* and *Dark Horizons)*, and co-edited with Pauline E Dungate the Joel Lane tribute anthology *Something Remains* in 2016. In in 2018 he co-edited with Jan Edwards the first volume of *The Alchemy Press Book of Horrors*. www.alchemypress.co.uk

Pauline E Dungate is a short story writer, reviewer and poet. She is co-editor (with Peter Coleborn) of *Something Remains,* a tribute to Joel Lane. When not reading, writing or pottering about in the garden she visits far-flung places in order to photograph butterflies – including distant lands such as Mexico and Colombia. She lives in Birmingham.

Jan Edwards is an editor of anthologies for The Alchemy Press, the British Fantasy Society, Fox Spirit and others. Her short fiction has appeared in many crime, horror and fantasy anthologies.

Some of those tales have been collected in *Leinster Gardens and Other Subtleties* and *Fables and Fabrications*. Her novels include *Sussex Tales* and *Winter Downs* (Bunch Courtney book one, and winner of the Arnold Bennett Book Prize) and its sequels: *In Her Defence* and *Listed Dead*. She is also a recipient of the BFS Karl Edward Wagner Award. http://janedwardsblog.wordpress.com

Bryn Fortey started publishing in the late 1960s with stories in anthologies such as *New Writings in Horror and the Supernatural* and *The Fontana Books of Great Horror Stories*. Because of real life issues Bryn's writing dried up until he was published again by The Alchemy Press in the 2000s. His stories have been collected in two volumes: *Merry-Go-Round and Other Words* and *Compromising the Truth*. He was passionate about music, especially jazz and Blues, which often features in his poetry. Bryn Fortey died on 21 July 2021 at the age of 83. He will be missed by his close family and friends.

Tim Jeffreys' short fiction has appeared in *Supernatural Tales, Not One of Us, The Alchemy Press Book of Horrors 2,* and *Nightscript,* among various other publications, and his latest collection of horror stories and strange tales *Black Masquerades* is now available. He lives in Bristol, England, with his partner and two children, and is currently at work on a novel. www.timjeffreys.blogspot.co.uk.

Tom Johnstone came to fiction writing rather late in life, and so pursues it with the quiet desperation of someone conscious of the relatively short time he has left. He is the author of the collection *Last Stop Wellsbourne* and two novellas, *The Monsters are Due in Madison Square Garden* and *Star Spangled Knuckle Duster.* His short stories have also appeared in or are forthcoming in such publications as *Black Static, Terror Tales of the Home Counties, Nightscript VI, Body Shocks* and *Best Horror of the Year Volume 13.* tomjohnstone.wordpress.com

Garry Kilworth was born in York in 1941. His father being regular RAF, he was an itinerant service brat until he himself joined at the age of 15. Childhood years were spent on remote overseas stations, the most exciting of which was South Yemen. There at the age of 14 Garry was first lost, then found after two days in the Hadhramaut Desert. There also began a love of the exotic, which has been an integral part of his fiction. His most recent efforts at entertaining the masses are *Elemental Tales* and *Blood Moon*, two collections of short stories. The first is a series of tales with a metal element at the heart of each. The second is a novella and eight short SF, fantasy and horror stories, one of which appeared in *Alchemy Press Book of Horrors 2*. www.garry-kilworth.co.uk

Johnny Mains lives in the South West with his wife and child. You can find him on Twitter as @ohsinnerman.

Ralph Robert Moore's fiction has appeared in America, Canada, England, Ireland, France, India and Australia in a wide variety of genre and literary magazines and anthologies, including *Cemetery Dance, Black Static, Shadows & Tall Trees, Nightscript, Midnight Street, ChiZine*, and others. He's been nominated twice for Best Story of the Year by The British Fantasy Society, in 2013 and again in 2016. Moore's books include the novels *Father Figure, As Dead As Me, Ghosters*, and *The Angry Red Planet*, and the story collections *Remove the Eyes, I Smell Blood, You Can Never Spit It All Out, Behind You, Breathing Through My Nose*, and *Our Elaborate Plans*. His website **Sentence** (see link below) features a wide selection of his writings; you can see what he's currently working on, and other aspects of his day to day life, by going to www.facebook.com/ralph.r.moore/. Moore and his wife Mary live outside Dallas, Texas. www.ralphrobertmoore.com

Marion Pitman read MR James and Algernon Blackwood at an impressionable age, which could explain a lot. She likes moving around, and regards herself as a Londoner. She has written poetry and fiction most of her life, and published it since the 1970s. She sells second-hand books, and has worked as an artists' model. She has no car, no television, no cats and no money. Her hobbies include folk-singing, watching cricket, and theological argument. Her short story collection *Music in the Bone* is available from The Alchemy Press. http://www.marionpitman.co.uk

John Llewellyn Probert latest book is the British Fantasy Award-nominated *The Last Temptation of Dr Valentine*, the second sequel to his British Fantasy Award winner *The Nine Deaths of Dr Valentine*. He won the Children of the Night Award for his portmanteau book *The Faculty of Terror* and his current projects include two more titles utilising the same structure. He is also at work on two novels and two non-fiction film books while continuing to write about current releases at his website House of Mortal Cinema. After all six books have been finished he intends to sleep for a bit. But he probably won't, because he has just got a major publisher interested in his memoirs.

Daniele Serra is an Italian illustrator and comic book artist. His main influences and inspirations are the weird/horror stories by HP Lovecraft, William H Hodgson and Clive Barker, Ridley Scott movies, and Japanese horror films. As a comic book artist he has worked for Image Comics, BOOM! Studios, Titan Comics, IDW Publishing, Seraphim INC and Short Scary Tales Publications. Serra's illustrations have featured in or on over 250 books by Stephen King, Ramsey Campbell, Clive Barker, Joe R Lansdale, William Hope Hodgson, Tim Waggoner, Brian Stableford, Alan Miller, Marcello Fois and many others, as well as for music and Blu-Ray releases. His illustrations have been used as the set dressing for the movie adaptation of Stephen King's *Cell*. Two-time winner of the British Fantasy Award for Best Artist (2012, 2017), Daniele Serra lives in Sardinia with his wife, his cats, a lot of exotic insects, and a huge collection of horror books and movies. www.danieleserra.com

Steve Rasnic Tem, a past winner of the Bram Stoker, World Fantasy, and British Fantasy Awards, has published 470+ short stories. Recent collections include *The Night Doctor & Other Tales* and *The Harvest Child and Other Fantasies*. His novel *Ubo* is a dark science fictional tale about violence and its origins, featuring such viewpoint characters as Jack the Ripper and Stalin. *Yours to Tell: Dialogues on the Art & Practice of Writing*, written with his late wife Melanie, is available from Apex Books. Valancourt Books published *Figures Unseen*, his selected stories, and will follow up with *Thanatrauma: Stories* this Fall. www.stevetem.com.

Surrounded by gnomes, gargoyles and poisonous plants, **KT Wagner** writes Gothic horror and op/ed pieces in the garden of her Maple Ridge, British Columbia home. She enjoys day-dreaming and is a collector of strange plants, weird trivia and obscure tomes. In her spare time, she organizes writer events and works to create literary community. KT graduated from Simon Fraser University's Writers Studio in 2015. A number of her short stories are published in magazines and anthologies. She's currently working on a scifi-horror novel. www.northernlightsgothic.com

Ashe Woodward has been writing stories since she could type on a Commodore 64. Monsters of all kinds are her jam and she loves the adventure of exploring the "where" and "why" they thrive in the human imagination. She lives in Ontario, Canada with her husband Tim and their two dogs, Jake and Bella, who (*she swears*) were accidentally named after *Twilight* characters. ashewoodward.com

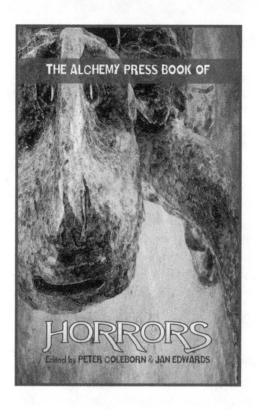

The Alchemy Press Book of Horrors

Edited by Peter Coleborn & Jan Edwards

The first volume in the series contains twenty-five tales of horror and the weird, stories that encapsulate the dark, the desolate and the downright creepy. Stories that will send that quiver of anticipation and dread down your spine and stay with you long after the lights have gone out. Who is Len Binn, a comedian or…? What secrets are locked away in Le Trénébreuse? The deadline for what? Who are the little people, the garbage men, the peelers? What lies behind the masks? And what horrors are found down along the backroads?

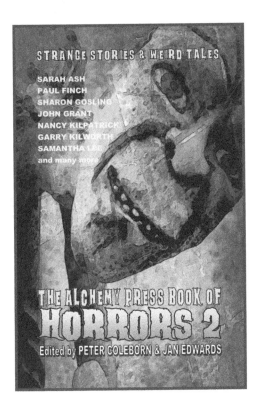

STRANGE STORIES & WEIRD TALES

SARAH ASH
PAUL FINCH
SHARON GOSLING
JOHN GRANT
NANCY KILPATRICK
GARRY KILWORTH
SAMANTHA LEE
and many more

THE ALCHEMY PRESS BOOK OF
HORRORS 2
Edited by PETER COLEBORN & JAN EDWARDS

The Alchemy Press Book of Horrors 2

Edited by Peter Coleborn & Jan Edwards

"Strange stories and weird tales and all of the creeping horrors in between."

Seventeen fabulous writers, including Sarah Ash, Paul Finch, John Grant, Nancy Kilpatrick, Garry Kilworth, Samantha Lee, lead you on a spine-tingling tour from seaside towns to grimy cities, to the lonely and secret places, from the fourteenth precinct to Namibia and so many other places along the way.

THE ALCHEMY PRESS
BOOK OF THE DEAD 2020

Celebrating the careers of more than 450 individuals who made significant contributions to the horror, science fiction and fantasy genres during their lifetimes. Compiled by award-winning writer and editor **Stephen Jones**, this first volume in a new annual series includes tributes to a trio of Hollywood legends ... possibly the last star of silent pictures ... the screen's best James Bond ... a pair of British actresses who were both "Bond girls" and *Avengers* ... two British actors who played – but did not voice – iconic *Star Wars* characters ... an author who did for crustaceans what James Herbert did for rodents ... and a forgotten pioneer of "sword and soul" fantasy ... all illustrated with numerous photographs and associated images.

This is not only a welcome reference volume, but also an informative and entertaining tribute to those we lost in 2020 and who left their mark on books, movies and popular culture in unusual and often fascinating ways.

The Alchemy Press Book of the Dead 2020
Compiled by Stephen Jones
ISBN 978-1-911034-12-4 £14.99

Available from Amazon and other good booksellers

alchemypress.wordpress.com/books-of-the-dead/botd2020/